The Crime of Julian Wells

THOMAS H. COOK won an Edgar award for his novel
The Chatham School Affair and has been shortlisted for the
award six times, most recently with *Red Leaves*, which was also
shortlisted for the Duncan Lawrie Gold Dagger award. Cook
lives with his family in Cape Cod and New York City.

Books by Thomas H. Cook

The Crime of Julian Wells

THOMAS H. COOK

A Mysterious Press book
for Head of Zeus

First published in the United States in 2012 by
Mysterious Press, an imprint of Grove/Atlantic.

This edition first published in the UK in 2012 by Head of Zeus Ltd.
This paperback edition first published in the UK in 2013
by Head of Zeus Ltd.

975312468

A CIP catalogue record for this book is available from the British Library.

Paperback ISBN: 9781908800657
eBook ISBN: 9781781850398

Printed and bound by CPI Group (UK) Ltd,
Croydon, CR0 4YY.

Head of Zeus Ltd
Clerkenwell House
45-47 Clerkenwell Green
London EC1R 0HT

www.headofzeus.com

For the women of Maui:
Ann Hood, Diane Lake, Annie LeClaire,
Jacquelyn Mitchard, Deborah Todd, and Sara Young.

And in loving memory of Heiman Zeidman.

The Curfew tolls the Knell of parting Day,
The lowing Herd winds slowly o'er the Lea,
The Plow-man homeward plods his weary Way,
And leaves the World to Darkness, and to me.

Thomas Gray, *Elegy Written in a Country
Church-Yard*

Before

He folds the map and puts it on the table beside his chair. Beyond the window, he sees the flat gray waters of the pond. The boat, its yellow paint long faded, rests beneath a weeping birch.

He rises, walks to the window, and looks out.

In the distance, a small breeze rustles the leaves of the birch and skirts along the green lawn and gently rocks the purple irises that grow beside the water. He has seen so many grasses, so many flowers. The lavender fields of France, the cloudberries of the Urals with their little orange petals, the feather grasses of the pampas swaying like dancers.

He will miss these things.

He considers the act, then its consequences.

He will make it clean.

There will be no fuss.

He turns and gives a final glance at the map. He has studied so many maps. He thinks of the water bearers of the world, almost always women, hauling their jerry jars to the river or the lake. His mind is like those jars, worn and dusty, scarred by use, but still able to hold its heavy store of memory.

And yet there is something he forgot.

He walks to the small desk in the corner, opens the notebook, and tears out the top sheet. He folds it carefully, without hurry, then sinks it deep into his pocket.

It is disturbance you must look for, the old trackers told him. Not prints. Not trails. But disturbance in the spear grass, a sense of reeds askew. Those will lead you to the one you seek.

He looks about the room for any hint of such disturbance, finds none, and with that assurance, walks to the door, then passes through it, and moves out onto the lawn. He feels the breeze whose movement he had sensed before, cool upon his face, a pressure on his shirt, a gentle movement in his hair.

He hears a bird call, glances up, and sees a gull as it crosses the lower sky. When was it he first saw the sunbirds of the Sudan, their sun-streaked, iridescent feathers?

He shakes his head. It doesn't matter now.

He draws down his gaze and with a steady stride makes his way to the boat. It is heavy, and he has been weakened, though less by his final work than by this final decision.

But the decision has been made.

The boat is weighty but he pulls it into the water. What was the lightest he ever knew? Oh yes, it was made of bulrushes. And what was the other word for bulrushes? Oh yes, it was tule.

The boat rocks violently as he climbs in, but he rights himself, grabs an oar, and pushes out into the water.

How far to go?

The center of the pond. Far enough that he will appear small and indistinct in the distance so that his sister cannot tell what he is doing, nor get to him before he can complete the task.

Seventy feet from shore now. Perhaps eighty. He has not rowed in a long time. Even now his arms are aching. But that will be over soon. He knows that he has grown weak in the Russian wastes, but he is surprised by just how weak he is. Or has his secret always worked upon him like a withering disease?

One hundred feet out from shore.

Enough.

He takes the folded paper from his pocket and sinks it into the water.

Done.

He sits quietly for a moment, then with his old resolve, he begins the process. First he rolls up his sleeves. For a few seconds he pumps his fist, squeezing in and out. The blue veins rise as if to his command.

He leans forward and picks up the knife. Its serrated edge will hurt, but he has all his life known pain.

No mess.

No fuss.

He holds one arm over the pale yellow port side and with a single slice opens up his vein. The blood flows down his hand and along his fingers in a steady stream that reddens the water below them. He brings the other arm and hangs it over the water, takes the knife with his bloodied hand and makes a second motion.

It is done.

At least the first phase.

Now there is only the will to wait.

He releases the knife and watches it splash into the red water. The wait is not long.

Soon he begins to lean forward as life flows out of him. He will think no more of sunbirds and bulrushes.

Finally, he droops over the port side, his arms now deep in the water.

Seconds later he is gone.

The wait was not long, but its solitariness is unimaginable.

Oh, if I had but been there, my dear friend.

Oh, if I had but been there in the boat with you.

Knowing what I know now.

PART I
The Tortures of Cuenca

1

There is no more haunting story than that of an unsolved crime, Julian had once written, but solutions, I was to discover, can be haunting, too.

To know the world, one must travel it in the third-class carriage, and I had little doubt that that was surely how Julian had come to know it. He was one of those for whom the usual comforts meant nothing. If the water was yellow, the walls laced with mold, if the sink was ringed in rust, or even if there was no sink at all, if the mosquito net was ripped and the cloaca full, it was the same to Julian. The deeds that drew him were the darkest that we know, and he'd pursued them with the urgency of a lover.

From his first trip abroad, I'd had little doubt that he would remain an expatriate all his life, which made it all the stranger that, in the end—that terrible, lonely end—he had died at home.

Now my thought, growing more insistent by the hour, was how I might have saved him.

"He was wizened," his sister, Loretta, said to me. "If you can say that about a man who was only in his fifties." She took a sip from her drink. "It's hard to imagine that he's gone."

3

We sat at a small square table in a quiet corner of what was still called an actors' bar, though now it catered mostly to Broadway tourists. I presumed that Loretta had chosen it because it returned her to the days when she'd struggled to be an actress, trudged that dreary path from audition to audition until rejection's blade had whittled away the last of that youthful hope. I'd seen her in two productions, both pretty far off Broadway. In the first, she'd played the object of desire in *A View from the Bridge*. In the second, the title role in *Hedda Gabler*. In both cases her talent had impressed me, especially the uneasy balance of pathos and simmering violence she'd brought to Hedda, which had also frightened me a little. She'd had every right to succeed on the stage, but hadn't. Watching her now, I decided that there was perhaps no ash quite so cold as the one left by an unrealized ambition, particularly an artistic one. But then, I thought, there is no such thing as a truly fulfilled ambition, is there? At twenty-three, Alexander the Great had bemoaned the fact that there were no more worlds for him to conquer. It seemed to me that we were all like poor thwarted Alexander, unsatisfied in one way or another. Some were dissatisfied with their choice of careers, others with their choice of mates, still others with their lack of money. My chief dissatisfactions were childlessness and widowhood, to which had now been added my failure to save my one true friend.

"Some people, when they die, bring more than themselves to an end," Loretta said. "The books I copyedit now are mostly happy talk. Tips on how to avoid thinking about the only things Julian ever thought about." She shook her head. "Half the time, I feel like a whore." Her smile carried the dogged effort of a lost cause. "Have you seen the new rewrite of *The Great Gatsby* for teen readers? It's sixty-seven pages long, and it seems that Fitzgerald intended the book to have a happy ending."

She was in her early fifties now, but her eyes were as sparkling as they'd ever been. In Egypt, Flaubert had encountered a woman whose exquisite beauty was marred only by that one bad incisor. I could find no such flaw in Loretta. She wore the beauty of her maturity as she had worn the beauty of her youth— easily, almost unconsciously, and with breathtaking grace. Time would do what time always does, but there would be no Botox in Loretta's future, no facelifts. She would move through the remaining seasons of her life as easily as she moved through the stages of a single day.

"Julian was an artist," Loretta said firmly.

An artist, yes, but with a curious obsession.

I thought of how he'd spent his last six years following the Russian serial killer Andrei Chikatilo's path through countless dismal towns, sleeping in the same railway stations, eating black bread and cheese, eyeing the vagabond children who had been Chikatilo's prey, *becoming* him, as Julian always seemed to do while writing about such villains.

"The last book really took it out of him," Loretta added. "But it wasn't just exhaustion."

"What was it?"

She thought a moment, then said, "He was like a man in a locked room, trying to get out."

Perhaps, but even so, Julian's mood hadn't troubled me, because I'd always thought that studying atrocities and detailing the outrages of serial killers would be a labor he would at some point seek to escape. Perhaps, at last, he was breaking free of all that, for there were times, such as when he described a sunset on the Atlas Mountains or a rainstorm in the Carpathians, when his love of the world cut through the darkness and he seemed, at least briefly, to soar above the grim nature of his subject matter. At such moments his spirits would lift, only to be dragged down again, as if by some invisible weight. Oh, what can you do, I had often thought, what can do you do with such a man?

"I had no inkling he might do what he did," Loretta said.

Nor had I, though only a week before, Julian had canceled a trip into the city. Two days after that, Loretta had called to say that he'd been unusually agitated. For that reason, she'd been surprised when she'd seen him calmly make his way toward the small pond that bordered the house, even more surprised that he'd climbed into the little boat the two of them had used as a child, and rowed away. A few minutes later she'd noticed the boat drifting toward shore with Julian leaning over the port side, his bare arms dangling in the water.

"I knew instantly that he was dead," Loretta said. "And that he'd done it to himself." She took another sip of wine. "But why?"

The tone of her question was quite different from any I'd heard in her voice before. She gave off the air of a person going through someone else's old papers, looking not for deeds or insurance policies but for the small journal with its cracked leather binding and rusty latch—an item of no value whatsoever, save that it was there, written on some faded page, that the dreadful secret lay.

But had Julian actually had any such dreadful secret? I had no idea. We'd lived very different lives, after all: he, the expatriate writer; I, the stay-at-home literary critic, whose primary gift was in dissecting novels that, no matter how awful, were certainly beyond my own creative powers. He'd settled in Paris, if you could call the apartment in Pigalle that he rarely used his permanent residence. But even when I'd met him in Paris, or London, or Madrid, he'd had the air of a man briefly stranded in a railway station. For Julian, the road was home, and he'd trudged down some of the worst ones on earth, writing articles about plague and famine and holocaust in addition to his five books. And his writing had been exquisite. Like Orpheus, he had brought music into hell, and like him, he had died in a world that no longer wished to hear it.

"I sometimes think of him as a fictional character," Loretta said. "An immortal detective in pursuit of some equally immortal arch villain." Something in her eyes shattered. "But he will be forgotten, won't he?"

"Probably," I answered frankly.

"Each book was like a nail in his coffin," Loretta said. "Even that first one."

She meant *The Tortures of Cuenca,* Julian's study of a fabled injustice that had been committed in Spain, in 1911. He'd never really returned after that book, save for short periods, during which he would search for his next book or article. After *Cuenca,* the pattern was always the same. Go away. Write. Return. Go away. Write. Return. I could not recall just how many times he'd left the Montauk farmhouse he and Loretta had inherited, then come back to it out of nowhere and with no advance word, like a body washed up onshore.

"He was already planning the next one, you know," Loretta said. "In a way, that's what threw me off, because Julian was the same as always. Sitting in the sunroom, planning his next move."

"Planning it how?" I asked.

"By studying a map," Loretta answered. "That's how he always began working on his next piece, by studying a map of the country he was going to. Then he'd start reading books about the place."

As a result of that research, there'd always been considerable sweep to Julian's work, as his friendlier reviewers had sometimes pointed out. No crime floated freely. It was always part of a larger disorder, one fiber sprung from a hideous cloth. In a passage on Henri Landru, for example, he'd managed to connect the serial killer's murders in Paris to the nearby slaughter on the Somme, and this while writing a curious meditation on one of Gilles de Rais's blood-spattered minions.

"It was going the way it always had, the circle of Julian's life," Loretta said. "Then suddenly he was dead."

I felt an inner jolt, not only at Julian's death, but at my own inevitable demise and everyone else's, the wheel of time, that ceaselessly revolving door that ushers you out and brings the one behind you in, life itself, the killer we can't catch.

"I keep imagining myself in the boat with him," I said. "I'm completely silent, but I'm searching for what I could say to him that would change his mind."

"Do you find the words?" Loretta asked.

I shook my head. "No."

Loretta cocked her head slightly, the way she did when an idea hit her. "Do you suppose he had a wife somewhere? Or a lover? Someone we should notify?"

The question took me off guard. I'd never considered such a thing.

"I would certainly doubt it," I answered, though it was conceivable that a rootless man might eventually have sunk secret roots.

"I always hoped that he had someone," Loretta said. "Some whore in Trieste, if nothing more. Just someone he was growing old with, someone who might comfort him."

"Then perhaps you should believe he did," I said.

Loretta's eyes flashed. "Is that what gets you through the night, Philip?" she asked. "Choosing to believe something, whether it's true or not?"

"In one way or another, Loretta, isn't that what gets everyone through the night?" I asked.

"You don't think he ever fell in love?" Loretta asked.

"No, I don't think he ever fell in love," I answered, and again felt the pain of losing my wife three years before, a hole in my heart I could find no way to heal.

Loretta reached for her drink but only stared into it. "It was Argentina," she said, her tone quite thoughtful. "The map Julian was looking at the day he died. Maybe he was thinking about that trip the two of you made down there."

"That was thirty years ago, Loretta," I said. "Why would he have been thinking about that?"

THOMAS H. COOK

She released a breath that was like a tired breeze, driven too far over rough terrain. "Like the winds from off the Karst," as Julian had once written in one of his college essays, "thirsting for the Adriatic." Such had been his style in the high days of his youth, his language predictably stilted, cluttered with allusions to places he'd never been. So different from what his work later became, those emaciated sentences, so darkly spare.

"A map of Argentina," Loretta said softly, almost to herself. "Do you think he was on the trail of something down there?"

"It's possible, I suppose."

But on the trail of what? I wondered, though there seemed no way to know in what direction Julian was heading when he decided to go to the pond instead.

"By the way," I said, "have you read the manuscript Julian brought back?"

"No," Loretta said as if my question had only drawn her deeper into Julian's mystery. "He cut out their eyes, you know, that Russian horror. And that's not all, of course."

"Yes, I know what Chikatilo did," I said with a wave of the hand.

Loretta's attention drifted toward the window. "We were in Rome, Julian and I. Just children. We were in that little piazza, the Campidoglio. He said it looked perfectly square because Michelangelo had designed it to look perfectly square by widening it here and elongating it there. It wasn't actually square at all. It was a masterful trick of perspective. 'It's distortion that creates perfection, Loretta,' he said."

10

She turned toward me and I saw a subtle shift in the mosaic of this woman, and with that shift I realized just how deeply Loretta had loved Julian, and that she always would. He'd been the older brother who had taken time with her, who had offered her his thoughts, his feelings, and then, for some reason she would never know, had chosen to remove himself for years on end, one of life's true vagabonds.

"Julian was good," she said softly. "That's what I'll miss. His goodness."

I felt a scuttling movement in the place where my youth lay like a discarded old traveling case, timeworn and battered, layered in gray dust. I glanced at my watch. "I'm sorry, but I have to look in on my father."

Loretta nodded. "How is he?"

For the first time in a long time, I felt an uneasy loosening in the grip I was careful to maintain upon myself.

"Fading," I said. I looked toward the window, where the rain had not let up. "Bad night." I rose, grabbed my coat, and drew it on. "Well, I'll see you at the service on Friday."

Loretta stared at her now-empty glass. "Do you think you knew him, Philip?"

"Not enough to have saved him, evidently," I answered. "Which means I'll always be silent in that boat."

She looked up at me. "I guess we all leave a trail of little pebbles scattered on the forest floor," she said. "But I'll always wonder where those pebbles would have led to with Julian."

I had no answer to this question, nor ever expected to have

one. She saw my retreat, and so offered her own admittedly inadequate one.

"Just to more pebbles, I suppose," she added with a small, sad smile.

I gathered up my coat. "I'm afraid so."

I expected this to be the end of it, but something behind Loretta's eyes darkened. "I'm silent in that boat, too, you know," she said.

The feeling I saw rise in her at that moment was striking in its subdued passion. She had worked at home for years and years, while nursing Colin through his long dying, and yet, for all that, something still sparkled in her, a fierce curiosity.

"And if I never find those words, I feel that I'll live a bit like poor Masha," she said. "Dressed in black, in mourning for my life."

They were dramatic words, of course, but the moment was dramatic, too, I thought, and in its aftermath, as I stepped outside and hailed a cab, it struck me that both for her and for me, what she'd said was true. A man we'd both loved had taken his own life. He had done so alone and had given neither of us a chance to stop him.

There are times when the very earth seems poised to move against us, and at that instant, I recalled Julian at Two Groves, playing croquet with my father, while Loretta and I looked on. He'd hit the ball with both verve and confidence, which had given his game a dead-on accuracy that even then I suspected he would later apply to whatever he chose to do. Upon his inevitable victory, he had leaped into a shimmering summer air that had seemed to embrace him.

How, from so bright a beginning, I wondered, had the world conspired to bring him to so black an end?

2

There are some bridges you cannot cross again, and so your only choice is simply to make the best of the shore you have chosen. And so, in the taxi, heading toward my father's apartment, I concentrated on my life's many satisfactions. The smaller ones, like good food, and the larger ones, like the years I'd had with my wife—comforts that Julian had not found in his youth and later chose not to seek.

For some reason, these thoughts brought to mind a passage from one of Julian's books, his description of Henri Landru. He'd written that the famous French serial killer had begun to talk as his date with the guillotine grew near, even going so far as to make a crude drawing of the kitchen where the bodies had been burned. Death's approach had turned him quite gossipy, Julian said, so that in the last days, Landru had been less the condemned man silently brooding on his crimes than a washerwoman chatting in the market square.

Not so Julian, I thought now, and instantly imagined him alone on the sunporch with his map of Argentina and God only knew what grim thoughts in his mind. Had he, in his last hours, inexplicably returned to the first tragedy that touched him? And if so, why?

There could be no answer to these questions, of course, so rather than pursue a fruitless trail, I drifted through the mundane details of Julian's early life.

He was born upper-middle-class, his father a State Department official who'd been one of my father's closest friends. His mother had died giving birth to Loretta, and after that Julian and his sister had been overseen by a series of nannies. By the time Julian and Loretta were in grade school, James Wells had retired because of a heart condition. A few years later, he'd bought the Montauk farmhouse, in which he had died at age fifty-five.

That death had devastated Julian, and something of his lost father settled over him for many months, a lingering presence, like the ghost of Hamlet's father, which is exactly how Julian once described it. In the wake of his father's death, he seemed ever more determined to make a mark in life. Even so, the space his father had occupied remained empty, a void never filled. "A little boy needs a hero," he once said to me, though without adding what I knew was on his mind, the fact that with his father gone, he'd lost that hero in his own life.

A cautious man, Julian's father had left his two children, Julian, fifteen, and Loretta, twelve, well fixed, mostly by means of a substantial life insurance policy, the proceeds from which had retired the Montauk mortgage. A bachelor uncle had promptly moved into the house and from there attempted to assume the role of father. Boarding school had taken up the remaining slack. College tuitions had later absorbed what was left of the inheritance, so that by the time Julian graduated from Columbia and Loretta from Barnard, only the Montauk house remained.

The surprise in all this was that despite the loss of his father and the rather haphazard and emotionally flat nature of his later upbringing, Julian had emerged with so solid, even sterling, a personal character. He had not received the intense moral education my father had provided for me—his many lectures on charity as the greatest of all virtues, his compassion for the poor and the disinherited, his deathless hope that the meek might one day inherit some portion of the earth. And yet, Julian appeared to have taught himself those very lessons, so that by the time he began to spend summers with me, he seemed already primed to receive the finishing touches of my father's table talk—that is to say, his ancestral tales of men who'd fought under the banner of some universal goodness.

But why was I recounting Julian's personal history? I wondered. What good would it do now?

None whatsoever, of course, and so I had no explanation for this bend in my mind, except that something in my latest exchange with Loretta had set me to considering Julian's life in the way a detective might, as if he were a mystery whose disparate clues I was now trying to puzzle out. No, not a detective exactly, I decided, more like a writer seized by a mysterious purpose: Charles Latimer in *A Coffin for Dimitrios* listening as Colonel Haki describes the nefarious career of a strange Greek swindler, wondering what he really was, this dead Dimitrios, and as he listens, growing slowly, haltingly, and against his own better judgment, ever more determined to find out.

I thought again of the summers Julian had spent at our home in Virginia while Loretta either attended a theater camp in upstate New York or stayed at her aunt's house in Connecticut. Those had been hot, languid days at Two Groves, days of fishing in the pond, canoeing down the river, reading together in the study, or listening as my father talked, mostly to Julian, about having a career in the State Department, one he expected to be very different from his own, Julian more what he called "the James Bond type" than he had ever been.

And this was true enough. There'd been a genuinely dashing quality to Julian. It was easy to imagine him swinging a polo mallet or leaping hedges on a black stallion. He had an ear for classical music and an eye for painting, but even these less muscular attributes did not detract from how very male he was. Both men and women loved him, and that, as my father once noted, cannot be said of many men. Sometimes he reminded me of Sebastian in *Brideshead Revisited*, equally favored by the stars. But Sebastian had lost himself to drink and thus lived his life in a blur of attenuated afternoons. Julian on the other hand was strictly spit-and-polish, ready to work and quick to pitch in, a young man who drank very little and whom I often found alone in our orchard, his back pressed against the trunk of a pecan tree, studying, it seemed, the crazy patchwork of the limbs.

From my great store of memories, I suddenly drew out the one of Julian visiting me at Princeton. It was a memory that lifted me, as if on the swell of some elegiac refrain, then drew me down again like sand in a wave, so that I was once again seated on my dormitory bed, alone, reading, of all things, *A Sentimental Journey*.

"Sterne hated Smollett, you know," Julian informed me as he swung a chair around and sat down before me. "He said his travel writing was all 'spleen and jaundice.'"

Tall and slender, he wore dark, well-pressed pants and a white shirt with both sleeves rolled up to just below the elbow. He'd done his share of sports at school, but what he gave off, more than health and raw competitiveness, was that confident American sense of not only getting what you want, but of getting it easily and, in a way, deservedly, as if it had been awaiting you all along.

"Are you really going to major in English, Philip?" he asked.

I turned to face him. "What's wrong with studying English?"

"Nothing at all," Julian answered. "But your life will be rather sedentary, don't you think?"

And so it had turned out, I thought now, my life just the sort Julian had never contemplated for himself any more than he would have contemplated the darker one that had come to him after Argentina.

After Argentina.

Had it begun there, I asked myself, the downward spiral of Julian's life?

The question brought up one of Julian's abiding themes, the fact that in each life there are confluences, currents, and undercurrents, and that in some swim the Graces—Splendor, Mirth, and Good Cheer—while in others there are surely monsters. So it was in much of Julian's writing, a chance encounter, a hastily spoken word, some idle conversation that might seem of no importance but which, for better or worse, changes a life forever. In *The Tortures of Cuenca*, it is the mundane selling of a lamb that ignites suspicions that ultimately lead to a great crime.

Crime, I repeated in my mind, then cut off any further thought along such lines as the corner of West End and Seventy-eighth Street came into view.

"That awning there," I said. "The blue one."

The cab drifted forward a few more yards, then stopped. I paid and got out. The building's uniformed doorman nodded as he approached. "How's your father?" he asked.

"Holding his own," I answered.

"Give him my regards."

The elevator was old and elegant, all dark paneling and brass, and in that way it struck me as oddly military, a device meant to convey the high command to some tower from which a general could survey the field. Curiously, this thought again returned me to Julian. This time it was his description of Waterloo, the day we'd walked the field together under the unblinking eyes of the Lion Monument. As we walked, he'd recounted the descriptions various travelers had written a few days after the battle, the field littered with bits of white paper, the stationery of two armies. They'd found blood-spattered love letters and letters to children, Julian told me, letters written by hands now severed by flashing sabers and cannon fire, a juxtaposition of images that suggested what his later writing would be like, slaughters, sometimes massive ones, described with a haunting poignancy.

This flash of memory made me briefly wonder if I were becoming a character out of Proust, poor melancholic Swann biting into a madeleine or tripping on an uneven paving stone and by that taste and brief imbalance propelled backward to times past. If so, I felt the need to shake it off, because at a certain point memory becomes a beach strewn with landmines, all life's many losses buried in those sands.

My father was seated by the window, peering down at the rain-soaked street when I stepped into the living room. If he heard the jangle of keys as I entered the apartment, he gave no sign of it. His body remained still, his shoulders squared, his head upright, his eyes flashing with their customary fire.

"You're tardy, Philip," he said.

Tardy was one of those quaint words my father refused to jettison. To do so, he said, would be to surrender language to the whims of mere novelty. It was important to keep old things, he insisted, because it was through them alone that new things could be judged. He said this without rancor, and nothing in his demeanor suggested the crankiness of some old geezer bemoaning the loss of the five-cent cigar. Yet he was someone who fancied himself a defender of ancient values, and he'd often spoken of such things to Julian during those evenings when the two of them smoked cigars and drank port in the library at Two Groves, my father in full Socratic pose, despite the fact that he was hardly a man of great intellect.

But the wish to be wise is almost as valuable in a man as wisdom itself, and so I'd always admired my father's goodness. Julian, more than anyone, had known the depth of my love for him. Once, as the two of us had walked the grounds of Two

Groves, he'd slung a brotherly arm over me. "You're lucky to feel the way you do about your father, Philip," he said to me. "A man needs to revere someone." Years later, in Salzburg, he talked about Mozart's contempt for lesser talents: "A man with no one to revere, Julian said, is a man alone." At that moment, he seemed to consider such loneliness the worst of fates, a sentence he would not have imposed upon the vilest man on earth. And yet, at times, I thought now, he had seemed to impose that very loneliness upon himself.

"So why were you late?" my father asked.

"I was with Loretta," I explained. "We met for a drink."

My father nodded softly. "So sad about Julian. Please give her my best at the service."

He had decided not to attend the upcoming memorial, and given his many aches and pains, I didn't press the issue, since I knew that his arthritis would make the ride to Montauk difficult for him.

"Did you hear what happened today?" my father asked. "More bombings in Europe. It's the price of colonialism. You should never invade another people's country if you don't expect to be invaded in return."

My father had toiled his life away as a State Department bureaucrat, his eyes forever glancing wistfully at the oversized globe he'd hauled from office to office during his long tenure in the old gray C Street building rightly situated, he'd once joked, in an area of the capital known as Foggy Bottom.

"When the Soviet Union fell, I thought we might have a few years of actual peace," he added. He shook his head in grim frustration. "But humanity isn't made for peace. It finds a hundred ways to keep itself riled up."

He'd hoped to devote his life to peace, an ambition that had foundered on the banks of Foggy Bottom at least in part because as a young man he'd made the mistake of joining a few ultraliberal organizations, though that was but the first of many problems that had stymied his career. Succinctly put, he'd had a warm heart during a Cold War, and for that reason he'd been shuttled from desk to desk, his hopes for an appointment that would give him genuine authority forever thwarted by his own fierce feeling that the human interest was larger than the national interest, a view that had won him many friends among the radical reformers of the Third World, but none in Washington.

It was a failure that struck deep, all the more so given that his own forefathers had been robust men of affairs, both soldiers and diplomats. Portraits of those men now lined the walls of his apartment, men in uniforms and formal dress who with equal courage had faced bullets on the field and bullying at the negotiating table.

Given the blighted nature of his career, I'd assumed that retirement would be a good thing for my father, but he hadn't taken to it very well. Certainly, he had not wanted to move to New York, but the last of his old friends had died, and he'd been left alone in his Tidewater house. At last he'd acquiesced to my repeated entreaties for him to move north, where he could enjoy the many diversions of the city, along with the company of his son. Nor did he seem to regret this move, though there were times when the pall of loneliness came over him and he stared out at a skyline he probably found as foreign as the minarets of Cairo.

"So how are you feeling?" I asked.

"Good enough," my father answered.

I glanced at the array of pill containers that sprouted like sickly orange growths from the top of the small, wooden table beside my father's chair. It's not that we grow old, I thought, but that we grow old in decline and discomfort, and these hardships are made worse by the awareness that nothing will improve. No coming days will dawn brighter than the last that dawned, and this sorrow is further deepened by a fear of death—one that I could on occasion see in my father's eyes. Those same eyes had some years before begun to fail, so he had given up reading spy novels and Westerns for watching movies of the same ilk, John Wayne and Gary Cooper the unlikely heroes of his waning years.

"Loretta and I talked about Julian, of course," I said. "She thought he was already planning his next book."

"Already at work on the next one?" my father asked. "I thought he'd just come back from Russia."

"He had, but rest was never Julian's thing," I said. "So, once he'd finished the book on Chikatilo, I suppose he just began to research the next one."

"Chikatilo?" my father asked. "Who is that?"

"A Russian serial killer."

My father shook his head. "I don't know how Julian lived with such people in his head."

"For some people, bad things are alluring, I suppose," I said. "Chekhov went all the way to Sakhalin, and Robert Louis Stevenson—"

"Well, it's unhealthy, if you ask me," my father interrupted with a quick wave of his hand. "Unhealthy to sink into that mire." He leaned forward and massaged one of his knees. "I remember that first summer when Julian came to stay with us. We fished all day, remember?"

I nodded. "Loretta stayed with an aunt that summer. In Chicago."

"But Julian came to Two Groves," my father said. His spirit lifted on a memory. "We took long walks in the orchard."

It was a fine house, to say the least, set upon substantial acreage, but hardly the Tara of *Gone with the Wind* that its grand title suggested. Still, Julian had made considerable sport of Two Groves before his visit there. "We come from houses that have addresses," he would tell some recent acquaintance, "but Philip here comes from TWO GROVES!"

"Julian saved your life that summer," my father added.

I saw him dive cleanly into the water, then swim furiously toward me. I'd tried to swim too far and had exhausted myself. Had Julian not been there, I would most certainly have drowned. Over the years, my father had mentioned this incident many times. Julian, of course, never had.

"Do you think he would have risen to the top at the State Department?" I asked.

"Probably not," my father answered. On that word, his mood abruptly soured. "Well, I should be off to bed now, Philip."

He rose with the help of a cane that was itself a part of his regalia, dark wood, with a brass eagle's head grip. Using it, he stood very erect, and in that proud stance, made his way slowly across the room, I at his side, but careful not to extend my hand or offer any unnecessary physical support. That would come at some point, I knew, but not yet, and as long as my father could make his way without assistance, I let him do so.

We were halfway down the corridor when he stopped and nodded toward a photograph of his father in his doughboy uniform.

"Julian noticed that picture," he said. "It was hanging in the library at Two Groves, and he asked me if my father had ever killed a man. I said he probably had, but that he'd been an artillery officer in the Great War, so he probably never saw the people he killed. I remember that Julian said he thought it must be quite different to kill close up, looking your victim directly in the eye."

"He described just that sort of close-up murder once," I said. "It's in *The Tortures of Cuenca*. He has a sister imagine the killing of her brother, how the murderer must have actually felt her brother's dying breath. On his face, I mean. I remember the phrase he used. He called it 'the last moist breath of life.'"

"Moist," my father whispered. "How would Julian have known that a last breath is moist?"

He moved forward again before he stopped, turned back and looked at me, a glance that alerted me that I'd unaccountably remained behind.

"Are you all right, Philip?" he asked.

"Yes, why?" I asked.

"You look odd, that's all."

I shook my head. "Not at all," I assured him. "I was just thinking of Julian, how deeply he sank into the crimes he described."

"Julian had a lot of feeling," my father said, "but too much of it was morbid."

He turned and made his way into the bedroom, I now at this side. He was already in his pajamas, and so, after taking off his robe, he eased himself into the bed, all of this done without my assistance, but under my watchful eye.

My mind was still on Julian. "He was like Mephistopheles," I said. "He took hell with him wherever he went."

My father waved his hand by way of dismissing such literary notions. He had always been impatient with my bookish talk, bookish ways, bookish life, so different from the one he'd sought but never achieved.

"It's a pity about Julian," he said softly and sadly. "No wife. No children. A wasted life in some ways." He shook his head at the hopeless extent of that waste. "Darkness was the only thing he knew."

3

A man is made by the questions he asks, and I found myself increasingly questioning my father's statement regarding Julian, that he had known only darkness. For I could remember my friend in the bright days of his youth, when he'd gone full speed at life. Like my father, he'd wished to change the world for the better. He'd known about history's many horrors, of course, but he hadn't focused on them. Life had seemed manageable to him then, its evils visible because they were so large: poverty, oppression, and the like. It was against these forces he would take up arms, a young Quixote. He'd been naive, of course, but that had made him genuine. He'd known that he was good, and this had been enough to make him happy.

When the best man you'd ever known, the one you'd loved the most, and of all the people you'd ever known, the one who'd had the greatest capacity for true achievement, when such a man later trudges to a pond, climbs into a boat, rows a hundred feet out into the water, rolls up his sleeves, and cuts his wrists, are you not called upon to ask what you might have said to him in that boat, how you might have saved him?

And if you do not ask this question, are you not, yourself, imperiled?

I would later consider the unsettling tremor I'd felt when I asked myself those very questions. It was as if I'd suddenly felt the bite of a blade, the warmth of my own blood now spilling down my arm.

Outside the building, the doorman was leaning against the wall, smoking a cigarette. "Rain's stopped," he said.

I stepped from beneath the awning and looked into a quickly clearing sky. There were wisps of dispersing clouds, and here and there the flicker of a star, a rare sight in Manhattan.

"Yes, it's quite nice now," I said. "I think I'll walk."

"They've already warned me," the doorman whispered with a sly wink and something vaguely sneering in his voice.

"Warned you?" I asked as if he'd just heard a sinister aside.

"About me smoking," the doorman explained. "The board don't like it when I smoke."

"Oh," I said.

He laughed. "But I do it out in the open, so the union says I can smoke if I want to."

"Yes, of course," I said. "Well, good night."

I walked to Broadway, then turned south, a route I'd taken many times, so the sights of this section of the world's longest street were familiar to me. And yet I felt that something had been minutely altered, and that this change had occurred in some part of me that I'd thought impenetrable since my wife's death, a wound I'd covered with a thick scar tissue that nothing had pierced until now.

Clearly Julian's death, the dread manner and heartbreaking loneliness of it, had opened me up both to questions and to memories, one of which came to me now.

We were in Greece, where Julian had come across the case of Antonis Daglis, the otherwise nondescript truck driver who had murdered several prostitutes. For Julian, such ordinary murderers were of no interest. Tracing their crimes, he said one day while we drank ouzo in an Athens taverna, was like following a shark through murky waters, dully recording that it ate this fish, then that one. It was evil he was after, I could tell, some core twist in the scheme of things.

In the end, Julian found nothing to write about in Greece, but while in the country, we wandered through various remote areas, notably the Mani. He was reading the great travel writer Patrick Fermor at the time, and one night, as we tented on a rocky cliff overlooking the Aegean, he told me about a funeral Fermor had attended in the same area. At the funeral, the dead man's soul had been commended to the Virgin Mary in strict Christian fashion, but a coin had also been placed in his coffin as payment to Charon for ferrying the dead man's soul across the Styx. To this incident Julian added a comment that now echoed through my mind: *All excavations lead to hell.*

Had Julian been clawing toward some fiery pit during those last days in the sunroom? I wondered.

This question, along with the memory that had just summoned it, added to the feeling of unease that was steadily gathering around me, and which I experienced as a shift in the axis of my life or, more precisely, as a faint, somewhat ghostly color added to a spectrum. It was as if Julian's death now called my own life into question, threw it off balance, so that I had to confront the stark fact of how little I had known the man I thought I'd known the most.

On that thought, another memory came to me, this time of Julian and me walking in Grosvenor Square in London. Julian had suddenly stopped and pointed up ahead. "That's where Adlai Stevenson died," he said.

He went on to tell me that Stevenson had been strolling with an acquaintance at the time, feeling old, talking of the war. "How many secrets must have died with him," Julian said.

Had secrets died with Julian, too?

I thought again of the agitation Loretta had noticed in him and that she'd previously described: Julian sleepless, pacing, a man who seemed not so much depressed as hounded. In every way, until that last moment, she told me, Julian had appeared less a man determined to die than one ceaselessly searching for a way to live.

I reached Lincoln Center a few minutes later and, still curiously unready to go directly to my apartment, sat down on the rim of the circular fountain and watched as the last of those bound for the symphony or the theater made their way across the plaza. It was here I'd met Julian a week after we'd graduated from college. He'd already sent in an application to work at the State Department, and I'd expected him to tell me a little more about the ground-level job he hoped to get, but instead he said,

"I want to go somewhere, Philip. Out of the country. And not Europe. Someplace that feels different."

"Where do you have in mind?"

Without the slightest hesitation, he said, "Your father suggested Argentina. He said I should see a country where the political situation is dangerous. Get a feel for what it's like to live in a place where everything is at risk."

I was, of course, aware that Argentina was still in the midst of very dark political repression, and for that reason, if for no other, it hadn't been on my "must-see" list.

"I'm not sure going to Argentina is a good thing," I said. "Or even a safe one."

"Do you always want to play it safe, Philip?"

"Yes," I answered.

"Oh, come on," Julian said. "You have a month before you start your job."

I remained unconvinced.

"Philip, for God's sake," Julian said. "Don't measure out your life in coffee spoons."

His allusion to poor, pathetic J. Alfred Prufrock was clearly meant to shock me into acquiescing to his idea of an Argentine adventure, but now, when I recalled that moment, it was Julian's energy and self-confidence rather than my hesitation that struck me, the sense that he could walk through a hail of bullets and emerge unscathed. He was rather like Aiden Pyle in *The Quiet American*, young and inexperienced in anything beyond the well-ordered life of a privileged American. Julian Wells, conqueror of worlds, shielded by his many gifts, destined for greatness. Like his country, invulnerable.

How quickly all that had changed. All of it. After Argentina.

I knew that in a novel it would be a woman who caused this change. But Julian hadn't fallen in love with the woman we'd met there. Even so, her sudden disappearance had turned our Argentine holiday into a bitter experience, one I'd long ago managed to put behind me, but which had lingered in Julian, so that over the years he often returned to it in our conversation. I thought of the map he'd laid on the little table in the sunroom. In his last hours had he been thinking of Argentina again?

I rose from the fountain and made my way to my apartment.

It was in a prewar building with high ceilings, one of the few such buildings whose upper floors still provided a view of Central Park. Once there, I dropped into a chair and let my gaze roam among the shelves of books that stood across from me until my attention was drawn to where Julian's books were arranged chronologically, beginning with *The Tortures of Cuenca*.

I drew the book from the shelf, opened it, and read the book's dedication: *For Philip, sole witness to my crime.*

The "crime," I always thought, was Julian's decision to write about what had happened in Cuenca, an effort I disparaged at the time because I could see no need to retell a story already well known. It would be a *crime* to waste his time on such a book, I told him, advice he'd obviously not taken, and of which his dedication had been meant to remind me.

31

I'd read this dedication many times, of course, always with a knowing smile, but now it returned me to the brief few days Julian and I had spent together in Cuenca. We'd met in Madrid, where Julian had been living, doing odd jobs, picking up the first of his many languages. We'd then driven around Spain for several days before reaching the town. Our month in Argentina was more than a year behind us by then, but Julian was still laboring under the effects of what he'd experienced there, all of which I'd expected to dissipate in time.

We'd arrived at Cuenca about midday, strolled the town's streets, then taken a table at a small café on the village square. Though a matter of dark renown in Spain, neither of us had ever heard of the crime that had occurred there some seventy years before. As I later discovered, it was briefly mentioned in the guidebook I'd bought in the airport before leaving New York, a book I'd intended to read on the flight but hadn't. In any event, an English-speaking former magistrate had given us the details, an old man who'd claimed to have seen the actual figures in the story—the guards, the prisoners, even the prosecutor.

"No one thought anything about the crime of Cuenca," he said. "I mean, that it would take so strange a turn."

The old man had then gone through the details of what had happened there, a story he told quite well but from which he drew a somewhat banal conclusion.

"So you see, it's quite possible for a person to disappear," he said.

I glanced at Julian and saw that he was deep in thought. "Yes," he said quietly, "It's quite possible."

32

The old man glanced about the village square, his gaze captured by a group of unruly teenagers, all of them speaking in loud voices, heedless of the disturbance they caused.

"*Vivíamos mejor cuando vivía Franco,*" he said, almost to himself, reverting to Spanish. "We lived better when Franco lived." With that he rose, bid us a polite good-bye, and left.

Seconds later, I noticed that Julian's attention was focused on two Guardia Civil lounging at the entrance to one of the town's official buildings, tall and dark, wearing their curiously winged black caps. It was such men as these who'd carried out the tortures of Cuenca, and for a moment Julian simply stared at them quietly.

Then, quite suddenly, a thought appeared to seize him.

"Let's go," he said.

We paid the bill, then rose, and moved along the town's dusty streets. The evening shade was descending, the first lights coming on.

"Someone once said to me that it's not what a man feels before he first wields the whip," Julian said as we closed in on the road that let out of the town, "it's what he feels after it." He stopped and looked at me. "But it's really what the person being whipped feels that matters. Guilt is a luxury, Philip."

I thought of a French painter, James Tissot, the way he'd portrayed the scourging of Christ from different angles, the faces of the men who'd beaten him, obscured in one, revealed in the other.

I described these paintings to Julian, then said, "The guilt of whipping a great man would be terrible."

"Or an innocent one," Julian said.

We continued on, now down the hill and toward the bridge below the town. I kept quiet for a time, but finally made an attempt to lighten the mood that had descended upon us.

"So, when are you coming back to the States?" I asked.

"Never," Julian answered so abruptly that I wondered if he had only just made that stark decision. "At least not to live."

And so there would be no brilliant career? No rising through the ranks of government? He would never be secretary of state? Wild and unreal as those dreams had been, were they truly to be abandoned now?

All of this I voiced in a simple question.

"Are you sure, Julian?"

He stopped and looked at me. "Yes."

His gaze had something in it that chilled me, something I expected him to voice, so that it surprised me when he said nothing more as we descended the slope that led to the river and the bridge.

I was still reliving that long-ago moment when the phone rang.

It was Loretta.

"Harry called," she said.

She meant Harry Gibbons, Julian's editor.

"We've agreed that you should deliver the eulogy at Julian's memorial service," Loretta said.

She repeated what she'd told me earlier: that it was to be a quiet affair, just a few friends and associates.

"Anyway, Harry has a few things you might want to include," she added. "He thought the two of you should discuss it at his office tomorrow afternoon."

"Okay," I said.

A pause, then, "Are you all right, Philip?"

It was the same question my father had asked only an hour or so before, and I gave the same answer. "I'm fine."

"You seem so . . . quiet."

"It's how I grieve, I suppose."

"Yes, I can see that in you," Loretta told me. A brief silence, then, "Well, good night, Philip."

"Good night."

I hung up the phone, glanced down at the book in my lap. *The Tortures of Cuenca* with its stark cover, a drawing of the two hapless victims of that crime huddled in the dusty corner of a Spanish prison, shackled hand and foot, waiting, as they eternally would be in this rendering, for the torturer's approach. I'd found the cover quite disturbing and said so to Julian. He'd replied with the tale of Ned Kelly's execution, how the murderous rogue had stood on his Australian gallows, peered down at the reveling crowd, then turned to the hangman and, with a shrug, uttered his last words. "Such is life."

I peered into the frightened eyes of these baffled and despairing men a moment longer. Had this, in the end, been Julian's only view of life?

I drew my gaze back to the window. The park beyond it was well lighted, as it had always been, a fact that made me wonder why its reaches seemed so much darker to me now.

Darker to me now?

Heavy-handed, I decided, now in critical judgment of my own last thought. Too much foreshadowing. In a novel, as the last line of a chapter, it would make a wary reader groan.

4

"When Bernal Díaz first came with Cortés to the central market in Mexico City, he found little bowls of human feces for sale," Harry said. "They were used in tanning leather, and Díaz said that the tanners were going around sniffing at these bowls to find the very best of the lot."

We were sitting in Harry's office on Sixth Avenue. It was spacious with a large window overlooking the street. From such a vantage point, I thought, you could actually think of yourself as a prince of the city, something Harry clearly did.

"That has always been my view of Julian," Harry continued. "That he was a very fine craftsman who worked with disgusting materials."

"Did you ever tell him that?" I asked.

"Of course not," Harry answered. "It wouldn't have mattered anyway. After that book about Cuenca, Julian never considered writing anything but that grim stuff." He shook his head as if in the face of such repellent work. "Like that African piece."

"The one he wrote about Swaziland," I said. "Yes, that was quite horrifying."

"No, not that one," Harry said. "The one about that French bastard." He shivered. "Julian really made you feel the misery in that one."

He meant Julian's account of Paul Voulet's vicious trek into the African interior.

"But at least that piece had a hero," Harry added.

This was true, and Julian had written quite beautifully of Lieutenant Colonel Klobb, the man who'd gone after Voulet, trailed him from one outrage to the next, an archipelago of razed villages, slaughtered men, women, and children, some still alive when Voulet hung them from trees low enough for the hyenas to eat their feet. Klobb emerged at last as a paragon of courage and nobility, and his death at the hands of Voulet's men generated a final scene of inevitable tragedy, life having once again turned its back upon the good.

Harry leaned back in his chair and folded his hands over a stomach much rounded by Grey Goose martinis. "I was quite shocked by Julian's death, of course," he said. "I suppose you were, too."

I nodded.

Harry drew in a somewhat labored breath and leaned back in his chair. "And so we have seen the last of Julian."

I found myself wary of closing the book on Julian so decisively, suspecting, as Loretta had, that the map of Argentina suggested a project Julian had been considering, but which he had, in the strongest possible terms, decided to abandon.

"Do you have any idea what his next book was going to be about?" I asked.

"No," Harry answered. "He hadn't mentioned any new ideas to me. Why do you ask?"

"He was looking at a map of Argentina," I said. "Loretta told me that this was the way he always began to research his next book."

Harry cocked his head to the right. "Why would the subject of Julian's next book matter now?'

"I don't know that it matters," I admitted. "But he seemed very agitated during those last days, and I can't help wondering what might have been on his mind. I suppose I've come to think of the map as a clue."

"A clue?" Harry asked. "You're a critic, Philip, not a detective. Julian's next book went with him." He clearly saw that I would not be so easily deterred. "All right, look," he said, "I have no idea why Julian was looking at a map of Argentina, but he might have been thinking about a book on Pedro Lopez, the 'Monster of the Andes.' Three hundred little girls, can you imagine?"

"When did this happen?" I asked.

"It may still be happening," Harry answered. "Because this Lopez fiend is still at large. So, maybe—perhaps like you, Philip— Julian had begun to fancy himself a detective, rather than a writer." He released the breath of someone chronically frustrated by an author whose unprofitable direction had never changed. "Now, let's forget about what Julian's next book might have been and focus on what will surely be his last one. He worked his ass off on it, after all, and it's going to be published posthumously, so we need to give it a little push." He looked at me pointedly. "And try not to make the book sound too grim. People don't like reading dark stuff."

"That's too bad," I said. "Because they're missing something."

"Really? What?"

"The gravity of life."

Harry sat back and folded his arms over his chest. "What's bothering you, Philip? Clearly something is."

With Harry's question, the actual nature of what was bothering me came clear for the first time.

"It bothers me that there might have been something Julian never told me," I said, "and that if he had, I might have saved his life."

But this was a notion I couldn't prove, and I had a job to do, so when I got back to my apartment, I considered what I could say at Julian's memorial service that might help him matter, at least in the eyes of those in attendance. It would need to be something unique to Julian, or at least some gift he'd used uniquely.

But what?

I didn't know, and so I let my mind drift toward other aspects of my remarks.

I'd need to mention the Russian book, of course. Harry had been right about that. I knew that people liked anecdotes at memorial services, and this realization allowed my mind to range without limit or direction over the years of my friendship with Julian. But soon I realized that to have such liberty was not altogether helpful in terms of organizing a eulogy, so I began to divide his life into the usual chronological segments: boyhood, early manhood, and the like. This was not helpful either, and in the end I found myself dividing Julian's life into the parts represented by his books. To prepare my talk, I decided to peruse them in hopes of finding something cogent to say about each one. This would allow me to end my talk by giving a plug to the Russian book, Julian's last and as yet unpublished work.

Later that evening, after I'd let time calm my mood a little more, I sat down in my favorite chair and again drew down the first of Julian's books.

The Tortures of Cuenca.

The facts of the crime had been well known long before Julian had written his book, but I'd forgotten most of them, so I took a few minutes to familiarize myself with them again:

On August 21, 1911, a man by the name of José Maria Lopez Grimaldos, twenty-eight, was seen walking alone on the road between Osa de la Vega, a small town, and the nearby village of Tresjuncos in the Spanish province of Cuenca. Grimaldos was known as "El Cepa," which means "the strain," an odd nickname, all but untranslatable, as Julian had noted, but it evidently referred to the fact that Grimaldos was short and something of a dullard, thus, presumably, a "strain" on those who knew him.

On that day in August, Grimaldos had been seen on the road that led from the farm of Francisco Ruiz, where he sometimes worked, to his small house. He never got home, however, and the following day, his sister reported his disappearance to the authorities. Her brother had sold a few sheep on the day of his disappearance, she told them, and at least two men would have been aware that he was in possession of the proceeds from that sale. Their names were Valero and Sanchez, and it just so happened that they had often treated Grimaldos quite badly, ridiculing and bullying him. Was it not possible that they had robbed and killed him, too?

An investigation ensued, with other witnesses also focusing the investigators' attention on Valero and Sanchez, but in the absence of Grimaldos's body or any actual proof of his murder, the case had been closed in September of 1911.

There is no more haunting story than that of an unsolved crime.

Thus Julian had declared in the first line of his first book, and thus it had proved for the Grimaldos family.

Julian's account of their relentless struggle for justice was the best part of the book, and as I read it again, I realized that it was there that Julian had found the beating heart of his narrative. It had not been in the aerial view of Spain with which he'd begun, suggestive though it was of his later sweep. Nor had it been in his meticulous rendering of the Spanish legal system, for that had been overelaborated and had at last grown rather tedious. It had not even been in Julian's rendering of the fierce emotions that had seethed beneath Cuenca's monochromatic landscape.

According to Julian, those emotions had been unearthed not only by the haunting nature of an unsolved crime, but because, for the people of Cuenca, all mysteries had to be solved, else demons would rule the world.

Armed by their unwavering faith, the Grimaldos family had refused to forget poor, lowly El Cepa. Holding him in their memory and seeking justice for his murder became their sole obsession, a work of the soul carried out in countless acts of remembrance, El Cepa the persistent subject of their daily conversation. But Julian had also recorded the family's endless chores—planting and harvesting, sweeping, washing, trudging to the well and back again, the backbreaking work their bodies had endured even as their minds continued to be ceaselessly tormented by their brother's vanishing—and with each day they grew more convinced that Valero and Sanchez, still their neighbors and men they saw each day, had murdered him.

They watched and waited, and in 1913, when a new judge was appointed over Cuenca, they seized the moment and drew their swords again, now hopeful that the earlier judge's dismissal of the case against Valero and Sanchez for lack of evidence might be overturned.

The new judge was young and zealous, and the specter of an unsolved crime, as Julian wrote, worked like a rattle in his brain.

Valero and Sanchez were rearrested, and this time the Guardia Civil was determined that the killing of José Maria Lopez Grimaldos, as well as the obvious torment it had caused his family, would not go unavenged.

The torture inflicted upon Valero and Sanchez was hideous, and Julian's account of it was highly detailed. Initial reviews of the book had noted, not always approvingly, the graphic nature of his description, but reading it now, I was struck by the fact that Julian had written of those torments through the eyes of the men who'd suffered them. In Cuenca, I had told him about a painting of men scourging Christ, the expressions on their faces as they'd tormented him. Julian had placed his emphasis on the suffering of the victims, and in reading it again, I found

THOMAS H. COOK

myself admiring how he made the lashes fly so that I heard their crack and felt their terrible bite as if entirely encased within the very flesh they tore.

Had this been Julian's greatest gift, I wondered, that he had been able to describe with such terrible depth, wounds he had neither felt himself nor inflicted upon another?

I wasn't sure, but for my little talk at Julian's memorial ceremony, it would have to do.

5

"It wasn't Julian's hard work that made him singular," I said. "Nor was it even the depth of his research. It was the way he made the reader feel the sting of the lash, the blunt force of the truncheon, the point of the knife. His books are the echoing cries of those whom time has silenced. He never turned away from pain, or cheapened it, or added to it the slightest degree of false amelioration. The purpose of an artist is to convey the harder truths so that we may understand them and learn from them and be less baffled by life. This is what Julian did because he was an artist."

Thus, with a thud, my little talk ended.

The people assembled beneath the white tent Loretta had had erected on the lawn of the Montauk house had listened respectfully, but they were clearly happy I was done. They'd thought me a windbag, I knew, and a boring one at that.

I glanced to the left, where the pond winked in the light, the yellow boat beside it.

I had failed Julian once again.

I recalled Harry's request for a plug.

"*The Commissar*, Julian's study of Andrei Chikatilo, will be published next fall," I added. "I hope you all will read it."

I waited a beat, added the required "Thank you," then stepped away from the lectern.

I was the last to speak, so the people now rose and made their way out of the tent and into the house, where Loretta had food and wine waiting for them. I trailed after the group, but stopped at the entrance of the tent and glanced back toward the lectern. Loretta had placed large photographs of Julian to the right and left of where I'd just spoken. The one to the right was of Julian standing in the snow, the great wall of the Kremlin rising behind him. In the photograph he wore a huge overcoat and an *ushanka*, a Russian fur cap with large flaps to cover the ears. In one of his letters, Julian had informed me that *ushanka* meant literally "ear cap." This had been typical of Julian. He'd known the word for the hippopotamus skin whip with which the Belgians had flayed open the backs of the Congolese, *chicotte*, and the word for the labyrinthine mines dug in search of water in the Sahara, *foggara*—words that had given his books a rare authenticity.

"Good job, Philip."

I turned to find Harry standing next to me, grinning cheerfully, clearly long past our difficult last encounter.

"And thanks for plugging the Russian book," Harry added. "Loretta finally sent it to me. It's pretty strange."

"In what way?" I asked.

"In that Julian focused on Chikatilo's fantasies," Harry said. "The way he assumes the part of a patriot when he kills these kids. They were spies. They were traitors. They had to be destroyed to protect Mother Russia." He glanced toward the house and now clearly wanted to push this unpleasantness aside. "So, you coming?" he asked.

"In a minute," I said, then turned back toward the front of the tent, my gaze now focused on the photograph to the left of the lectern.

I had no trouble placing the photo, of course. I'd taken it when we were in Buenos Aires, the Río de la Plata behind him, the two of us about to take a boat to Montevideo with our guide. I'd left Argentina a week later, but Julian had stayed on.

For the first time in a long time, I thought of the grave purpose that had kept Julian in Argentina, the many leads he'd followed, the growing sense of futility as each led nowhere. He had looked everywhere, but had failed to find her. Had he been thinking of that failure while he studied the map of Argentina on that last day? Had he still been thinking of it as he later walked to that little yellow boat?

Loretta had thrown open the windows of the sunroom, and I could hear the white noise of muffled voices, along with the strains of Mahler's *Kindertotenlieder,* which Julian had first heard at Two Groves and he later called the saddest music in the world.

For the next hour or so I mingled with the guests, most of whom were friends of Loretta's who'd come to pay their respects to her departed brother but hadn't actually known Julian.

By evening everyone had left, so Loretta and I sat alone, still in the sunroom but no longer in the sun. Loretta lit a few candles. They aged the air to a pale yellow, rather than turning the atmosphere romantic. But this perception, I thought, was actually a misperception, a little elegiac twist of mind.

"Julian liked candles," she said as she poured herself a scotch. "Scotch for you, too, Philip?"

"No, I still have a little wine," I said.

While Loretta poured herself a drink, I let my eyes roam the bookshelves that lined the adjoining room, the library she'd built some years before. They were filled with books on every imaginable subject, and in that way they suggested the range of Loretta's mind. For most of her life she'd worked as a freelance copy editor while taking care of her son, Colin, who had died at sixteen from the degenerative disease he'd been born with and which had slowly removed first his ability to stand, then to walk, then to speak, and at last, to breathe. Her husband had left her not long after Colin's birth, and after that, she'd moved into the Montauk house.

"Did Harry give you Julian's latest?" she asked as she took a seat across from me.

"No, but he's sending it to me."

Loretta lifted her glass. "Well, to Julian's last book," she said.

A thought occurred to me. "Do you have the map?" I asked. "The one Julian was looking at before he died?"

"Of course," Loretta said.

"May I see it?"

She gave me a quizzical look, then got to her feet, walked over to a nearby table, and drew the map from one of its drawers.

"Argentina, like I said," she said, handing it to me.

I took the map from her and unfolded it.

"What are you looking for?" Loretta asked.

"I'm not sure," I admitted.

I did not have to be Sherlock Holmes to see that Julian had focused his attention quite narrowly on a small area of Argentina, the sparsely populated region tucked near the conjoining borders of Paraguay and Brazil, very near the great falls at Iguazú. In pencil, he'd traced a route from the falls to the small village of Clara Vista, which he'd circled, and which lay just across the Paraguayan border. It was a town I'd never heard of and we hadn't visited it during our trip to Argentina.

"He may simply have been reminiscing," Loretta said. "It wasn't all bad, his time in Argentina. He always described Buenos Aires as quite beautiful. And, of course, there was that guide who so impressed him."

I glanced up from the map and for the first time in many years, said her name.

"Marisol."

Loretta nodded softly. "By the way, I called René today," she said.

She meant René Brossard, who had served in one way or another as Julian's assistant, first as his French interpreter, then by means of small tasks, collecting his mail and paying the bills on the apartment in Paris during the long periods when Julian was away.

"I'd already told him about Julian, of course," Loretta said. "But today I told him that I wanted him to have something of Julian's. Just a little token. His pen."

"I'm sure René will appreciate that."

"And I have something for you," Loretta said.

With that, she rose and left the room. I heard her footsteps as she made her way up the stairs to the little room that had been Julian's office.

She came back down the stairs a few minutes later, carrying an old leather briefcase.

"It was Julian's one true traveling companion," she said as she handed it to me. "It went all over the world with him."

The briefcase was old and discolored, its seams frayed here and there, and it gave off a powerful sense of Julian's life, how he'd lived it like a man on the run.

"Thank you, Loretta," I said as I took it from her. "I will treasure it, believe me."

Later, back at my apartment, I put Julian's briefcase beside my reading chair, then picked up *The Tortures of Cuenca*, determined, perhaps as a final act of homage to my best friend's life and work, to finish it before going to bed.

Under torture, Valero and Sanchez had confessed to killing José Grimaldos and destroying his body. Oddly, they'd been unable to designate where his body lay, a fact, as Julian noted, that should have called their confessions into question, but which, in a strange reversal, had served instead as further evidence of their guilt:

> *Valero and Sanchez had refused to locate the body because the death of Grimaldos had been long and terrible, so the town believed. They had refused because, once unearthed,*

*Grimaldos's body would reveal what had been inflicted
upon it while poor, bullied El Cepa had still lived: a body
beaten, slashed, burned, with eyes plucked out and ears cut
off, with knees bashed and fingers severed, and everywhere,
everywhere, sliced-away flaps of skin. So runs the imagina-
tion, as greater guilt is made certain by the uncertainty
of the evidence. By this means, the lack of a body merely
deepened the crime of Cuenca, multiplied its offense, and
made Grimaldos's murder yet more cruel, sprouting new
snakes from Medusa's head.*

For these many crimes, the prosecuting attorney asked for
the death penalty, but the case dragged on through the labyrinthine chambers of the Spanish judicial system, until, in 1918,
the accused were at last sentenced, each to eighteen years.

They were released six years later, and two years after that,
in the spring of 1926, as Julian wrote, "poor, bullied El Cepa, so
long assumed hideously murdered, suddenly appeared."

He had been living in a nearby village all those many years,
and in the final passage of his book, Julian takes his readers from
the eagle-eye roost of the Casas Colgadas, over the twining river
and scrub brush and the bare rocks of the plain, then eastward,
toward the coast, along the shabby roads of rural Spain, on and
on, until he brings them to the flowered streets of Valencia and
at last into the shadowy interior of a small kiosk, where . . .

*. . . during the last years of his life, El Cepa, the unmur-
dered, toiled in his tiny, suffocating space, remembering or*

not the dusty streets of Cuenca, and selling lottery tickets for life's least deadly game of chance. And thus did he remain, El Cepa, still undead, but locked in the casket of his booth, and with each hot breath, struggling in that darkness to outlive his crime.

I closed the book and recalled that when I'd first read it all those many years ago, I'd found nothing particularly striking in that final passage. For that reason it seemed strange to me that these same stark words now quite inexplicably moved me. For here was Julian's sense of life's cruel randomness, life a lottery upon whose uncontrollable outcome everything depended, how because this streetcar stopped on this particular corner at this particular moment, nothing for this particular human being would ever be the same.

But was this all that was to be found at the end of Julian's first book?

I considered all the books and articles that had followed *The Tortures of Cuenca,* a life's work whose dark subject matter I had always laid at the foot of some mental oddity little different from the obsession of stamp collectors or people who grow orchids.

Loretta had once said that Julian's books always ended like the tolling of a bell. But had that really been his concluding mood? Or was it rather, as it seemed at the end of *The Tortures of Cuenca,* a sense of life as a grim trickster whose cruel twists and turns none of us can avoid.

I closed the book, then, on impulse opened it again, this time to the dedication Julian had written so many years before:

For Philip, sole witness to my crime. I had always thought this entirely tongue-in-cheek. But now, given the life that had subsequently come to my friend, and the terrible way by which he'd ended it, I couldn't help but wonder if this strange dedication, haunting as it seemed to me now, pointed to some different, darker, and perhaps still-unsolved crime.

I recalled the final passage once again, my mind now focused on its concluding line: *to outlive his crime.*

In the book's dedication I'd been singled out as the sole witness to Julian's crime, but I could think of no such offense, no crime I'd ever witnessed. But had there been one that I hadn't recognized or discovered, a crime that Julian, too, had struggled to outlive but failed?

PART II
The Eyes of Oradour

6

"I can't stop thinking about Julian," I told Loretta.

She'd come into the city as she always did on the anniversary of her son's death. He'd loved Central Park, and during the earlier stages of his illness, before he'd been confined to a wheelchair, they'd sometimes come here to sit and watch passersby, and even from time to time, when he'd still been able to do it, to stroll around the pond, as Loretta and I were now doing.

"It feels like I'm always in the presence of an unquiet ghost," I added as we walked over to a nearby bench and sat down.

"Well, he was unquiet, that's for sure," Loretta said. "Usually he came home quite tired, but this time was different. It was as if some vicious little animal were clawing around inside him."

I glanced out into the park, where scores of strollers were making their way along its deeply shaded paths. "My mind keeps bringing things to the surface. Little bits of memory that swirl and coalesce and pick up other little bits."

She clearly saw the troubling aspect of this. "What little bits?" she asked.

"That dedication in his first book, for example," I said. "That I was the 'sole witness' to his crime." I shrugged. "I don't remember witnessing any crime. I thought he meant his writing of the book, which I'd advised against. But now, I'm not so sure that that's the 'crime' Julian meant."

This last remark clearly connected to something in Loretta's mind.

"You know, it's strange, but for all the dreadful acts Julian wrote about, I don't think he ever witnessed a crime of any sort." Her gaze drifted over to one of the great gray stones of the park, children scooting down its smoothly rounded surface. "I wonder how he would have reacted if he'd ever actually seen an atrocity like the one at Oradour." She looked at me. "Psychologically, he might not have been able to survive it. Primo Levi killed himself, remember? Tadeusz Borowski, too."

"But they were the victims of a great crime," I reminded her. "Not people who had done some awful thing. They didn't die of guilt. They died because they were unable to bear the suffering they'd seen."

"Well, Julian had certainly seen plenty of suffering," Loretta said. "But I don't think that was the source of his agitation."

"Then what was?" I asked.

Loretta remained silent for a time, thinking something through. Then she said, "Julian and I were sitting in the yard at Montauk a few days before he died. I looked over at him. Looked closely at his face. There were these deep lines. And his eyes looked sunken. I said, 'You know, Julian, the crimes you've written about are carved into your face.'"

Loretta was right. Julian's features did seem to bear the imprint of Cuenca and Oradour, the castle ruins of Brittany and Čachtice, the bleak wastes of the Ukraine.

"His response was strange," Loretta said. "He said, 'No, only the one I'll never write about.'"

As if once again on that rainy street, I saw Julian turn up his collar, pull down his hat, and wave me under the awning of a small store on Avenida de la Republique. He'd grasped my arm fiercely, then asked if I'd heard from Marisol."

"Do you suppose it could have been Marisol's disappearance?" I asked. "I mean, he was looking at a map of Argentina, after all."

"I suppose that could have been the crime," Loretta said.

"But what would keep him from writing about that?" I asked.

Loretta's look reminded me of a fictional detective in some old noir classic.

"Did Julian love her?" she asked.

"No," I answered. "He cared for her, certainly. But he didn't fall in love with her."

"Did you?"

"No," I said.

With that answer, I heard Marisol's voice again: *Our time on earth is divvied out like stolen things, a booty of nights and days.*

"But there was something compelling about her," I added.

"That Julian saw?"

"Yes, of course," I said. "And he did everything he could to find her. But people simply vanished in those days."

Vanished, yes, I thought, but why had she vanished? For me, this had always been the mysterious part of Marisol's disappearance, that it had remained so thoroughly unaccountable. Her body had never been found, and thus it was unlikely that she'd been the victim of an ordinary murder. But neither would she have been a likely target of the country's political repression. What had she done, after all, except work as a guide and study dress design and occasionally express some opinion about a writer or a style of dance? Of all the people I had ever known, she had seemed to me the most innocent.

"The thing about Marisol," I said, "is that she wasn't at all political. She was smart and ambitious, a hard worker. She had a way about her, a knowingness, but in every other way, there were thousands like her in Buenos Aires at that time."

"Thousands who were like her but who didn't disappear," Loretta said.

I nodded. "Yes."

With that answer, there seemed little to do but change the subject.

"Anything more from René?" I asked.

"Yes," Loretta said. "An e-mail, if you can believe it. I never met him, but Julian's description didn't suggest a man who's ever been computer savvy." She looked somewhat puzzled. "He wasn't at all surprised by Julian's death. That he killed himself. René likes to use English phrases. He said Julian was 'a burned-out case.'"

Suddenly, I felt somewhat like one myself, a man who'd lost his wife to disease and his friend to suicide, both irreplaceable, a childless man whose father would soon be passing, a man with a small apartment who practiced a dying profession.

I tried to shrug off the darkness that settled over me with these thoughts. "So, what else did René say?"

"He wanted to know what he should do with Julian's stuff," Loretta answered. "Whatever he had in his apartment."

The thought of René rifling through Julian's possessions struck me as profoundly wrong. Should it not be someone else, someone close to Julian, who did this? These were the personal possessions of a very private person, after all, a man I'd loved and whose work I'd admired and with whom I'd traveled some small portion of the world.

"Would you mind if I did it?" I asked Loretta.

She leaned back slightly. "You mean go to Paris?"

I nodded. "René will just throw everything into the garbage," I said. "And somehow that just doesn't seem the right end for Julian's things."

Loretta smiled softly. "You truly loved him, didn't you?" she asked.

A fierce emotion stirred in me.

"I did, yes," I said. "And more than anything, Loretta, I wish I could have been with him in that little boat."

"I'm going to Paris," I told my father the next day.

The two of us were sitting at the small breakfast table over morning coffee.

"I need to go through Julian's things," I added.

It surprised me that in response to this, my father abruptly sank directly back to his own past.

"I never got to travel much in my job," he said quietly, then drew in a long breath and released it slowly, "but I did find myself at the Nile Hotel once. In Kambala. Idi Amin was still in power in those days."

Something in his recollection of that time clearly pained him, but he faced it bravely and went on.

"Everybody knew that Amin had several suites in the hotel," he said. "Some were for his whores. Others were torture chambers."

It was the latter rooms he appeared to visualize now, and I found myself seeing them, too: walls splattered with dried blood, a straight-back chair, a naked lightbulb hanging from a black cord, a metal table fitted with drains. Hell is not other people, I thought, in opposition to Sartre's famous line; it is what we do to other people.

"I was at the hotel when he put Archbishop Luwum on trial there," my father continued. "I tried to get my superiors to intervene, but they said it was none of our affair, and besides, dreadful as Amin was, he was no different from others. 'The Africans don't have presidents,' one of them told me. 'They have chiefs.' Mobutu said that, too, by the way, as justification for his own slaughters." He shrugged. "Well, Amin charged Luwum with smuggling guns, if you can believe that, and tried him out in the open, African-style, in the courtyard of the hotel. He'd filled the place with his rabble of soldiers. They were drinking whiskey and chewing khat, and they kept screaming, 'Kill him!

Kill him!' Luwum just stood there, not saying a word, just staring that fat, whoremongering Kakwa thug right in the eye." His gaze intensified and bore into me. "That's what Julian should have looked for and written about, Philip," he said. "Men like Luwum. Men who were doing some good in the world."He shrugged. "Julian's tragedy is that he only looked at the dark side, and it weakened him and made him sick."

My father had never indicated such qualms about Julian's work, so it had never occurred to me that he thought it so misdirected.

"In my opinion, it's the good people who deserve to be written about," he added softly.

This called into question the whole of Julian's work, how relentlessly dark it had been. I recalled an article on bastinado he'd once written, the beating of the feet, its different names, *falanga*, *falaka*, where and when it had been practiced, and with what instruments. He'd even meticulously described the physical structure of the feet, the large number of small bones, the nerves that cluster in the soles, how painful it must be to suffer such assault.

My father shrugged. "But that was Julian," he said in a way that made it clear he had no intention of dwelling further on the grim nature of his books. "So you'll be going away."

"For a little while," I said. "But I'll stay in touch. With Skype, we can even see each other. And if anything . . . comes up, I can fly back in no time."

"Of course," my father said, though he was clearly reticent to see me go, feeling vulnerable as old people inevitably do.

"I have to do this, Dad," I said.

My father smiled, then reached over and touched my hand. "I can see that," he said. Something inexpressibly sad drifted into his eyes. "It's a good thing to have a mission."

I considered all the futile missions my father had undertaken. He'd worked for fresh water in lands ravaged by cholera, for regional clinics in jungle redoubts, for irrigation in regions made barren by drought. In every case, as he'd long ago admitted, he'd been thwarted by the "big picture" at the State Department, global strategies of containment, domino theories, the specter of mutually assured destruction.

"Yes," I said, then changed the subject, and for the next hour or so we talked of old films he'd watched on television lately. In addition to Westerns and spy movies, he'd begun to watch the noir movies of the forties, Humphrey Bogart and Alan Ladd, and when he spoke of them I could hear a strange longing in his voice, his old desire to be a man of action still pursuing him and accusing him and tainting his memory with failure.

"Do you want to watch a movie?" I asked in hopes of stopping the downward slant of his mood.

"No," my father answered. He seemed to go deep inside himself, then return slowly, like a diver resurfacing. "It's the dusty people, Philip, too small for us to notice," he said, "the little dusty people who bear the brunt of our mistakes."

His mood was quite obviously descending, so I gently urged him toward his youth, and for the next few minutes he talked rather nostalgically about his own father, then his college years, then about my mother, who, like my own wife, had died before her time.

"You should be getting home now," he said at last. "I could go on for hours."

"Yes, I probably should," I said.

My father looked like one who'd once been offered a mission not unlike my own, but had either refused it or failed to achieve it. "Good luck," was all he said.

7

There is no substitute for meaning, and the luckiest of us are those who have felt the spur of a grave commitment. I couldn't possibly include myself among the men who hung in dark frames from the walls of my father's apartment. They had been warriors and diplomats, and a few, as my father had once reluctantly admitted, had been spies. I knew that my own life would never be as charged with mission as theirs. Even so, that map of Argentina, the grim fact of Marisol's disappearance, and finally Julian's curious mention of some crime I had witnessed—*his* crime—had joined together to provide a purpose to my going to Paris that was larger than any I had known in a long time.

This purpose was still in my mind when I got back to my apartment.

I poured a glass of brandy, took my usual seat at the window, and looked out over the park, a glance into the night that loosened the bonds of recollection, and took me back to Berlin with Julian more than twenty years before.

He'd gone there in an effort to track down and interview some of the surviving German soldiers who had massacred the

villagers of Oradour-sur-Glane in June of 1944. He had decided
to write an account of this atrocity, and on the train from Paris
to Berlin, he'd gone through its terrible details.

He was twenty-seven at the time, and although we had regu-
larly exchanged letters, it had been well over a year since I'd seen
him. By then, a certain texture had been added to him by his
travels and his studies, and his voice bore a gravity that I associated with the knowledge and experiences he had accumulated
since last we'd met.

"So, how is the new book coming?" I asked him.

"Oradour is hard to write about," he said.

His eyes were still blue, but their shade seemed deeper,
though I doubt their color had actually changed. Still, there was
an incontestable depth in those eyes, something that spoke of
the charred village whose tragedy he had chosen as the subject
of his next book.

"Yes, it was terrible what happened at Oradour," I said.

"I don't mean that it's hard to write about in that way,"
Julian said. "It's that there's a kind of voyeurism involved, a
peep-show quality."

I looked at him, puzzled, and at that instant, the train entered a tunnel that threw us into shadow, so that we sat in silence,
rumbling on, until the train passed out of the darkness and we
were bathed in light again.

Something in Julian's face had changed. It was as if, during
the brief darkness of the tunnel, some other, deeper darkness
had fallen upon him.

"The pain of others should not be made thrilling," he said softly. "There should be no intellectual sadism in reading about Oradour."

Had that been the moment when it first occurred to him to write his book as he'd later written it? I wondered now.

One thing was clear: In *The Eyes of Oradour,* Julian had focused exclusively on the victims, all 642 of them, each given a single page to bear witness, a kind of *Spoon River Anthology* for the members of that murdered village. That was the magisterial oddity of the book, the way Julian had managed to see the massacre through the eyes of those who'd suffered it. To write of the atrocity at Oradour in so strange a way had been a brave choice, and at times—when a little girl used her own body to shield her doll from the attack, for example—he had brought a heartrending vividness to the victims' deaths.

But in that same narrative, he'd refused to name either the men who ordered the massacre or those who carried it out. Even as unnamed figures, the Germans are glimpsed only at quick moments when the crowd breaks and the back of a soldier, or perhaps only a boot or uniformed leg, is glimpsed in what amounts to a photo flash. At other times the soldiers are disembodied voices, shouting commands or gently deceiving the villagers of Oradour as to their real intent. In other instances, they appear only as the blurry hint of a figure, a brushstroke of helmeted gray.

On the whole, I thought the book extraordinarily accomplished, worthy of the many years it had taken Julian to write it, though a few reviewers had complained that he had concealed the methodical human agency behind the massacre too much, making the innocent of Oradour seem less like the victims of actual cruelty than of the touching down of a storm.

At the time, even though I greatly admired the book, I also thought this criticism not altogether unfair. It was a monumental crime, after all, and Julian had determinedly concealed the men who had carried it out.

Why had he done that?

We were sitting on a bench behind the great library on Fifth Avenue when I posed that very question. It was winter, and we were both wrapped in our overcoats. It had snowed the day before, and the bare limbs of the trees were laced in white. Julian remained silent for a long time before explaining why he hadn't identified any of the German soldiers. "They deserve to be forgotten," he said, as if shielding the murderers had been one of the book's metaphorical devices. "It's the innocent who deserve to be remembered."

"But don't you think the perpetrators need to be remembered, too?" I asked.

He turned to me and something in his eyes told me that this was a subject that pained him.

"What would be the point of telling some little boy that on a particular day, in a particular place, his father was complicit in a terrible crime?" he demanded. "What good would come of it?"

"But otherwise the father would get away with it," I

answered. "And a man who does a terrible thing should be identified."

Julian gave no response, so I hammered home the point.

"Like whoever killed Marisol," I added because the unsolved crime of her disappearance suddenly occurred to me. "He got away with it."

One of Julian's gloved hands wrapped around the other. "Yes," he muttered.

He seemed so abruptly moved by the mention of Marisol that I quickly added, "You did your best to find her, Julian."

Then, to change the subject, I glanced at the book peeking out from the pocket of his coat.

"What are you reading?" I asked. He drew the book from his pocket and I looked at the title, quite surprised by what I saw.

"Eric Ambler, I see. So, you're reading spy fiction now?"

"It helps to pass the time," Julian said.

"Betrayal and false identities," I said jokingly. "People who are not what they appear. Thrilling stuff," I added with a laugh, "but not the stuff of great literature."

"You might be surprised," Julian said softly. "Life is a shadow game, after all."

I absently opened the book and saw that he'd underlined its most famous line. "It's not who fires the shot," I read, "but who pays for the bullet."

He removed the book from my hands and returned it to his pocket. "It helps to pass the time," he repeated. "And I don't read Borges anymore."

Borges, I thought, and felt the dust of the Chaco settle over us once again, a place I'd never seen, but which our guide had called home.

Borges.

A sure sign, I knew, that Julian's mind remained on Marisol.

8

In the great tales, she is always beautiful, of course, the one whose loss torments a man. Since Helen walked the ramparts of Sparta and equally dazzled the men of two opposing armies, we have given little value, in literature at least, to a plain-looking girl.

That is not to say that Marisol was plain, but simply to say that she was by no means a dazzling Helen or a fiery Antigone. She was Cordelia, the loyal daughter of King Lear, quiet, modest, motionless at her center, a pendulum at rest.

She came into the lobby of the hotel like a small breeze off the pampas, the sort that barely moves the grasses.

"I am Marisol," she said in her softly accented English. "I am pleased to meet with you." Her eyes were black, but striking, and her skin brown, but with a golden undertone, so that in a certain light, as Julian once observed, she seemed carved from a muted amber.

A week before, my father had contacted the American consulate in Buenos Aires, and someone in that office had recommended Marisol as a guide. She was fluent in English, according to the consulate, and others had been satisfied with her services. With a slightly comic edge, my father had added that Marisol had been properly vetted by the consulate, which meant, of course, that she was no female Che Guevara.

On that first morning, she wore a dark gray skirt that fell just below the knee, with a matching jacket. Her blouse was white, with a tailored collar, and she wore it open at the throat. The shoes were black and well polished, with a modest, business-like heel. But such gestures toward urbanity did not conceal the depth of her indigenous roots. These were in the oval shape of her eyes and the width of her nose and the black panther sheen of her hair. Europe had made no invasion of her blood. For that reason one sensed in her, as I'm sure Julian did, a strange and unconquerable purity.

"I welcome you to Buenos Aires," she added with a quick smile.

Where many of the women of the city wore a crucifix on a gold or silver chain, Marisol wore a simple string of wooden beads. From the beginning, Julian said, there was a no-nonsense quality about her, something steady, down-to-business, and in a way profoundly conservative, a brick in the sturdy wall, as he would later write of those who resist the excesses of revolutionary fervor, that slows the violent winds of change.

Julian offered his hand. "I'm Julian Wells, and this is Philip Anders."

"*Un placer*," Marisol said as she shook our hands. "I will teach you a little Spanish while you are here." She gave each of us an evaluating glance. "That is okay?"

"Absolutely," Julian told her. "Right, Philip?"

"Of course."

She swept her arm toward the entrance to the hotel. "Come then. There is much to see in Buenos Aires."

The day's tour began with a long walk that took us from Casa Rosada all the way to La Boca, by which Marisol hoped, as she said in one of her rare misuses of English, "to integrate us."

She was a woman of extended silences, I noticed, and she said very little as we walked the streets of La Boca, looking at its brightly colored houses. It was as if she understood that quiet observation was the key to knowing a place, perhaps even the key to life. In any event, she was careful to allow space for standing, sitting, seeing, so that we never felt rushed. Nor did she engage in the guidebook patter that can be so annoying. Marisol, as I would come to understand, was a shaded pond, calm and unruffled.

By evening we had found our way back to the hotel. The restaurant, Marisol said, had a good reputation, though she had never eaten there.

We took a table outside. It was early evening, that twilight interval between a city's working day and its nocturnal life.

"By the way, where are you from?" Julian asked her at one point.

"I was always moving between Argentina and Paraguay," Marisol answered. "I crossed this border many times as a child."

"Why?" I asked.

"When my mother died, I was sent to my father in Paraguay," Marisol answered. "At this moment, my father died, and I was sent to an aunt back in Argentina. When she was also dying, she took me to a priest, and it was this man who cared for me."

The priest had lived in a part of northern Argentina that bordered on the Gran Chaco.

"It is very dry, with nothing, and for many years no one cared about it," Marisol informed us. "Then they found oil."

It was the struggle to possess this oil that had generated the Chaco War, she said, a conflict that had been unimaginably brutal.

"They died in great numbers, the soldiers," she said. "So much sickness, and no doctors. You have not heard of it, this war?"

"No," Julian answered.

Marisol didn't seem surprised. "We are unknown to you, we who live down here," she said. "To you, we are fallen off the earth."

A silence settled over her, both somber and serene, from which emerged what seemed to be the central hope she had for her people, their one quite justified aim.

"All we want is a fighting chance," she added softly.

Then her eyes abruptly brightened and she was our professional guide again.

"You must have a taste of Argentina," she said. "Of our wine. It is called Malbec, and the difference in taste between the cheap and the not cheap, it is not so big." She smiled softly, but it seemed an actress's smile. "You will like it, I think. But just in case, you should order the cheap one."

Only once more during that day did Marisol again leave her role as cheerful, uncomplicated guide. It was in answer to Julian's question about her feelings concerning the current state of Argentina, then in the final throes of its Dirty War.

In response, Marisol's gaze grew tense. "Here we say that Argentina *es un país perdido,*" she said softly. "A lost country." She shrugged. "And we have another saying. A funny answer when we are asked how we are doing." She glanced about to make sure she could not be heard, then whispered, "*Jodido pero contento.*"

"What does that mean?" I asked.

She was suddenly hesitant. "I do not wish to be vulgar."

"Oh, come on, Marisol," Julian said. "We're all adults here."

"Okay," she said, then laughed. "It means 'screwed but happy.'"

We parted at around nine that evening, then met again the next morning, mostly for a tour of various museums, during which Marisol was very much the professional guide, talking of this artist or that one in the fashion of a museum brochure. There were also walks along the canals, a visit to Teatro Colón, Buenos Aires's famed opera house. Our third day involved a ferry to Montevideo followed by a boat ride to the estuary where the Germans had scuttled the *Graf Spee* in December of 1939. Marisol was surprisingly knowledgeable and knew the exact coordinates beneath which the doomed vessel lay.

"The English tourists like to come here," she told Julian by way of explanation. "Sometimes the Germans, too. So I discovered where it is and we are now exactly at this place." She smiled brightly. "Knowing such a thing makes me a better guide, no?"

On the fourth day Marisol took us to the cemetery in Recoleta.

"This is a very quiet place," Marisol said as she led us beneath the dazzlingly white arched entrance.

For a time we wandered silently among the mausoleums, moving slowly, but without a stop, until we reached Evita's tomb.

"Eva Perón was a poor girl," Marisol said softly when we paused before it. "Just another poor girl from Los Toldos."

"Would you have voted for her?" Julian asked.

Marisol shrugged. "Now there is no voting here," she said. "It is only between two bad things that we must choose." She peered at the small plaque attached to the tomb. "Sometimes, when I bring the people here, I tell them what Borges said about life," she went on. "This adds to me as a guide."

"What did Borges say?" Julian asked.

Marisol, honest to the quick, said, "The English, it is not my translation."

"Still, I'd like to hear it," Julian insisted.

Marisol summoned this translation that was not hers, then said, "Okay, Borges said: 'Our time on earth is divvied out like stolen things: a booty of nights and days.'"

Her eyes darkened slightly, and then, as if by an act of will, they brightened again, though this time something behind them remained in shadow. "Come," she said. Then, very quickly, she turned and headed out among the tombs. "Come," she repeated as she waved us forward. "A guide should be always smiling."

She had only contracted for a set number of hours each day, but she went off the clock at six that evening, so we remained in the restaurant for a long time. We had dinner, then strolled along Calle Florida for a time, where we stopped to watch a couple of street performers dance the tango.

Marisol watched them for a little while, and during that interval I noticed her mood descending. "I do not like the tango," she said as she turned and led us away from the dancers. "The man rushes forward. The woman pushes him away, then turns her back to him. The man rushes to her again and jerks her around with violence. It is disturbing to me, this dance. It is not romantic. It is—what is the English word?—prelude. Yes, it is the prelude to a beating."

We returned to the hotel at around eight in the evening. I was tired, but Julian was full of energy, so we went to the lounge for a nightcap, where he talked of nothing but Marisol. He had seldom traveled since his father's death, and I could see that her foreignness appealed to him: the fact that she was bilingual, which he was not, and perhaps even her indigenous facial features.

"Do you suppose she really isn't political?" he asked. "That business of having only two bad things to choose from?"

"That's what she said."

"But coming from that poor background, she must hate the junta," Julian said.

"Yes, but maybe she's one of those people who look within themselves for a way out of oppression," I told him. "That's why they get on boats and sail to new worlds."

Julian hesitated briefly, then said, "If someone like Marisol doesn't have a fighting chance, then something's very wrong, Philip."

I smiled. "You'll fix that when you're secretary of state," I assured him.

I'd meant this only half jokingly for at that moment it seemed quite possible.

"That's not for me," Julian said. "It's all politics. Your father knows that. He's had plenty of experience with it. You want to do good, but the policy is evil, and you must serve the policy."

"What then?" I asked. "You have to do something with your life."

"Something behind the scenes, I guess," Julian said. "The secret gears."

"The secret gears?" I asked, rather amused by how vague, yet adventurous it seemed. "You mean dark alleys and notes slipped into drop boxes? That's the work of spies, Julian."

"I suppose it is," Julian said. "But it would be better than an office at Foggy Bottom."

"It would also be more dangerous," I reminded him.

"More dangerous, yes," Julian agreed. "But only for me."

And with that, he laughed.

9

"Laughed?" Loretta asked when I told her this.

It was the day I was to leave for Paris, and she'd insisted on taking me to the airport. She'd arrived late in the afternoon, dressed in a dark green pants suit and looking so surprisingly rested that I'd have sworn she'd spent time in a spa.

"Laughed, yes," I told her. "So I didn't take him seriously."

She was seated by the window, the park to her back, the light quite bright, so that she was half in silhouette. "Julian would have made a good spy," she said. "That's clear from his books, how good he was at integrating information, making connections, seeing the big picture."

"That's true," I said. "He did that in *The Eyes of Oradour*. In one passage you're not even in France. He takes you to the sarcophagi of Cozumel, describes how small the people of that island were, and from there to how small all the Indians of South America must have seemed to the likes of Cortés and Pizarro."

"It's a great skill, putting such details together," Loretta said. "And of course the clandestine part of it would have appealed to Julian when he was a young man, the secret devices."

Like one seated in a dark movie house, I unexpectedly imagined Julian as precisely that, a figure in a rainy alleyway, dressed in a trench coat, the brim of his hat pulled low, smoking a Gauloise as he waited for his beautiful female contact.

No, that would not have been it, I thought.

Julian would have been waiting for something else.

But what?

On the heels of that question, a strange anxiety swept down upon me, and as if from a great height, I saw Julian lean over the side of the boat and make those two horrible motions, and then a circle of blood sweep out from the boat, deep and red, flowing out and widening until the whole pond was a deep, thick, impenetrable red.

Loretta's voice suddenly brought me back.

"I have something for you," she said, then reached into her pocket, drew out a photograph, and handed it to me. "It was in Julian's notebook. The one I gave him the morning he died. I found this picture tucked inside, so I think he must have been thinking of that first trip."

In the photograph Julian and Marisol were posed before the Obelisk, a place we'd often used as a point of rendezvous. It was around noon, the sun directly overhead so that it hardly cast a shadow. Marisol stood to Julian's left, and he'd put his arm around her waist and was gently drawing her toward him.

"You took that picture, didn't you, Philip?" Loretta asked.

"Yes," I answered. "It was our last day together." I stared at the picture a moment longer, then looked at Loretta.

"How very odd," she said. "Julian had the same expression on his face as the one you just had."

"What expression?"

"Dread," Loretta answered. "We were having dinner three days before he died. I'd been editing a book on Soviet espionage. There was an agent with the code name Beaker, quite a clever agent. He was a double agent, actually, working for one side while pretending to work for the other. Beaker was a very gifted little actor, but at one point, when he is sitting with another agent, he knows this other agent is trying to determine if Beaker, himself, is a spy. So Beaker is trying very hard to appear completely non-chalant, give no hint that he even knows that this other guy is out to get him. In the past he has always been able to completely conceal his terror of being discovered, but this time, his nerves give way . . . and he turns the corner of napkin. It's a tiny little movement, but it's a nervous movement, and at that moment Beaker knows absolutely that the other guy has seen it, and has read it for what it is." She smiled, but cheerlessly. "It was as if a tiny bead of sweat had just popped onto his brow, but it was enough for the other man to see the jumpy little spy beneath the mask."

"It's almost comic," I said.

"I thought so, too," Loretta said. "But it wasn't comic to Julian. I could tell by the look on his face. His mind was going somewhere. And one thing was clear. He understood Beaker. I could see that. He understood how his nerves had cracked. He didn't talk for a second or two, then he said, 'When your life is a lie, the truth has high stakes.'"

We watched each other silently for a moment, a time during which a dark cord seemed to draw us closer to each other.

"One more thing," she said. "Another little anecdote. Then you'll have all I have to give you about Julian."

She appeared somewhat reluctant to tell me the story.

"The day before he died, he went into the sunroom after dinner," she said. "There was a notebook on the little table beside his chair. I saw him take it up and write something in it. Then he put it back down and after a while he dozed off. When I went in to wake him, I saw what he'd written. A single sentence, but I remember it because it was so strange."

Briefly she seemed captured in that very strangeness.

"He'd written, 'Life is, at last, a Saturn Turn.'"

I had no idea what this meant, and told her so.

"I have no idea either," Loretta said. "But it must have meant something to Julian, because after his death, when I found that little notebook, I saw that he'd torn out that page. I couldn't find it anywhere, and it was summer, so there was no fire. I looked in all the places he might have tried to discard or hide it. I never found it, so there was only one place he could have put it."

"The pond," I said.

She nodded. "Hiding that note was his penultimate act."

"And it was an act of subterfuge," I added. "Of concealment." I felt the soft click of a tumbler. "One of his themes."

Now the dread that had earlier marked Julian's face, and more recently my own, settled upon Loretta's features, too.

"Julian once told me about a myth he'd come across," she said. "It came from the Pacific Islands. It was called the 'Myth of the Reeds.' It says that at death, the soul of each man is bound by his hidden crimes, each one wrapped around him like a reed. And it is only as these crimes are solved that he is freed." She let this settle in before she added, "I sometimes thought that Julian was tangled up in a reed."

"And died that way?" I asked.

"Unless that's what he was cutting," Loretta said. "Metaphorically, at least."

I could find nothing illuminating to add to this, and so we talked of other things until the hour came, and we set off for the airport.

Evening was beginning to drift down over the city by then, lights coming on, both in the buildings and in the traffic. The time had come for me to leave.

At the airport, I pulled my luggage from the back of the car. "When will you be back?" Loretta asked.

"I haven't booked the return yet," I answered.

"Does that feel good?" Loretta asked.

"I suppose it does, but at the same time I know that I'm a little at sea in all this," I admitted. "Let's face it, I was never trained in finding anything but metaphors and symbols."

She smiled. "Julian used to say that you find more when you don't know what you're looking for."

I felt a wave of admiration for my lost friend, the random riches of his work. Harry had often complained that he could not be categorized. Was he writing about crime or was he writing about history? Did you put him in "General Nonfiction" or did you put him in "True Crime"? His books had been strewn with little nuggets of everything: history, science, philosophy, a vast number of quotations, all of which made it nearly impossible for booksellers to find a slot on the shelf. I'd even found his books tucked hopelessly in "Travel" and even once in "Vampires."

"He found a great deal," I said.

"And so will you, Philip," Loretta assured me.

I thought of all the many years during which she had accumulated her own great store of knowledge and experience, all she had read and all she had endured, a bounty I found myself wanting to share.

"I hope so," I told her, "because I think something very important depends upon it."

"What?" she asked.

"Us," I answered softly, and knew that in some inexpressible way this was true.

Loretta came forward and kissed me on the cheek. "Julian could not have had a better friend," she said.

10

But Julian had had perhaps as good a friend in René Brossard.

They'd met in Africa, when Julian was researching the Paul Voulet outrages, and had subsequently traveled together to some of the remote outposts where those atrocities had been committed. According to Julian, Brossard had a lingering aura of old crimes, though the nature of those crimes had never been revealed. Even so, there was a hint of violence both suffered and inflicted, Brossard's one of those lives that had both struck and received a blow.

I'd met him in Julian's company a few times, though he'd made certain to remain in the background on those occasions. Whether this had been the product of Gallic manners or simply that he was slow to warm to strangers had never been clear. Of course, it might equally have been the outward evidence of some inner furtiveness, for there was surely something veiled about Brossard.

He had aged quite a bit during the intervening years. Where before his hair had been sprinkled with gray, it had now gone white. His eyes were more webbed and the lines in his long face had deepened. The muted light of Charles de Gaulle Airport added a layer of grayness to his unexpected pallor.

"I was very sad to hear of Julian," he said as he offered his hand.

"It came as quite a shock."

"Hmm," René said.

We exchanged a few pleasantries, then René led me to his car, and we set off for Paris, where I'd booked a small hotel not far from l'Opéra.

It was early in the morning, but I'd slept on the plane, so rather than bid René a quick farewell and go up to bed, I asked him to join me for a cup of coffee so that we could begin to discuss whatever itinerary he thought appropriate for my stay.

"I am sorry to say, but there is a delay in getting you into Julian's apartment," he informed me. "It is my fault that I did not tell you before, but I did not learn of it until this morning."

"What's the problem?" I asked.

"The one who owns the building, he has gone from the city for a few days, and I cannot get the key," René said. He shrugged. "I only come to the building to get Julian's mail. I never have a key to go inside." He smiled. "Perhaps he was not so good at the keeping house." He drew a pack of cigarettes from his jacket pocket, thumped one out, and lit it. "But he was a good writer, Julian. Very good." He seemed at the end of what he knew of Julian. "Always writing. Tap, tap, tap. Day and night."

"But no one can write twenty-four hours a day," I said. "He must have gone out from time to time."

"Sometimes, yes," René said. "Mostly to this little bar, Le Chapeau Noir. In Pigalle."

"Yes, I remember Julian writing about that place," I said. "He seems to have gone there quite a lot."

"It has cheap wine, and Julian was always lacking in the money," René told me. "But, me, I do not like it. It is full of refugees and émigrés. Africans and Arabs, people on the run from bad things."

"What kind of bad things?" I asked.

"Crimes," Brossard answered. "There were such places in Algiers. Criminals are like chickens, they crowd in upon each other. In a place like Le Chapeau Noir, there is blood on every hand."

"Except for Julian's, of course," I said.

"Except for Julian's, yes," Brossard agreed.

"Then why did he choose such a place?" I asked.

"It was near his apartment," Brossard said. "Perhaps it was the first door that opened to him." He shrugged. "He was a sad man, Julian. They are often in this way, such people. I saw it early. He was drawn to darkness. This I saw at Oradour."

"Oradour," I said as an idea occurred to me. "Since I can't get into Julian's apartment, would you mind taking me there?"

"It is only a destroyed village," René said. "But, okay, when do you want to go?"

"Tomorrow morning?"

"So fast? You are not wanting to sleep tomorrow, for the jet lag?"

"No," I answered. "I'll be rested by morning."

"Okay, tomorrow we go to Oradour," René said. He took a draw on his cigarette, then crushed it out. "I remember that

Julian, he was not so interested in the Germans. But the Malgré-nous, these interested him."

He saw that I did not speak a word of French.

"It means 'despite ourselves.' The Malgré-nous were from Alsace, these men, but the Germans drafted them. A few were at Oradour, and so they were made to do what they did, as they say, 'despite themselves.'"

It struck me that this was one of Julian's abiding themes, the sudden intervention of some event that without warning reveals a previously hidden element of character and by that means leaves a man forever the victim of a dark surprise.

"He talked to a few of them," René continued. "Old men. Dead now." His smile was wily, a ferret's grin. "It would be just so in one of those books, no? A thriller? The hero seeks a witness, but when he finds him, this witness is dead?"

"In pulp fiction, yes," I said. "But about that bar, the one Julian frequented, was there anyone he spent time with?"

René thought a moment, then said, "A priest. They spoke Spanish. This man, he was from Argentina. Julian said that he had been to his country during a bad time."

"The Dirty War, yes," I said.

René nodded. "I remember one night, Julian spoke of a woman he met there. He was very moved by this woman. Julian did not often show his feelings, but this night, I saw that for this one, a pain was left with him."

"Her name was Marisol," I told René. "She disappeared while Julian and I were in Buenos Aires."

René shrugged. "Lots of women disappeared during that time, no?"

"Yes, but they were kidnapped by the junta," I told him. "Marisol, on the other hand, wasn't in the least political."

René laughed at what he seemed to consider my naïveté. "Not political? How do you know?"

The question was simple, but it surprised me anyway, for, in fact, I didn't know whether Marisol had or had not been political. At least, not for sure.

With that recognition, a small crack appeared in the wall of what I'd always assumed about her. True, she'd only once mentioned the situation in Argentina, and even then only generally: *Argentina es un país perdido*.

But in what way had she thought it lost? I wondered now.

Marisol had never said.

One thing was clear, however. Although she always listened attentively when Julian spoke, it had been with an air of critical attunement, as if, because he was a privileged American, she should be wary of him and his worldview.

It was a distrust that surfaced one afternoon as we strolled down Calle Florida. Julian had begun to talk about the many far-flung places he hoped to visit in the future, one of which was Calcutta.

"The Black Hole of Calcutta is one of the places I'd like to see," he said. "I always thought that phrase referred to the city itself, that it was hopeless and impoverished. A pit."

Marisol listened to him in that highly attentive way of hers, as if seeking to understand not only the words, but what might lie between them, in the manner of a translator always in search of some new idiom or nuance in a language not yet fully mastered.

"But it was really an event," Julian added. "A mass murder, really."

Then, with characteristic detail, giving the precise date and location, Julian told us how Indian troops had crammed scores of British subjects into an unventilated room, where they'd died of suffocation or been trampled to death during one long night's ordeal.

"What did the British do after that?" Marisol asked.

"They decided that the Indians were savages," Julian answered. "And the subjugation of India became less—"

"Gentle?" Marisol interrupted softly.

I'd never heard her interrupt anyone. It simply wasn't her style. There was an unmistakable edge in her tone, too, though one so subtle I couldn't tell if it reflected anything more than the general anticolonialism any young person might have embraced at the time. Certainly it was not enough for me to conclude that Marisol was political in the sense that I'd used the word with René, something that would have caused her to be a target of the Dirty War.

René was quiet for a time after I related this small exchange to him. Then he said, "Anyway, you were safe. You and Julian, I mean. He made much of this, that despite all that was going on in Argentina, the two of you were safe."

"Yes, Julian and I were safe," I said, and thought of the legions of the disappeared, the marches their mothers made each day in the Plaza de Mayo. Still, I could not place the Marisol I'd known—so very quiet and lacking any visible political position—among the ranks of those who'd later been caught up in the Dirty War's repression. From those clutches, she'd always seemed as safe as Julian and I, and because of that, it had never occurred to me that she might have ended up in some dank cell, bruised and battered and lying in her own excrement, listening, with whatever consciousness remained to her, for the dreadful footfall of her torturer's approach.

"You have been silent for a long time," René said.

His voice seemed to come to me from a far less perilous world.

"Really?" I said. "I didn't realize."

René drained the rest of his coffee. "Tomorrow we go to Oradour."

We left Paris the next morning, a warm day but rainy, the city streets shrouded in a gray mist that gradually dissipated, so that we were in bright sun within an hour or so.

The way to Oradour was south from Paris, and it led into the heart of what had once been Vichy France, where the French had been permitted to rule—or pretend to rule—during the German occupation. Here Pierre Laval had signed the infamous order deporting non-French Jews to their deaths, for which, among other of his collaborationist acts, he had been executed by firing squad after the war.

Julian had touched on all this in a letter written while work-ing on Oradour, and in recounting Laval's death, he had offered an unexpectedly sympathetic portrait of Laval's final hours, how he'd bungled a suicide attempt by not shaking the bottle before drinking the poison it contained, the way he'd worn a tricolor scarf to the execution site in a twelfth-hour effort to grasp the laurel of patriotism, his final love-of-country declaration, shouted just before the shots rang out: *Vive la France!*

It was the seamless combination of scope and detail that Julian brought to all his later books, and thinking of it as we closed in upon Oradour, it renewed my admiration for him as a writer, one all the more fortified by what I'd learned from René the day before: the solitary life Julian had led in France, the habitué of a seedy bar in Pigalle, the way he'd made himself companion to the alien and the lost.

We reached Oradour in the early afternoon. My plan was to walk through it slowly, absorbing the place in increments as the day waned, so that I would reach the end of my tour at the very time of day when, according to the final passage of his book, Julian had left it for the last time, his research completed, his many hours of interviews and of walking the town's ghostly streets finally come to their end.

We parked just outside the town by the visitors' center, and for the next few hours I carried Julian's book with me as I slowly ambled among its ruined streets, René at my side, look-ing faintly bored. Along with a scattering of other tourists, we strolled among the shattered buildings and stood in the charred nave of the church in which so many had been burned alive, the rest shot as they attempted to escape. I paused at Hotel Avril, where the three Pinède children had hidden, their village burning around them, its smoke and fire finally driving them from their hiding places. Behind the hotel, I saw where, in the midst of their flight, they had encountered an SS soldier who had unaccountably permitted them to escape.

Toward the end of my walk, I paused at the well into which the bodies of several villagers had been tossed. Julian had no doubt stood here, and so I tried to imagine what he might have been thinking as from this vantage point his own eyes had observed the ruins of Oradour.

Surely he would have considered how, for a few hours on June 10, 1944, Oradour had truly been a hell on earth, for in his account of it nothing of that horror had been lost. He'd tried to see the tragedy from 642 angles, but it was his own eyes, at the end of the book, that had seen the town in its grief-stricken repose. That final view had been glimpsed on the Champ de Foire, so when I at last came to that part of town, I opened Julian's book and read, softly but aloud, its concluding passage:

> Twilight fell on the Champ de Foire. The car Dr. Desourteaux drove into Oradour that afternoon still rests where he left it, though no longer in the same state. Time has stripped away its paint and its metal has gone to rust, for even a ruin cannot be spared the assault of further ruin. So also fade the killing sites, the barns at Laudy, Milord, and Bouchole, the Beaulieu forge, the Desourteaux garage,

the little wine store on the road to St. Junien, the church
where the women and children were gathered, and whose
shattered belfry still looks down upon the road that, but
for the terrors of that day, those same women and children
might later have taken to distant, spared Limoges. The signs
that designate these once unheralded spots have begun to
peel and soon must be repainted. The bolts that hold them
to Oradour's stone walls will likewise need to be replaced.
For ruins, too, must be restored, and with every restoration,
Oradour, the town, slips further into Oradour, the event,
a process that will reach its end when the last of those who
survived those fearful hours pass beyond all further restora-
tion, and the last eyes to have seen Oradour as something
other than a martyred village will at last be closed.

After a dramatic pause, I closed the book and looked at René.

"Okay," he said. "So, we go now?"

A few minutes later we reached the hotel René had booked
for us. It was in a neighboring village, small, quiet, with a restaurant that served us politely, though the waitress appeared
somewhat surprised when René, so thoroughly French, asked
for ketchup for his *pommes frites*.

"A self-conscious American in France would never do that,"
I told him.

He laughed. "Yes, but I am French, so I can do what I want."

He ate with great relish, like a man accustomed to answer-
ing his appetites without reserve, and in that way quite the opposite of Julian, who had lived a far more Spartan life.

"Did you ever see Julian happy?" I asked. "Did you ever see him laugh uncontrollably?"

"He had only black thoughts," René answered. "That was his nature."

"No, it wasn't," I said. "When he was a young man, he was happy and self-confident. He had lots of romances. He would horse around like anyone else."

"Horse around?"

"Joke with people, that sort of thing."

"This is what it means, 'horse around'?"

"Yes."

René took out a pad and made a note. "Julian, yes, you are right, he did not, as you say, 'horse around,'" he said as he returned the pad to his pocket. "Only sometimes he went to Le Chapeau Noir." He placed the bowl of his glass between his large hands and rolled it back and forth. "It is like a place from a movie, this bar," he said.

"In what way?" I asked.

The glass stilled, as did René's usually darting eyes. "If you go there, you will see," he said.

11

But why should I go there? Julian had never written about Le Chapeau Noir in any of his books. From time to time it had made an appearance in his letters, though rather sketchily, a line here, a line there. Still, he'd written about it enough for me to have gathered that it was typical of Pigalle, that is to say, rather seedy. I'd imagined it with a cement floor, its tables and chairs a mismatched assemblage. Julian had once described its clientele as a ragged array of expatriates. He'd probably said other things about it, too, though only one of them had stuck, the fact that it was the sort of place where, even when men talk of love, they seem to talk of murder. That had been a telling phrase, which no doubt accounted for the fact that I'd remembered it.

Clearly, Julian had gone to Le Chapeau Noir quite often, and perhaps for that reason, I found myself imagining him as a lone figure, dressed in a worn trench coat, moving down a deserted, rain-slicked street, the lights of Pigalle's famous windmill shining dimly through a mist.

This was a purely fanciful portrait, of course, and yet, in imagining such a scene, my curiosity was heightened, particularly as to why Julian had described Le Chapeau Noir in a way that was so incontestably sinister, a bar where love and murder mingled with the smoke, curled and twined and became entangled.

"It was like places in those spy books he was reading," René told me when I mentioned this to him the next morning over breakfast. "There was still the Cold War in those days, and this bar, it was maybe a little like Vienna in that movie." He began to hum the theme of *The Third Man*. "And now you are maybe a little like the American in that movie, no?" he asked with a short laugh. "Searching for your dead friend?"

I'd never thought of myself as a character in a film, especially one written by Graham Greene, and yet, I had to admit that I did feel a little like Martins in *The Third Man*. I wasn't a penniless pulp writer, as he'd been, and I didn't expect to meet a mysterious woman in a cemetery, but, as a man who'd lived a relatively safe life, experienced only the most commonplace adventures, risked nothing except on the stock market, there was something in Martins's steadily intensifying investigation of the mysterious Harry Lime that was not unlike my own.

But I could also feel Martins's confidence that no matter what he discovered about Harry Lime, it would do nothing to undermine his love or admiration for him. Anna Schmidt had assured him of exactly that in one of the movie's most quoted lines: "A person doesn't change just because you find out more." I felt no doubt that it would be the same with Julian, for it seemed to me at the time that the goodness of a man was like a vein of gold that only widens as it deepens, then dazzles at the core.

My walk through Oradour had only increased my confidence in his essential goodness because it was here that Julian had made innocents the focus of his art by giving them voice, while at the same time, in a single, extraordinary artistic choice, he had denied any voice to their tormenters, so that while the villagers had emerged as individuals, the Germans had all but disappeared.

Disappeared.

Strange how that word brought Marisol back into my mind, she whose disappearance had so disturbed Julian, his search for her one of his life's distinct failures, a dark end to his Argentine adventure that could not have been predicted by its bright beginning.

And it had been very bright, indeed, that beginning. We were often together, the three of us a faintly *Jules and Jim* trio of young people, though it was never a love triangle.

But though Julian was not in love with Marisol in that fiercely romantic way, he had certainly searched for her as if she'd been a lost lover, journeying all the way to the Chaco to see the priest who'd raised her.

He was in his midsixties, this priest, but he looked much older. His hair was gray, his face deeply lined, so that upon first impression he seemed to be as weathered as the destitute parish in which he'd labored all his life.

"He was already old when my aunt brought me to him," Marisol said as we made our way to meet him that afternoon. "But he took in this little girl he did not know."

She was dressed less stylishly than usual and had added a small white flower to her hair, a touch of the indigene that you never saw in worldly Buenos Aires. A nod to the priest, I supposed, proof that her heart—or at least part of it—remained with him in the Chaco.

The old priest was sitting alone on a bench as we approached him. He did not see us but continued to stare straight ahead while he fingered a wooden rosary.

"It is Father Rodrigo who sent me to Buenos Aires," Marisol said, her gaze more intently on Julian than on me. "He is the saint of the Chaco."

He was now only a few feet away, and it seemed to me that he was older than the color of his hair or the texture of his skin suggested. There was a spiritual quality to his agedness, a sense that he was as old as his faith, a witness to that first crucifixion.

We were almost upon him before he caught Marisol in his eye and struggled to his feet.

"Ah, my sweet daughter," he said as he drew her into his arms.

She kissed him on both cheeks, then turned and introduced us.

The priest shook Julian's hand first, then turned to me.

"I have heard of your father," he said. He stretched his hand toward me and I took it. "He is said to be a good American. A friend. *Hermano en la lucha.*"

"I don't know what that means," I confessed.

"A brother in the struggle," Marisol informed me.

Brother in the struggle?

I couldn't imagine what Father Rodrigo was talking about.

"He is a man of the people, your father," Rodrigo added. "This is what I have heard. He is known as our friend in your capital. The poor do not have many friends there."

He had been gently pumping my hand during all this, and only now released it. "So, how do you know my Marisol?"

Though the question had been addressed to me, it was Julian who answered it.

"By way of the American consulate," he said.

Father Rodrigo's expression soured as he turned toward Julian. "They are working with the bad men of this country," he said firmly, then looked at Marisol. "Be careful what you say, my child. It is known that they are spies."

Spies. The word clearly caught Julian's attention.

"Really?" he asked. "Spies for whom?"

"For Casa Rosada," Rodrigo answered. "They give them names. Then these people disappear." He looked at Marisol and placed a single, jagged finger at his lips. "Careful," he said, then glanced toward a nearby bench. "Come, let us sit down."

Once seated, Father Rodrigo took a moment to observe his surroundings. "Ah, how beautiful is San Martín. I have not seen it since I was a boy."

He meant Plaza San Martín, a lovely park in the heart of the city, where Marisol had earlier instructed us to meet her. It was close to Retiro Station, she said, and Father Rodrigo was scheduled to leave the city that evening. I'd had little interest in coming, but Julian had insisted. Clearly he had indicated to Marisol that he considered it important to meet this old priest.

At rest, Father Rodrigo seemed even older, but also he looked neglected. His clerical collar was slightly frayed and there were a few small tears in his cassock. This suggested that no help was being provided to him, no Gran Chaco equivalent to those formidable ladies of my boyhood parish, women who kept their priests tidy down to the neatly folded underwear.

My father had explained that South American clergy who subscribed to revolution theology were being punished by what he called "the powers that be," but on Father Rodrigo such imposed deprivations had created an aura of saintliness. Here was the Church as it should be, I thought, not a thing clothed in robes and adorned by jewels and housed in splendid cathedrals, but a country priest in a worn cassock.

"So," Father Rodrigo said, glancing first to Julian, then back to me, "has Marisol told you of the place where she grew up?"

She had, as a matter of fact, but for the next few minutes, we listened politely as Father Rodrigo detailed the sad life of the Chaco, the poverty and poor education, young lives doomed to nothing else. It was this doom that he'd wanted Marisol to escape. He'd seen her intelligence, her will, the fact that she would grasp whatever opportunity came her way.

"Which she has done," he said proudly, then drew Marisol beneath his arm. "She is no longer a girl from the Chaco."

Marisol plucked the small white flower from her hair and gave it to Rodrigo. "I will always be a girl from the Chaco," she said.

By then, night had begun to fall over Plaza San Martín. Father Rodrigo struggled to his feet.

"I must go now," he said. "The bus home leaves soon."

Marisol tucked her hand beneath the old man's arm. "I will go with you to the station," she said.

"I'll come, too," Julian volunteered immediately.

"No," Marisol said softly. "It is for me to do this."

And I thought, here is the soul of goodness: love, duty, sacrifice, and atonement, all combined to form something for which no word exists in English, save perhaps *grace*.

"No, I want to go with you," Julian said insistently, like one who wished to share this service with Marisol.

Marisol appeared uncertain of accepting Julian's offer and surprised by his adamance.

"Let these good boys come with us," Father Rodrigo said to Marisol. He pressed his sunbaked hand against her immaculate skin. "We must learn the many roads into each other."

Had it not been for the utter sincerity in the old man's eyes, I would have thought that final line scripted, a homily only a Barry Fitzgerald could have delivered without provoking laughter. As a statement, it was at once profound and corny, as true as it was impossible, and yet, as an expression of the old man's Christian perfectionism, it seemed entirely sincere.

The old man smiled. "Come then," he said, now looking at Julian and me and nodding forward, his signal that we were to come with them to the station.

It was only a short distance to the train station, but much of it was down a long sweep of concrete stairs, which made our progress slow and halting, Father Rodrigo somewhat unsteady on his feet, so that often Marisol took one arm and Julian the other.

At Retiro, crowds of people gathered in great, noisy throngs. Some carried cardboard boxes tied with twine rather than luggage, but this was Buenos Aires in the eighties, not some distant jungle outpost of a century before, and so the vast majority carried simple, battered suitcases and valises not very different from what would have been seen in any American bus station.

If the bus to the Chaco was different from the others, it was only in that those who waited for it looked poorer and more resigned than those on their way to less distant and impoverished shores. They were farmworkers, as Father Rodrigo noted, toilers in soy and sorghum and maize.

The bus pulled in after a few minutes.

Father Rodrigo got to his feet. "God be with you all," he said, then turned to Marisol, and drew out a strand of dark beads. "I brought these from the Chaco," he said.

Marisol took the beads and hung them around her neck. "I will wear them every day," she said.

The old priest smiled. "Be kind to yourself, my daughter," he said to her, "and remember me."

Marisol faced the bus as it pulled away, her hand raised, waving, craning her neck, trying for one last glimpse of Father Rodrigo. But he had taken a seat on the opposite side, and so she did not see him again, though she didn't give up her effort until the bus had disappeared into the night.

"He could easily be arrested," Julian said firmly and in a way that gave his words a distinct authority. Then he looked at Marisol pointedly. "Talking the way he does about spies in the

American consulate. If there were such people, spying for Casa Rosada, they might feel threatened."

Marisol's eyes shot over to Julian, and I could see that his remark had struck her as very serious indeed.

"Threatened? But he is just a country priest," she said. She began to toy with the beads the old priest had just given her. "He is nothing to the ones in Casa Rosada. Who would listen to a priest from the Chaco? He is dust to them."

Julian's voice was full of warning. "Even dust gets trampled," he said. He looked out toward the distant and still-departing bus. "No one is too small to be noticed by the generals at Casa Rosada," he added.

He spoke with great authority, as if he had knowledge of secret connections between the American consulate and the masters of Casa Rosada, which, of course, he did not have. And yet, as I could see, Marisol took his words to heart, though she added nothing to the exchange that had just taken place and instead nodded toward the stairs that led back to San Marco.

"There is a nice little restaurant there," she said. "It is called La Flora."

A few minutes later we were seated at an outdoor table of the little café she'd mentioned. For no apparent reason, Julian began to talk about a book I was reading, arguing with me over a certain point. He was almost never wrong in such matters, but on this point I knew he was, which rather pleased me, and so to prove that I was right, I went back to the hotel to get the book. It was a chance, however juvenile, to one-up my always completely confident friend. The hotel was only a block away, so I was back very quickly, moving briskly toward the café because I knew I was right and couldn't wait to prove it. But as I closed in upon their table, I saw that Julian and Marisol were talking very intently. Julian was leaning forward, and Marisol looked extraordinarily grave, like one who's just been given a dreadful warning. They both shrugged off this seriousness as I approached, however, and it wasn't until after Marisol had left us that I brought the scene up with Julian.

"What were you talking about with Marisol?" I asked.

"Nothing," Julian answered.

He said nothing more, but the troubled mood of that earlier conversation returned and seemed to haunt him, and he appeared to be questioning himself rather like a little boy who'd done something wrong.

"Marisol loves Father Rodrigo," he said.

"Yes, she does," I said. "I hope he's not in danger. But who knows? You're right, they could do anything to a man like Rodrigo." I looked out over the street. "It's a lost country, just like Marisol says. Because if it gained power, the left would be just as oppressive as the right is now."

Julian nodded softly.

"Marisol's right to stay out of it," I said. "Because they're crazy on both sides."

We sat in silence for a time, Julian's gaze curiously unsettled, like a man trying to find his way in a dark wood.

Finally, I said, "What's the matter, Julian?"

He looked at me and his lips parted, but he didn't speak. Instead, he turned away again, now looking out in the nightbound depths of San Martín.

"Nothing," he said softly.

I sensed that if I chose to pursue the matter, Julian would probably tell me what was on his mind. But it had been a long day and I was tired.

"Well, I'm heading for bed," I said.

Julian continued to face the park. "Good night," he said.

I went to my room and prepared for bed, but just before climbing into it, I glanced out the window, down to the little bar seven flights below. Julian was still sitting, just as he'd been when I left him, still peering out toward San Martín. Even from that distance, I could sense that something was troubling him.

I thought now, I should have gone down to him. If life knew only happy endings, a friend would have done just that. He would have looked down from the window, seen his friend in the shadowy light, understood, if not the cause of his trouble, then at least the fact that the trouble was there. He would have looked at his bed and felt a great need to climb into it. He would have thought of the soft pillows and the caressing sheets. He would have yearned for sleep and dreams and in his bone tiredness, he would have recognized his need for both. But in the end, this friend would have dressed himself and gone back downstairs, taken a seat at his friend's table and said to him, simply, "Tell me." He would have done all this because despite his youth and inexperience, he would have understood that sometimes it is simply such a gesture that makes the difference.

I knew that in any view of life designed to put a better face on man, this friend would have known these things and done them.

But I had not.

Now, however, with that scene playing in my mind, the question rose again as to whether Julian had been right in thinking that Father Rodrigo was going to be arrested. Therefore, when I got back to Paris, I decided to see if I could answer it.

12

I dialed the number almost immediately after returning to my hotel in Paris, then waited the usual protracted amount of time it took my father to answer, longer this time than when I'd called him on my first night in Paris.

But at last he appeared on my computer screen, already dressed for bed, though it was late afternoon in New York.

"I can see you very clearly," I told him.

He smiled. "You, too. It's really quite amazing."

We talked about trivial matters for a time, the weather in New York and Paris, a smattering of world and national news, then on to my impression of René and our visit to Oradour-sur-Glane.

At last I said, "Do you remember that when Julian and I were in Buenos Aires we met an old priest named Father Rodrigo?"

"Of course," my father answered. "You said he'd heard of me. I was surprised by that."

"Do you have any idea whatever happened to him?"

"Only that when Julian went down to the Chaco, he was no longer there," my father answered. "But I'm sure Julian told you that."

"Another of the disappeared," I said.

"So Julian thought," my father answered.

"He spoke to you about it?"

"Yes," my father answered. "Evidently this priest had said some fairly dangerous things when they met. Julian told me what he'd said, but I didn't see it as all that dangerous. It was common knowledge, after all, that we were more or less in cahoots with the junta."

"But what else could explain the fact that Rodrigo went missing?" I asked.

"Well, sometimes people vanish of their own accord," my father told me. "In a place like Argentina at that time, there were many reasons a man might want to make himself scarce."

"What would have made Father Rodrigo leave Argentina?" I asked.

"Nothing, if he was what he seemed," my father said.

"A country priest, you mean?"

My father nodded. "Even one with a loose tongue."

"You're saying Father Rodrigo might have been more than that?" I asked.

"I'm saying it's possible that in Argentina at that time such a priest might have been used."

"By whom?"

"The Montoneros, of course," my father answered. "Lots of priests were working for the Montoneros."

He saw that I had no idea what he was talking about.

"They were pretty much finished by the time you went to Argentina," he explained. "But before the junta, they murdered anyone who opposed them. And if Rodrigo were a Montonero, and he got wind that he had been discovered or was about to be discovered, then he might have found it a very good idea to leave the country."

"How could he have escaped?" I asked. "He was a poor parish priest."

"Yes, but if he were a Montonero, they could have financed his departure from Argentina," my father told me.

"What money would the Montoneros have had?"

"They would have had the millions they got from kidnappings and bank robberies," my father answered. "One kidnapping alone brought in sixty million dollars. It was the largest ransom ever paid. It's in the *Guinness Book of Records*."

"Would Julian have known any of this?" I asked.

"I doubt it," my father answered. "Why do you ask?"

"Because he seemed to think that Rodrigo was going to be arrested," I answered. "He told this to Marisol."

My father suddenly grew very still. "I didn't know that," he said quietly, and for a moment looked like a man sitting in a darkened theater, awaiting a film whose story he dreaded.

"He never mentioned it?" I asked. "Not even after he got back from Argentina?"

My father shook his head. "Of course, we rarely talked after that."

This was true. Julian had but rarely seen my father after Argentina, and even then only at what were more or less public gatherings, Loretta's wedding, for example, and Colin's funeral.

"Good people like this Father Rodrigo can be manipulated, Philip," my father said quietly, like a man considering the treacheries of life.

"But Julian couldn't have known that Rodrigo might be a Montonero operative," I said.

"That's true," my father said firmly. "The only way he could have had intelligence of that sort was if he had some contact at Casa Rosada."

"Which, of course, he didn't," I said.

"No, of course not," my father said. "They were absolute evil." His eyes appeared to see that evil quite clearly. "They tortured people mercilessly."

I saw that his mood was blackening, so I moved to change the subject.

"You know, it's interesting to think that Rodrigo might still be alive," I said, almost lightly. "And if the Montoneros wanted to get him out of Argentina, he could be anywhere."

Now my mind fixed on the shadowy priest with whom Julian had often been seen at Le Chapeau Noir. "Anywhere at all," I said, almost to myself.

"Anywhere at all," my father repeated. The darkness fell upon him again. "It's a twisted world, Philip," he said, "the one you're touching now."

"At the end of the conversation, my father said that I was getting into a twisted world," I told Loretta when I called her later that night.

She had listened silently, and when I finished, she took a moment before she spoke.

"Do you think that priest might actually have been a Montonero?" she asked.

"I don't know," I said, though I immediately began to consider the possibility. Certainly it was possible that Rodrigo might have gotten carried away with some form of revolutionary theology, agreed to help the Montoneros in some way, and then, with the junta on his trail, found it necessary to flee the country.

I shared this with Loretta, then added as if I half believed it, "He might even be in Paris. Maybe even at this little bar Julian frequented. René said that Julian often talked with a priest there."

I said this jokingly, as if describing the elements of a pot-boiler plot, but Loretta's tone turned serious.

"Your father's right," she said. "It is a twisted world." A pause, then, "Be careful, Philip."

Some warnings come like the tolling of a bell, and thus it was with Loretta's.

For that reason, if for no other, I should have heeded what she said to me and thus anticipated the terrors that awaited. But the Saturn Turn twists for all, as Julian had already learned, and so I moved unknowingly ahead.

PART III
The Terror

13

In *The Terror*, Julian's curious meditation on one of Gilles de Rais's awful minions, he wrote:

> *The route to moral horror is never direct. There are always ramps and stairs, corridors and tunnels, the secret chamber forever concealed from those who would be appalled by what they found there.*

We all had secret chambers, I thought, though most chambers probably harbored nothing more fearful than some peculiar desire, or if not that, then perhaps simply the sad awareness of an inexplicable inadequacy we dared not reveal. Even so, Julian would have been the last I'd have suspected of having such a place. At his father's death, he had been deeply stricken, but he had rallied even from this loss, regained his footing, and proceeded on, his confidence returning with each passing day, so that within a month or so, he seemed once again the boy of old, though perhaps even more determined to make a mark in the world.

For his spiritual resilience alone, I had admired him. But later, as his life took shape, I had also thought him physically brave. He'd been an intrepid traveler, after all, with the courage to cross fields so foreign he must have thought himself on the moon at times. Rimbaud, stranded in Egypt, had written stinging letters of regret, his pen crying out, *why, oh why, am I here?* I had little doubt that Julian had often found himself floating in some similar sea of strangeness, isolated, friendless, knowing little of the language and customs, short of money, with only history's most vile miscreants to occupy his mind. It takes courage to roam the world in that way, and roam it Julian certainly had.

But this same physical courage had sometimes struck me as reckless and foolhardy. I'd seen scars on his arms, bruises on his body. He never mentioned these injuries, but on one occasion, I got a hint about how he'd received them.

We were walking in Chueca, at that time one of Madrid's most dangerous neighborhoods, when two young men staggered out of a bar, headed for the bright lights of Gran Via. On the way, they came across a young gypsy woman crumpled against a building in a common beggarly pose. Normally such people were passed without a nod, but on this occasion, the men stopped to taunt her. "Look at this gitana," they said. "Can you smell this filthy whore?"

By the time Julian and I reached them, the insults had escalated into a physical assault, one of the men lifting his leg to press the toe of his shoe against the woman's breast while calling her names—*puta, coño,* and the like.

In Spanish, Julian said, "Leave her alone."

He said it quietly, but before the man could draw back his foot, Julian rushed forward and plowed into him, and they both went sprawling into the street. I didn't try to intervene, but neither did the other man's friend, so Julian and the man simply rolled around for a bit before getting to their feet, the Spaniard muttering curses as he staggered away.

That night, Julian emerged more or less unharmed, and we went on our way. But I suspected that on other occasions he'd done the same and gotten a thorough beating as a result. I idealized those confrontations in a way that ennobled Julian, cast him as a selfless defender of the weak, and yet, at the same time, I sometimes wondered what his motives were. Was he driven to test his courage? Had he decided that the grand work he once dreamed of could only be realized in small acts of self-sacrifice? I knew that martyrdom was sometimes less the product of saintliness than of spiritual ambition, so had Julian from time to time felt the pinch of his own shrunken hope of doing some great work and for that reason lashed out in acts of reckless altruism?

I had no answer to this question, of course. Yet, the more I pondered it, the more I felt that something was buried in Julian, a need, a remorse, something that held the key to him. I had no place to go for an answer, but nevertheless I decided to drop in on Le Chapeau Noir. Perhaps, with a little luck, I might run into the man Julian had spoken with there, the one with whom he appeared to have discussed Marisol.

René was right, as it turned out. Le Chapeau Noir was indeed a good deal like the sort of place one would find in novels of intrigue. In fact, it was less a place than an atmosphere, and even if its shadowy interior were not clouded with cigarette smoke, you would add this smoke to any description of it. You would also include a dim, oddly undulating light that throws this mysterious figure into half shadow, that one into silhouette, by turns revealing or concealing a forehead, a jaw, an eye with a patch, each face broken into puzzle pieces. You would add a random arrangement of wooden tables, and over there, huddled in a corner, you would put two men in linen suits, one with a very thin moustache, the other clean shaven, wearing a panama hat. Snatches of many languages would come at you like bats. Spanish answered by Greek, a hint of German from behind a curtain, Turkish over there, where a man in a red fez drinks tea from a white china cup. To his left, an Englishman in evening dress, come to sample the demimonde after a dazzling night at the embassy. No doubt there'd be an American, too, wearing a dark suit, off in a distant corner, seemingly naive and deceptively trusting, but with a revolver close at hand.

That would be me, I thought, as I slouched, minus the revolver, in a distant corner and silently watched the regulars at Le Chapeau Noir.

René had told me that the place was dead until around midnight, so I'd dutifully showed up at just after twelve. By then, a few of the tables were taken, though hardly by the throng of shady characters I'd anticipated. True, the majority of the customers were foreigners, just as René had described, but of these, only a few looked like thieves or black marketers. There were a few Algerians, but they were off by themselves, closely huddled around a small table. A tight group of East Indians had claimed the far end of the bar, their eyes glancing about rather nervously, though it was unclear whether it was the police or the Algerians they feared. The rest were French or Eastern Europeans, though at one point I thought I heard a bit of German.

Le Chapeau Noir was, of course, a thoroughly landlocked bar, and yet something about it had the moldering dankness of a harbor. I might have thought of Marseille or Naples, but for some reason—perhaps it was the presence of those few North Africans—I found myself associating it in full literary fashion with ancient Cádiz, known by the Phoenicians, an immemorial coastal trading post, populated by every kind of adventurer and deserter, safe haven for the criminal flotsam of two continents; perhaps in all the world, the first true city of intrigue.

I'd come here in hopes of encountering the priest with whom Julian had often been seen in what René called—with his usual melodrama and showy English—"dark conclave." With a little probing, René had gone on to describe the man and even volunteered to accompany me to the bar, for which I thanked him but declined. I needed to be alone, I thought, to experience Le Chapeau Noir in the solitary way I assumed Julian must first have encountered it. I suppose that I'd come to feel that I needed to see what Julian had seen, talk to the people he'd talked to, go where he'd gone, *become* him in the way he sought to become the great criminals he studied. Such a route is always dangerous, of course, like shooting the rapids of another's neural pathways. And yet, step by step, I'd come to feel myself drawn—perhaps lured—deeper and deeper into Julian's mind and character. It was as if I were once again following him into the caves we'd sometimes explored in the hills around Two Groves, Julian always in the lead, beckoning me forward with an "Oh, come on, Philip, what's to fear?" I dragging reluctantly behind him, refusing to give the answer that came to me: "Everything."

Suddenly I felt that I was once again trailing after him in just that way, going deeper and into yet more narrow spaces, caverns that were dark and cramped and airless, and in that way not unlike Le Chapeau Noir.

No one spoke to me, of course, but that hardly mattered, because my French was very bad, and so it would have been impossible for me to have a conversation with any of the bar's clientele, save to inform them that *"le plume est sur la table."*

Even so, I felt that my nights at Le Chapeau Noir provided a feeling for the dispossessed that was akin to Julian's. For there was something about this bar that gave off an aura of precious things irretrievably lost. For some it had been a homeland, for others, a political ideal. For yet others, it was some romantic dream the intransigent facts of life had indefinitely deferred.

Without telling me, René had been more practical in his research, and he had located the priest Julian had sometimes spoken with at Le Chapeau Noir, a man who had recently been detained for what René called "a document problem." He was now at liberty, however, and René assured me that he would appear at the bar the following night.

And so he did.

After talking with my father, I'd actually entertained the faint hope that this priest might be Father Rodrigo, a hope encouraged by René's description of an old man with leathery brown skin, very thin, quite stooped. Such a person might turn out to be Marisol's beloved priest, now in his eighties, and perhaps, if my father's vague suggestion turned out to be true, still withdrawing modest sums from God knows how much Montonero money. I imagined him as essentially unchanged, except physically, and therefore, with secular communism now in tatters, still dreamily devoted to some Christian version of the same radical, and to my mind naive, egalitarianism.

But the man I met at Le Chapeau Noir that evening was considerably younger than Rodrigo would have been. He was shorter than Rodrigo, too, and a tad rounder, with dark skin and black hair that had thinned a great deal and which he parted on the left side just above his ear.

"Ah, so you are a friend of Julian," he said as I approached him.

His accent was predominately Spanish, though there were hints of other lands, which gave the impression that he'd lived somewhat nomadically, his speech now marked with the fingerprints of his travels.

"When I met him, he had just returned from Bretagne," the man said.

He offered a smile that was rather rueful and suggested that his journey through life had been a difficult one, a smile that ran counter to his eyes.

"Julian noticed that I was drinking Malbec, the wine of Argentina," the man said. "He came to me and introduced himself." He thrust out his hand. "I am Eduardo."

"Philip Anders," I said, hoping to elicit Eduardo's last name.

He did not respond, however, and we took our seats at a small table near the back of the bar, Eduardo quick to position himself with his back to the wall, clearly a man long accustomed to keeping an eye on both the front door and the exits.

"We talked first of Cuenca," Eduardo said. "Julian had spent much time in that part of Spain." His smile was quite warm, but that warmth ran counter to what he said next. "Years before, when I was young and angry, I had gone to Cuenca to kill a man. He had wronged my sister in Zaragoza. He brought drugs into her life, and they killed her. Everywhere he spread this poison. Pity another's knife found his heart before mine could. I wanted my face to be the last he saw." He waved to the barman and ordered a bottle of wine, though not a Malbec. When it came, he poured each of us a round, then lifted his glass. "Do you know the fascist toast?"

"I'm afraid not."

"It comes from the Spanish Civil War," Eduardo said. "It was first made in Salamanca. Imagine that? Spain's ancient seat of learning. In the presence of Miguel de Unamuno, our country's greatest philosopher. Made by a one-eyed, one-armed general of Franco's army." He touched his glass to mine. "Long live death."

It was not a pleasing toast, but I drank to it anyway.

"He was an interesting man, Julian," Eduardo said as he set down his drink. "I enjoyed very much talking to him."

"What did you talk about?" I asked.

Eduardo smiled. "Many things. Julian was very learned. He had read a great deal. But, at the time, he was mostly thinking about evil women."

I thought of the evil women Julian had written about: La Meffraye, Countess Báthory.

"Yes," I said, "he wrote about such women."

"This he did, yes, but the one he spoke of most, this woman he never wrote about," Eduardo said. "But he was much interested in her and often he spoke of this woman."

"Who?"

"Her name was Ilse Grese."

When he saw that I'd never heard the name he said, "She was a guard at Ravensbrück."

"The concentration camp?"

Eduardo nodded. "Yes."

Irma Ida Ilse Grese, I found out later, was born in Wrechen, Germany, in 1923. Her father was a dairy worker who joined the Nazi Party early and, presumably, passed his political views on to his young daughter. At fifteen, she quit school as a result of poor grades and because she'd been bullied, particularly for her already fanatical devotion to the League of German Girls, a Nazi youth organization. After leaving school, she worked as an assistant nurse at an SS sanatorium. Later, she tried to apprentice as a nurse but was blocked by the German Labor Exchange, so she worked as a shop girl for a time, then drifted through a series of lowly agricultural jobs until she found her true calling as a guard, first at Ravensbrück, then at Auschwitz, where, given more power than a lowly milkmaid could ever imagine, she added her own peculiar heat to that hell.

"She was very cruel, this woman," Eduardo went on to say. "Julian told me of the many terrible things she did. How she wore heavy boots and carried a riding crop. She starved her dogs until they were crazed with hunger, he said, and then she set them on her prisoners. She enjoyed their pain. A true monster, this woman."

"Why did he never write about her?" I asked.

Eduardo shrugged. "Perhaps she was too simple. He said that she was just a thug. It was the other one who had captured him by then. The one he called 'The Terror.'"

Her real name was Perrine Martin, but she was known as La Meffraye, which in French means "the terror." Julian described her as being an old woman and longtime assistant to the serial killer Gilles de Rais. In his service, she proved herself very adept at procuring young children, despite her vaguely sinister clothing—a long gray robe with a black hood. Her actual involvement in the many murders recounted in Gilles's trial was, according to Julian's book, perhaps as much dark fairy tale as truth, but his writing suggested that she possessed demonic qualities well beyond her crimes—chief among them, I remembered now, was her capacity for deception.

Still, it was for murder that she was arrested and to which she later confessed, giving some of the most graphic and horrifying testimony of Gilles de Rais's trial. After that, she was imprisoned in Nantes, where, presumably at a very old age, she died. Thus her story ended, at least as far as Julian had followed it in his book.

"This woman who was a terror," Eduardo said, "Julian had a big interest in her."

"He did, yes," I agreed. "But in the book he sometimes seemed less concerned with her crimes than in the clever way she disguised herself."

Eduardo laughed. "A nice old grandmother, yes. You are right, it was in this that Julian found her true evil. This is what he said to me. Before the crime, there was the disguise."

"Disguise," I repeated softly, and with that word recalled something Julian had written in his book on La Meffraye, the telling phrase he'd used, how the woman's kindness, simplicity, devotion, and humility were nothing more than serrated notches in the blade she held.

Eduardo seemed to glimpse the dark and unsettling recollection that had suddenly come into my mind. "It sometimes caused me to wonder if perhaps someone had deceived Julian in his youth," he said. "Could this be so? Was there such a one?"

"Not that I know of," I said, then added what seemed to me an ever-deepening truth. "But I suppose there's a lot about Julian that I don't know."

We talked on for a time, and as we did, it became clear that Julian had shared a great deal with Eduardo: his early life, his father's death, the great emptiness he'd felt at this loss, and how, from then on, he believed that to kill a father was to a kill a son. He had also related a few stories about his travels with Loretta and his days at Two Groves.

By then I'd learned a few things about Eduardo, as well, most notably that he had never been a priest but had used that disguise, along with false papers, to move more or less undetected throughout Europe. Those movements had interested Julian, he said, and he had questioned him about them quite relentlessly. It was during those conversations that Eduardo had inquired about Julian's earliest travels. In response, Julian had first described the happy journeys he'd taken with his father and Loretta; then, quite reluctantly, according to Eduardo, he had at last spoken of Argentina.

"It was not a happy place for Julian," Eduardo told me. "He told me that Buenos Aires was a place that swarmed with agents and secret agents."

"That's true," I said. "The Dirty War was still going on when we were there."

Eduardo nodded. "Julian said a bad thing happened there. It was to a woman he knew."

"Our guide, yes," I said. "While we were in Buenos Aires, she disappeared. She was never found."

"And Julian loved this woman?" Eduardo answered.

"No," I answered. "At least not romantically. But he cared for her."

Eduardo looked puzzled. "Then there was perhaps another woman in his life?"

"Not one he ever spoke of," I said. "Why do you ask?"

"Because Julian seemed like a man betrayed," Eduardo said.

"In what way?" I asked.

"In the way of one who cannot forget his betrayal," Eduardo said. "For most men, it is a woman who leaves this stain. Perhaps this was not so with Julian."

He was silent for a moment, clearly thinking of Julian. At last he said, "Julian told me that on the walls of Russian prison cells, the prisoners of the gulag had written one word more than any other. It was not what you would expect it to be, this word. It was not *mother* or *father* or *God*." He seemed once again to be with my old friend, peering into the gravity of his face. "It was *zachem*."

"What does *zachem* mean?" I asked.

"It means 'why.'" Eduardo answered. His gaze became quite quizzical, but with a somberness that deepened it. "I think this was written also in Julian's mind. And that it was written there by betrayal."

14

Later that night, sleepless in my bed, I remembered Julian during our flight to Buenos Aires, how boyishly excited he was at the time, and how different from the man he later became, isolated and reclusive, the habitué of a Pigalle bar, talking of evil women who brilliantly disguised their vile crimes, with *zachem*, as Eduardo said, somehow carved into his mind.

Now, recalling the eerie sensation I felt at his mention of this word, I remembered my first meeting with Julian after he returned from France with the completed manuscript of *The Terror* and, in particular, a remark he made during our conversation, the fact that he considered deception to be life's cruelest act. El Cepa had deceived his neighbors into believing he was dead. The German soldiers had deceived the villagers of Oradour into believing they were only to have their identities checked. La Meffraye had deceived the children she brought to Gilles de Rais for slaughter.

"So is that your theme, Julian?" I asked him. "Deception?"

I sensed a defensive hardening within him at that moment, a wall going up. He glanced about and looked at his hands before he said, "I often think of something Thoreau wrote, that although children kill frogs in play, the frogs die in earnest."

Odd though this remark was, it seemed like an opening up, a chance to speak of whatever was so clearly troubling him, but in a moment of supreme insensitivity, I became pedantic.

"Thoreau took that from Plutarch," I told him in a little show of erudition, "who took it from Bion."

Julian nodded. "We're all thieves, I suppose," he said. "Spies and secret agents."

"Magicians of manipulation," René said the next morning when we had breakfast together in the hotel dining room. "That's what Julian called spies and secret agents."

"He told Eduardo that Buenos Aires had been full of such people when we were there," I said. "Which it probably was, though Julian couldn't have known much about such things."

"Then why does what he said trouble you?" René asked. "I can see that it does."

And he was right. Even now, I suddenly felt a twinge of uneasiness, the sense that I could no longer be certain of what Julian had or had not known about anything.

"It troubles me because Julian seems to have believed that he was betrayed at some point in his life," I said. "At least that's what Eduardo told me. And he seemed quite sure of it."

I related the memory that had returned to me the night before, the vaguely enigmatic conversation I'd had with Julian the day he turned in the manuscript of *The Terror*, how troubled he looked when he talked briefly about deception as the chief of crimes, the way it seemed to open the door into some darker room.

"He never worked on a book about spies, did he?" I asked. "I mean, for all his talk about spies and agents, he never wrote about them."

"No, he didn't," René said. He lit his usual after-breakfast cigarette. "I think he was not so much interested in spies. But, as you say, perhaps in disguise he was interested. We spoke of this from time to time. Deception was something I knew about from my time in Algiers. They were great deceivers, those terrorists in Algeria. I told Julian this. They passed codes during prayers, reciting the Koran but making a mistake. The mistake was the code." He laughed. "And sometimes even their ailments they used as code. A stomach problem was a man who got scared and had to drop out of a plot. A headache was a new development or maybe some technical matter that had to be figured out before those fucking bastards could blow up the next building or shoot the next policemen."

He laughed. "Half the time, it seemed like child's play."

"Child's play," I repeated, struck by the fact that so dangerous an endeavor could be thought of in such a way.

René took a long draw on his cigarette. "Child's play, yes," he said. "Julian knew this. He even spoke of Mata Hari in this way. That she was just a woman playing a game. Until they shot her, of course. He said once, 'But it is no longer a game when the bullet strikes.'" He looked at me quite starkly. "Julian believed they do many horrible things, the ones who don't grow up. Not to grow up, he said, was a kind of crime."

"What did he mean by that?"

René crushed out his cigarette with a violence that seemed to come from something deep within him. "We were talking

132

about Algeria, those girls who planted bombs. I say to him, they were like kids in a playground, those terrorists. Only throwing bombs instead of balls."

Suddenly, he stopped, and I saw that this memory had brought something abruptly to mind.

"What is it, René?" I asked.

With a curious gravity, René said, "He looked very strange, Julian. When I said this to him. He looked like maybe this was a truth he knew and which he did not like."

"What did he say?"

"The thing I told you, that not to grow up was maybe also a crime," René answered.

He sat back, lit another cigarette, and drew in several deep puffs before speaking. "He was a sad fellow, Julian."

"Maybe he was a classic romantic," I said. "In his youth, he wanted to change the world."

René shook his head. "No, Julian had clear eyes. Once he said to me, 'Do you know what love is, René? A failure of perspective.'" He shifted slightly. "Such things are not said by romantics."

I considered how very dark this remark was, the notion that no love could withstand the inquiry of clear minds, love itself a clever deceiver.

"He thought we all dangled in a great web of illusion, didn't he?" I asked.

René nodded.

"Illusions we had to have in order to be happy," I added.

René stared at the tip of his cigarette for a moment, then looked up at me. "These he hid from you, his sad truths."

A somewhat painful recognition hit me. "Perhaps he thought I was too soft to bear them."

René smiled. "He said to me once, 'It is not what you tell a friend but what you refrain from telling him that shows your love for him.'"

A single strand broke in the web that I had perhaps long dangled in.

"So Julian would deceive his friend," I said. "For his own good."

René shrugged, took a final puff of his cigarette. "So," he said. "He is back now in Paris, the landlord."

I looked at him quizzically.

"To Julian's apartment," René explained.

"Oh."

René watched me darkly. "You do not want this key?" he asked. "Perhaps you do not wish to go through Julian's things?"

"Why wouldn't I?" I asked.

René shrugged. "In a man's room, there are always secrets. I learned this in Algeria. Always secret things, and some of them, not so nice."

I waved my hand. "I'm not afraid of anything I might find in Julian's room. Besides, it's the reason I came to Paris."

René crushed out his cigarette like a man who'd given his prisoner one last opportunity to avoid a grim fate. "Okay," he said. "You have made your choice."

* * *

"But, you know, at that moment, I wasn't sure I truly wanted to go to Julian's room or go through his things," I confessed to Loretta when I called her that same night, recounted my conversations with Eduardo and the one I subsequently had with René, his final warning, all of it oddly disturbing.

"And yet, at the same time, I can't stop myself from taking a look inside Julian's apartment," I added. "I see him in that boat, and that compelling urge comes over me again, the need to stop him, to find out if there was some way I could have stopped him."

"You're like one of those obsessed detectives searching through a cold-case folder," Loretta said. "Only with you, the file you're looking through has Julian's name written on it."

"Yes," I said. "That's exactly how I feel. But all this talk of deception, of hiding things from his friends, it's very disquieting, Loretta." I smiled, but edgily. "In a thriller it would be others who are trying to keep me from finding things out. They'd be shooting at me or trying to run me down in a car. But in this case, it seems to be Julian who's covering his tracks." I considered what I just said, then asked, "Did he ever mention a woman named Ilse Grese?"

"No," Loretta said.

"He never wrote about her, but he seems to have been quite interested in her," I said. "She was a guard at Ravensbrück. A very cruel one."

Loretta said nothing, but I sensed a troubling ripple in her mind.

"He once talked about what he called 'beautiful beasts,'" she said. "Women who used their beauty or their innocence to deceive people."

I thought again of Julian's interest in Ilse Grese and others like her, women who'd committed their crimes partly by means of clever disguises. In *The Terror*, he had digressed into a discussion of Charlotte Corday, the murderer of Marat, her certainty that by killing one man she had saved a hundred thousand. He'd made similar points about Mata Hari in that same book, with lengthy discourses on women as revolutionaries, assassins, and spies—in every case, deceptive women. Women who had hidden their true motives, often behind masks of beauty, but sometimes behind masks of kindness, simplicity, innocence. Women who, for all their evil, appeared to be no more dangerous than a . . .

The name that suddenly popped into my mind stopped me cold.

Marisol.

15

It struck me as quite strange that late in the night when I thought of Marisol again, it was not Argentina that came to mind but a scene in *The Terror*, one I later looked up to make sure I'd remembered it correctly.

La Meffraye stands beside a forest woodshed, watching as a small boy skips playfully down a narrow, overgrown path. She is carrying a basket filled with baked goods, and as the boy draws near, she uncovers them just enough to release their fragrance into "the famished air." She does not let go of the cloth, however, but holds it—"with fingers not yet talons"—ready to cover the cakes, and in that gesture make it plain that she will offer none of her sweets to this little boy. For a single, heart-stopping instant, the cloth remains as suspended as her goodness, for this is the first of La Meffraye's potential victims. She wavers as the boy grows near, thinking now that it is only a game, that she will offer the sweet, but the boy will refuse. She convinces herself that this is true, and with that conviction she draws back the cloth and stretches out her hand and offers a sweet, which the boy immediately takes. At that moment, it is life itself that appears to betray La Meffraye by concealing the moral precipice even as she approaches it, a deception that continues until the instant of her fall.

The passage was primarily about La Meffraye, of course, but rereading it I found myself putting Julian in the place of the little boy she coaxes to his death. It was a nightmare scenario that had no doubt been generated by Loretta's mention of "beautiful beasts" and probably would have tormented me all night had I not finally escaped into a book I'd been asked to review. To my great relief, it was something entirely the opposite of Julian's dark tomes, sweet and light and at last uplifting, something completely forgettable, about a blind schoolteacher and a talking dog.

"When can we get into Julian's apartment?" I asked René the next morning when we met at the tiny breakfast room where the hotel served its far from well-heeled guests weak coffee and an even worse bread.

It was the bread René eyed suspiciously. "I would not have thought it possible to find bad bread in Paris," he said. "Perhaps it comes from England?" He stirred a coffee he also appeared to find far from his liking. "We can go today."

I took a sip of coffee. "This morning?"

"If you wish," René said.

"I presume Julian's things are still there?"

"Where else would they be?" René said. "It is on Rue Saint-Denis, as you must know." He smiled. "Julian was always near the prostitutes, but I don't think he enjoyed their pleasures."

"You obviously think he should have," I said. "Why?"

René considered my question for a moment, then lifted his right hand and curled his fingers into a fist. "When you are with your wife, your children, even your friends, you are like this," he said. "But when you are with a whore, you are like this." He opened his hand like one freeing a caged bird. "You can say to her the truths you hide from others. That you hate your life, that your friends are stupid, that your work destroys you, that you are a joke to yourself." A vague sorrow swam into his eyes. "Julian understood this. 'With the fallen,' he said to me once, 'you can be fallen, too.'" He drew his fingers once again into a fist. "But even so, Julian was always like this, clenched, holding on to himself."

René's observation was like him, I thought, a tad over-the-top, and yet I couldn't help but wonder if it truly might be the thing that Julian held within the tightly curled fist of himself that had finally drawn the blade across his veins.

We arrived at Julian's apartment an hour later. René had arranged for the owner of the building to leave the key with an old woman who lived on the first floor. She was North African, and I could see that René immediately regarded her with suspicion, as if he were still in Algiers, where every woman carried a bomb in her basket.

"Okay, we can go up now," he said as he ushered me toward the stairs. "But be careful. As we say, 'Napoleon pissed here.' You cannot trust the wood."

Despite my earlier reservations, I now felt a curious anticipation as I mounted the stairs, a sense that I was coming nearer to Julian. For it was to this one space on earth that, after all his many and extended travels, he had always been drawn back.

So why, I asked myself, as I stepped inside it, did it feel so lost and cheerless, so devoid of the homey quality one associates with decades of living in a space? In this room I'd expected to glimpse at least some small aspect of the devotion I thought Julian must have had for his work. Instead, I saw only evidence of his loneliness and isolation. There were no pictures to brighten the room's dim light, nor even so much as a calendar by which he might have recorded an upcoming rendezvous. There was no radio or television. Evidently, he did not listen to music either while he worked or to relax when his work was done.

What I found was a garret five floors above a dismal street. It had small windows kept tightly shuttered for so long that I had trouble prying them open. When I did, the light revealed the full austerity of the room, the iron bed, the small wooden desk, no element of which was in the least unexpected. Julian had lived like a monk, and on that thought I remembered the day we visited Mont Saint-Michel. We had climbed the stairs to its uppermost tower, where the monks had once sat exposed to the frigid winds of the Normandy coast. In that icy, windswept scriptorium, they'd spent their lives copying manuscripts, using small metal rods to break the ice-encrusted ink, and in this one, almost as uncomfortable and psychologically no less isolated, Julian, the secular anchorite, had written his dark books.

The materials he used in his research filled the bookshelves that covered almost every wall. There were probably around five hundred books, most of them about the eras during which the crimes he studied had taken place. There were books on Spain when the crime of Cuenca had occurred, and on the rest of Europe, particularly Germany and France, at the time of Oradour. Several shelves were devoted to his study of La Meffraye, and he had grouped a number of biographies of Elizabeth Báthory together, along with general histories of Hungary at the time of her crimes, though there were far fewer research materials having to do with her case. One bookcase held works that dealt with Andrei Chikatilo, interspersed with books on Russia during the time of the killer's life span, the dark age of Stalinism.

"Was this the only place Julian had?" I asked René, hoping that perhaps somewhere on earth Julian had found a less gloomy place to live.

"The only one I know about," René answered. He glanced about, clearly repulsed by the bleakness of the room.

"What's in there?" I asked.

He looked at the squat metal filing cabinet I indicated and shrugged.

I was not amused by René's indifference, so I ignored him and walked over and opened the cabinet's only drawer.

In a novel it would be Julian's "secret chamber" I found inside the drawer, and in a single, riveting instant, everything would be revealed, and I would subsequently return to New York knowing what I should have known to save Julian from himself.

But life holds its trump cards more closely to the vest, and what I found was five folders, each identified by a location: Cuenca, Oradour, Brittany, Čachtice, Rostov, places that like dark magnets had irresistibly drawn Julian to them. A sixth file lay beneath the others, but without an identifying label.

I turned to René. "You don't have to stay while I go through this," I told him.

René plopped down in one of the room's two chairs. "I can wait."

"Okay," I said, and with that I took the folders over to the desk and turned the switch on the small lamp I found there, though I expected that René had already arranged for the electricity to be turned off, since Julian had been gone for well over a month by then. But the light came on and in its dim glow I opened the first of the files.

There were mostly photographs Julian had taken in and around Cuenca of the various locations he would later describe in his book, pictures of its dusty plaza, the bridge, the roads that led out of the town, along with various municipal buildings. There was one of the two of us, as well. It had been taken by a passerby, and in the picture Julian was curiously focused, his gaze drawn, as I now recalled, to the Guardia Civil officer who was standing a few feet away talking to a well-dressed American whom we had encountered only minutes before. It was the only photograph with either of us in it, and I could find no reason, save sheer accident, that it had been included with the others. It was also the only picture Julian had failed to identify in his usual way by writing the name of the place on the back.

The photographs in the file marked "Oradour" were of the same sort, all of them taken at the site of the massacre and clearly meant to jog Julian's memory as he wrote. I had not gone with

Julian to the town, so there could be no pictures of the two of us there. Nor were there any photographs of Julian himself or of René, who had accompanied him there several times during the years he'd been writing his book on the massacre. Instead, there was a photograph of a man in his midseventies, dressed in the clothes of a rural laborer and standing beside a horse-drawn cart, with a grove of trees behind him. It was not a particularly striking picture; it was slightly out of focus and no attempt had been made to frame it in an interesting way.

Following Oradour and his work in Bretagne, Julian had gone to Hungary, where he'd spent a considerable amount of time in the area over which the castle of Countess Báthory loomed. In the file marked "Čachtice," as in the others, there were only pictures, and as before, most were of the castle ruins in which her crimes had been committed. But there were also views of the landscape that fell away on every side from the castle mount, and of the small villages that dotted the area, from which many of Elizabeth's victims had been drawn. The only difference in this case was that he had included four portraits that he'd evidently photocopied from various sources; one of them I recognized as the countess, and the other three Julian had identified on the back of the photocopies. The first portrait was of Dorottya Szentes, called "Dorka," according to Julian's note. The others were identified as Ilona Joo and János Ujvary, known as "Ficko." All had been accomplices in the crimes, and on the back of each photocopy Julian had noted their punishments. Dorka and Ilona had each had their fingernails ripped out before being burned alive. Ficko had simply been beheaded.

The fourth file contained exactly what I expected, a short stack of photographs of what were obviously the train and railway stations where Andrei Chikatilo had identified his victims, usually teenage runaways, both boys and girls, of which a collapsing Soviet Union had provided a continuous supply.

Julian had not identified the fifth file, but given what I found inside, its label instantly occurred to me: *Argentina*.

Marisol was in each of the photographs I found inside this file, and in each she was the same age she'd been during our time in Buenos Aires, her hair the same length, and she was even wearing, in one of the photographs, the same clothes she'd worn on the day she first met us.

None of the photographs was the sort normally taken by tourists. Save for one, they were all black-and-white and appeared to have been shot from a considerable distance, no doubt by someone who did not want to be seen, and clearly without Marisol's knowledge.

The exception, in color and quite the sort one would expect from a tourist, was a picture I'd taken in San Martín. In the photograph Marisol was seated next to Father Rodrigo. The two of them appeared to be locked in an intense conversation. Rodrigo had his hand in the air, his finger pointed upward, as if making a crucial point. I had taken it as Julian and I closed in upon them and had only gotten it developed after returning home. When I showed it to Julian, he peered at it for a long time, then said simply, "May I have this?" I'd given it to him, of course, and had never seen it again until now.

I had no idea who might have taken the remaining pictures.

In the first, Marisol is alone, this time in the Plaza de Mayo, the Casa Rosada behind her. In the picture she stares off to the right. Her expression is curiously troubled, and anxiety shows in her posture, suggesting that she might have been waiting for someone who had not appeared.

The second photograph shows Marisol on what is clearly a different day. It is raining and she is drawing in her umbrella as she prepares to board a bus.

In the third photograph Marisol is sitting with a young man near the entrance to Recoleta. His features are indigenous, like Marisol's. But his hair is black and curly, and even though he is sitting, it is obvious that he is quite tall. He is wearing jeans and a sweatshirt, and something in his manner seems wary. Marisol is leaning toward him, the black beads Father Rodrigo had given her hanging loosely from her throat. Her lips are at the young man's ear, parted slightly, so that she is clearly speaking. When I turned it over, I found a typed inscription: *Marisol Menendez y Emilio Vargas*.

"Look at these," I said to René.

He stepped over and looked at the pictures I'd spread out before him.

"I took that one," I told him, "but I don't know where the others came from. The young woman is Marisol. She was our guide in Argentina, the young woman who disappeared."

"Ah," René said softly. "Pretty, but not my type." He smiled. "Too small. Not enough meat. Who is the guy?"

"Someone named Emilio Vargas," I said. "At least that's what it says on the back of the picture."

René continued to stare at the pictures. "They look like surveillance photographs," he said. "They remind me of the old days in Algiers." He took out a cigarette and lit it. "There are eyes upon these two."

"Police surveillance, you mean," I said.

"Police, army, intelligence operatives," René said. "What's the difference?" He smiled, but rather mirthlessly, like one recalling a memory that still troubled him. "There was a young woman in Algiers," he said. "Her name was Khalida. It means 'eternal' in Arabic, but it didn't turn out to be so with this girl." Something in René's eyes shifted to the dark side. "By what you call coincidence, one of our men—"

"Our men?" I interrupted.

"A cop, like me," René answered casually, then continued. "Anyway, he took a picture outside the Milk Bar Café a few minutes before the bombing. Khalida was in this picture, standing a few feet from the door, looking nervous." He tapped the face of Emilio Vargas in the photograph. "Like this one. You can see it in his eyes. He is not at rest, this fellow. His mind is busy. With Khalida, we thought she was this way because she knew about the bomb, that she was maybe a lookout, waiting for the man who was to bring it, but it turned out to be a boy she was waiting for, a boy her father didn't like." He shrugged. "But it was too late before we found this out."

That outcome seemed to strike René as one of life's cruel turns, a twist in events that had swept poor innocent Khalida into the maelstrom of the Algerian revolt.

René laughed, but dryly. "In those days, we did what we did to whoever we thought deserved it." He laughed again, no less humorlessly. "Revolution is not a kind mother to its children."

"What happened to Khalida?" I asked.

"We followed her," René answered. "We thought maybe she would lead us to the big boss. But this girl, she goes to the casbah to buy vegetables; then she goes home with her little basket. She lives with her stupid father, who fills her mind with the massacre at Setif, how the Pieds-Noirs must all be killed, the usual 'Allahu Akbar' bullshit."

"She told you what her father said to her?" I asked.

"Not for a while," René answered with a casual shrug of the shoulders. "But like I said, we did what we did. And by the time we finished, it was too late for little Khalida." He picked up the picture of Marisol and Emilio Vargas and looked at it closely. "Their hands are touching."

I glanced at the photograph, and it was true. On the bench between them, they'd rested their hands in such a way that their fingers touched.

René continued to stare at the picture. "Betrayal is like a landslide in your soul, no?" he said. "After it, you cannot regain your footing." When I gave no response to this, he looked at me. "Perhaps this boy was Marisol's lover," he said. "It is an old story, no? The secret lover. It would have made Julian very jealous, no?"

I shook my head. "Not at all, because Julian was never in love with Marisol," I said. "You've read too many bodice rippers, René."

He was clearly puzzled by the phrase. "Bodice rippers?"

"Romance novels," I explained.

René dutifully drew out his notebook and added the phrase to it. "Very good," he said with small laugh. "I like the English language." His lingering smile coiled into a grimace. "The people, not so much."

16

We left Julian's place a few minutes later. René had obviously found Julian's apartment depressing. But so had I, and thus, with no reason to linger, I had already returned to my hotel later that afternoon when the phone rang.

"Philip Anders?"

"Yes."

"My name is Walter Hendricks. Your father asked me to call you. He said that you were investigating a friend of yours."

Investigating?

Was that truly what I was doing now? I asked myself.

"Your friend was Julian Carlton Wells, I believe?" Hendricks asked.

He had pronounced Julian's full name in the way of a man reading it from a dossier, but I only said, "Yes."

"I live in London now," Hendricks said. "But in the early eighties I was stationed in Buenos Aires. Your father thought I might be of help since I was in charge of the Argentine desk at the time that Mr. Wells became involved with a young woman who worked as a guide for the consulate."

"Marisol," I said. "What do you mean by 'became involved'?"

"Well, at least to the extent that after her disappearance, he inquired about her at Casa Rosada," Hendricks said.

"Julian went to Casa Rosada? I didn't know that."

"It's a matter of record," Hendricks said.

"What kind of record?"

"Well, I'm sure you're aware that dictatorships keep good records on people who visit the seat of government."

"Yes, of course."

"They record their names, their addresses, and if a flag is raised, they investigate them."

"Did Casa Rosada investigate Julian?" I asked.

"No, he wasn't investigated," Hendricks said. "But he was noted. Anyone connected to Ms. Menendez would have been noted."

"Anyone connected with Marisol?" I asked. "Why?"

"Because she had gotten the government's attention, evidently," Hendricks replied. "At least enough for them to have done a background check on her."

"But she seemed so uninvolved in politics," I said. "She seemed quite innocent, actually."

Hendricks laughed. "Well, there's an old line in intelligence work," he said lightly. "Play the kitten. Conceal the tigress." He seemed rather like a man who had completed a small task and was now anxious to move on. "In any event, Casa Rosada had a report on Marisol. There was nothing of intelligence value in it. Hundreds, perhaps thousands, of such reports were compiled during the Dirty War. Marisol's is no different from the others."

"May I see it?" I asked cautiously.

"I see no reason why not," Hendricks said. "But you'd have to come here. It's not something I could just put in the mail." He offered a small laugh. "It's of no importance to anyone, but procedure is a form of paranoia, as I'm sure you know."

"Of course," I said. "I could be in London by Monday if that's convenient for you."

"Monday is fine," Hendricks said. "If you're sure you want to make that effort."

He seemed genuinely surprised that I would pursue the matter any further.

"You thought I wouldn't want to see the report?" I asked.

"Frankly, yes," Hendricks answered.

"Why?"

"Oh, nothing, really," Hendricks said. "Just something your father said."

"Which was?"

"That you were the opposite of Julian."

"In what way?"

"That you had no taste for the 'cloak-and-dagger' life," Hendricks said.

"And Julian did?" I asked.

"Your father seemed to think so," Hendricks admitted.

"But Julian was just a writer," I said.

This was clearly a line of conversation that Hendricks had no interest in pursuing. "So, I'll see you in London, on Monday, right?" he asked.

"Yes."

"Meet me in the bar at Durrants Hotel," Hendricks said, and gave me the address. "Say four in the afternoon?"

"See you on Monday," I said firmly, then, rather than dwell on my father's curious comment about Julian, I decided to go out into the Parisian night, where I found a small café, took a table outside, and ordered a glass of red wine.

It was a warm summer evening, and given my visit to Julian's garret earlier in the day, it inevitably reminded me of Buenos Aires, the similar nights I spent there, often at an outdoor café, all of us talking about whatever came to mind, but almost never politics. It was the one subject Marisol carefully avoided, though at the time I noticed that Julian often tried to move the topic of conversation in that direction. Why had he done that? I wondered now, and on that thought, I recalled the few occasions when he abruptly canceled meeting me at one place or another, times when I didn't know where he was, and during which I now imagined him skulking behind some street kiosk, taking pictures of Marisol.

It was an almost comic notion of Julian as a spy, but a tiny shift in perception can sometimes bring about a seismic shift in suspicion, and in thinking through all this, I felt just such a shift and remembered a particular evening when we were all seated at a small café.

It was more or less at the corner of Avenida de Mayo and the wide boulevard of 9 de Julio, the obelisk at Plaza de la República rising like a gigantic needle in the distance. The night before, one of the junta's notorious Ford Falcon trucks had screeched to a halt before the obelisk. According to several witnesses, four men had leaped out, seized a young couple who were standing at the monument, thrown them into the back, and then jumped in after them as the truck sped away.

The abduction was so blatant, and occurred in the presence of so many witnesses, that the government had issued a statement decrying the kidnapping, though everyone knew that the government's own paramilitary thugs had carried it out and that these latest victims of the repression would likely never be seen again.

"But where do they take them?" Julian asked. "I mean, in the middle of a huge city, hundreds of people will see them."

"And hundreds will say nothing, so some little house in La Boca will do," Marisol answered in that nonpolitical way of hers, as if it were merely a matter of convenience that such people might disappear into one of Buenos Aires's most colorful neighborhoods.

"But they have to take them somewhere," Julian insisted.

"But why to some secret place?" Marisol said. "If they can take them in the middle of a city in the middle of the day, why should they need some cave in a faraway place to put them in?"

She saw that Julian was taken aback by what she said.

"It is before such men have the power that your courage should make you act," she said. "Once they have the power, your fear will control you."

"So you would do nothing to find this young man and woman?" Julian demanded, as if now accusing her of complicity in these crimes.

In response, and for the first and only time, Marisol's eyes flashed with anger, and with the force of a wind she shot forward.

"How would you find these two people, Julian?" she fired back. "Would you take some other man or woman from the street? Would you bring them to some place and torture them or maybe torture their children before their eyes? For, this you would have to do. Do you know why this is true? It is because once a monster has the power, to destroy this monster, you must become a monster, too."

With that, she sat back and with an unexpected violence drained the last of the wine. "There is no blood in your politics. But down here, it is always blood."

Julian said nothing as Marisol drew her hands from the table and let them fall into her lap, a gesture that told me she regretted her outburst because it was not how a guide should act.

Yes, Julian said nothing, but now I recalled that something in his eyes had glimmered darkly, as if, deep inside some secret chamber, a door had opened up.

I had taken the photographs of Marisol that I'd found in Julian's garret with me, and now I drew them from my jacket pocket and looked through them again. The one on top was the one I'd taken, and for a moment, I studied Marisol's face, her quiet features, her gentle eyes.

Play the kitten, conceal the tigress, I heard Hendricks say, and with those words I drew my gaze away from Marisol's face and settled it on her hands. To me, they seemed soft and delicate. I could not imagine them with claws.

PART IV
The Tigress

17

We must imagine a little girl looking up from her man-acled hands, seeing a woman approach, and believing in that instant that she is surely saved. For this woman is the mistress of the castle, she whose delicate white fingers hold authority over the secret chambers of Čachtice. With a gesture, she can open every barred door, pull down all the ropes and chains, order Ficko to the gallows and Dorottya to the pyre for what they have done: stripped her naked, forced her onto this sticky straw mat, and placed the manacles on her wrists and ankles, crimes for which she knows they will now be punished. It is beautiful Elizabeth she sees enter her cell, approach her, and, after a short pause and with a gaze no innocent should ever face, bid Ficko fetch her whip.

It was not Julian's words that awakened me, but my visual-ization of what the passage described: I'd seen Countess Báthory in her gown, weighted with jewels, her fingers sprouting pre-cious stones, drawing nearer to me, her deception so perfect and so humbling. I'd glanced down, like one presented to royalty.

I was not prone to nightmares. In fact, I couldn't remember the last time one had shaken me from sleep. But this one had been extraordinarily vivid, and I'd felt the manacles around my wrists, the gummy straw beneath my feet.

In memory, I thought the scene was much longer and more detailed, but in one of Julian's surprises, as I saw when I found the passage in the book, he had cut it short, then gone into a brief meditation on the added horror, as he supposed it, of being tortured by a woman rather than a man, the ordeal intensified, he said, by a horrifying turn in which humanity's oldest vision of female comfort is suddenly and terrifyingly reversed.

René arrived at the hotel just after nine, looking quite rested, clearly a man who never did battle with himself or questioned his past deeds, even the dark ones he'd probably committed in Algeria.

"You look like Julian," he said when I joined him at the little outdoor café not far from my hotel. "In the morning, he looked like a man who'd spent his night being chased by dogs."

"This happened often?" I asked.

"Many nights, yes," René answered. "Nightmares." He lit his breakfast cigarette, though I suspected it was not his first of the day. There'd probably been one when he rose, one before he shaved and one after, one before he dressed, one on the way out into the morning light. "Julian had terrible ones."

"I had a nightmare of my own last night," I told him. "It had to do with Julian's book *The Tigress*. The scene where we see the countess through one of the girls' eyes, a girl she is about to torture and murder."

"Julian was always doing that," René said absently. "Putting himself in the place of the victim." He glanced toward the street and seemed to lose himself in the traffic, until he said, "Perhaps he did not like to live in his own skin." He shrugged. "But we can live only in the one we have, no?"

The question was so rhetorical I felt no need to answer it.

"Last night, I got a call from a man in London," I told him. "He had a file on Marisol. He implied—well, a bit more than implied—that Marisol was something more than a guide."

René blew a column of smoke out of the right side of his mouth. "Perhaps a dangerous woman? We had one in Algeria. She was called 'the Blade,' and we feared her more than any of the men."

"Feared that she would do to you what you did to Khalida?" I asked cautiously.

"Algeria was a bad place, and in such places, bad things happen," René said. He looked at the lit end of his cigarette like one considering an ember from hell. "She was a torturer and an assassin, this one. These things she did, as you say in English, 'by night.'" He smiled as if admiring of her cunning. "By day, she was an ordinary woman. A teacher in a school." His smile widened and became more cutting. "She deceived everyone. Only her lover knew. And he was as bad as she was. They were—what do you say—'partners in crime'?"

I thought of the pictures of Marisol that Julian had placed in that unmarked file, Marisol looking entirely unaware, going about her business, except when she was with Emilio Vargas. In that picture she had looked quite intense. Had she lived a secret life? I wondered, with Emilio Vargas her partner?

* * *

I left Paris by way of Gare du Nord the next morning. On the high-speed train it was a journey of a little more than two hours, a pleasant ride through the French countryside, then under the channel and on to London. On the way, I thought of nothing but Marisol, though it was one particular memory that triumphed over all the rest.

Julian and I had gone to the Gran Café Tortini to meet her. It was on one of Avenida de Mayo's busy corners and had been long favored by Argentina's greatest artists and performers. Before more or less leaving the country, Borges had been a frequent visitor, along with a number of playwrights and actresses less well known to the outside world. The tavern had even gone so far as to commission wax figures of its most famous customers, so there was Borges, frozen in time, seated at a small table, in conversation with Carlos Gardel, the renowned tango singer, the great writer rendered so peacefully that I could hardly imagine him in the Argentina that now swirled around this serene representation of himself, the violence and the chaos, his beloved country very much in the turmoil my father had recommended that we see.

Marisol, so very punctual on all other occasions, was late. Her failure to appear shook Julian in a way that surprised me, and he'd begun to fidget and glance about.

"She's always on time," he said.

"She's only five minutes late," I reminded him.

"But she's always on time."

"I think you're overreacting a little, Julian," I said. "It's only five minutes."

"Yes," Julian said pointedly, "but it's five minutes in Argentina."

He meant in a country where anything could happen, of course, where a couple could be seized in broad daylight at the obelisk, where in La Plata ten high school students could be kidnapped, raped, and tortured, as they had been some years before in what was known as "The Night of the Pencils."

"Borges at first favored the junta," I said, "but now he attacks it. Usually from Europe."

"Where it's safe," Julian said. He peered out over the avenue, searching the morning crowds for Marisol.

"Sometimes that's the only choice," I said. "What would be the point of staying here?"

"To fight," Julian answered in a way that made me wonder if he'd begun to entertain the romantic notion of adopting Argentina, making its struggle his struggle, Julian a one-man international brigade.

I might have said something to that effect, but then Marisol came rushing up from behind us, looking a bit in disarray, but with her customary energy and good cheer.

"Ah," she said brightly, but with a smile that seemed painted on. "So we have arrived at the cultural center of the city." She glanced toward the wax figures, Borges, blind, holding his cane, and with that glimpse, an uncharacteristic shadow passed over her. "He wrote once that 'the present is alone,'" she said, then looked about at the other customers, most of them well dressed,

161

smoking quietly, sipping coffee. "He was not so blind that he could not see the junta's knife coming for him."

Never until that moment had I seen a trace of mockery in Marisol, and although she quickly brushed it aside and assumed her apolitical station as a cheerful guide, her disdain for Argentina's greatest living writer was clear.

"He wrote that kindness is not what a dagger wants," Julian said, his gaze quite intense.

Marisol looked at him in a way that suggested she had never seen him in exactly the same light. "You are reading Borges?" she asked.

"After you quoted him in Recoleta, how could I not?" Julian said.

"What did you read last?" Marisol asked.

"A short story called 'The Zahir,'" Julian answered.

Then he smiled softly and repeated a line from the story: "In the drawer of my writing table, among draft pages and old letters, the dagger dreams over and over its simple tiger's dream."

Tiger.

Dagger.

What in the name of heaven, I wondered as my train hurtled toward London, did any of it mean?

18

It was around noon when I arrived in London, several hours before I was scheduled to meet Hendricks at Durrants, the small hotel he'd recommended because it was near the American embassy. Durrants had often been used by American officials during the war, a time, spy novelists often pointed out, when the line between the good guys and the bad guys was clearly drawn.

London had changed considerably since my last visit, the influx of immigrants having put its mark on such places as Oxford Street, where Middle Eastern men now smoked hookahs in sidewalk cafés and women strolled about in full burkas. These were changes that gave the city a deeper sense of intrigue, or so it seemed. For I couldn't be sure that my present view of London as a place of plots and counterplots came from the actual changes I noted in the city itself or from the troubling details that were emerging from Julian's life—especially the preoccupation with betrayal that marked both his books and his conversation.

Durrants was on a side street not far from Hyde Park. By the time I got there, one of London's famous drizzles had settled in, along with a touch of fog. Beyond the bar's small windows, I could see black umbrellas sprouting like dark flowers on the street.

"You must be Philip."

I turned from the window to see a man standing at my table.

"Walter Hendricks," he said. "I trust your father is well?"

"As well as can be expected," I told him.

"For a man his age, you mean," Hendricks said with a knowing grin. "And mine, too, for that matter."

Hendricks, however, appeared far less frail than my father. In fact, there was something rough-and-tumble about him, a sense that he could still handle other men with a sure hand. His accent was Southern, of the type that held the soft twang of the Appalachians rather than the rounded o's of the Tidewater. Here was one whose ancestors had fought under Lee, rather than beside him, I thought, men who staggered back from Pickett's charge to hear their general's apology while trying hard not to notice that there was no blood on his sleek lapels.

"I would have expected you and Julian to have gone on the grand tour after college," he said as he sat down opposite me. "Argentina always seemed to be an odd choice." He smiled quite warmly. "'The dusty places,' your father used to call them. He had a soft spot for the people of those regions." His smile grew into a soft chuckle. "I told him that he should spend some time in Timbuktu, where even the food tastes like dirt."

"I'm sure he would have loved a posting like that," I said in defense of my father. "To face that kind of reality."

Hendricks's laughter trailed away. "Not for long," he said with the certainty of one who'd experienced such places. "No one likes that kind of reality for long."

He glanced about the bar. "Have you ever been here?"

"No."

He smiled. "Well, my guess is that many a plot was hatched in this place," he said. We were sitting at a small, round table clearly meant to accommodate drinks only. "It wouldn't surprise me if Reilly, Prince of Spies, once sat right in this corner, at this little table, and wondered if it might be possible to have Lenin assassinated."

Even in such casual conversation, Hendricks's eyes remained penetrating, the gaze of a man to whom one should not lie.

"I love history," he added. "It's the reason I retired to London, the sheer history of the place. I read history all the time. Probably as much as your father reads spy novels. He seemed to live in books back then." He laughed. "He was reading *The Thirty-Nine Steps* the day I met him."

"He doesn't read now," I said. "He watches old movies. Black-and-white mostly. From the forties."

"Yes," Hendricks said. "That would be his type." His smile bore the usual indulgence that men of the world accord their dreamier compatriots, and in it I saw the most that was likely ever given to my father by the sturdier and far less idealistic souls who'd pulled the strings at Foggy Bottom. "Stories about lone heroes. That was what he wanted to be, I think."

"But instead he lived his life behind a desk," I said.

Hendricks nodded. "That's true," he admitted. "But I'm not sure your father would have functioned very effectively beyond a desk."

"Really?"

Hendricks nodded. "As a matter of fact, he sometimes reminded me of what Trotsky said about Czar Nicholas."

"Which was?"

"That he should have been a kindly neighborhood grocer or something of that sort," Hendricks said. "A simple tradesman, invisible to history. But your father not only wanted to change the world, he wanted to do it by means of derring-do." He laughed. "In C Building, he was the resident Walter Mitty."

The resident Walter Mitty.

That was both the saddest and truest thing anyone had ever said about my father, that he had lived his life behind a desk while watching spy movies and reading spy books and dreaming of the romantic secret-agent life he would never have.

To think of my father in such a way pained me, so I turned the conversation away from him.

"So, the report on Marisol," I said as a reminder of why I'd come to London.

"Marisol, yes," Hendricks said. "I have to say that I am a bit curious as to why you're so interested in your friend's quixotic effort to find this young woman."

"Was it quixotic?" I asked.

"I would call it that, yes," Hendricks answered flatly. "He was trying to find someone he didn't know much about in a country about which he knew even less. He had no connections in Argentina and no authority to conduct any sort of inquiry into this young woman's whereabouts. And yet, he felt that he could simply and quite brazenly walk into Casa Rosada and ask whatever questions he liked." He shook his head gravely. "Such a little boy."

I recalled something Julian had said many years before. I'd been talking about Mussolini, how amazingly childlike he'd been, his love for mounting white horses and prancing about, his comical strut. The whole story had seemed to darken Julian's mood, his voice very serious when he said, "He wasn't funny to the Ethiopians." With that, he'd shaken his head softly, then added, "Men with power shouldn't be little boys."

Hendricks's gaze took on an added seriousness. "How could he have possibly expected anyone in authority to tell him anything? Not only where Marisol was or what had happened to her, but who she was?"

"Who she was?" I asked by way of directing the conversation back to her.

Hendricks smiled. "Nowadays they'd call her a 'person of interest,'" he said.

"To Casa Rosada," I added.

"Yes."

"Why?"

"Because she was evidently working for a well-known Montonero named Emilio Vargas," Hendricks answered matter-of-factly.

I tried to conceal my surprise. "Julian had a picture of Marisol with him," I said. "Where would he have gotten it?"

"Perhaps he was more successful at Casa Rosada than I thought," Hendricks answered with a shrug. "Anyway, as to Vargas. He was called 'the Hook.' It was his method of choice. To hang people on meat hooks."

I remembered an atrocity Julian had once mentioned, an entire Balkan village rounded up and loaded onto trucks, then transported to the local abattoir, where every man, woman, and child was put through all the stages of animal slaughter. He had described the process so vividly and with such detail that I'd finally skipped ahead.

"Vargas was as vicious as they come," Hendricks said. "Names were given to him and he had those people kidnapped. Their children, too, sometimes. Torturing them was Vargas's specialty. He would have justified it, of course. And it's true, there are people who can't be broken by torture. But when they see their children, naked, strapped to a bed beside a small electric generator . . ." He stopped. "I'm sure you get the picture."

I nodded.

"He operated a torture farm in the Chaco," Hendricks added.

"That's where Marisol was from," I told him.

Hendricks nodded. "Yes. I saw that when I read the report."

"What happened to Vargas?" I asked.

"He was shot eventually," Hendricks answered. "It was quite clear that before he died, he'd been rather badly treated."

"What does that mean?"

"That he'd been tortured for a long time," Hendricks said. "Missing some important parts, if you know what I mean." A smile slithered onto his face. "He deserved every cut, if you ask me."

"Where was he found?"

"Floating in the Plata," Hendricks answered.

"I can't imagine Marisol having anything to do with a man like that," I said.

"Then how do you explain the picture?" Hendricks asked. "I don't know how Julian got that picture, but I do know this: Casa Rosada had come to suspect that Marisol was a spy for Vargas and that she was primarily trying to find information while working as a guide for the American consulate."

I had briefly imagined Marisol in this cloak-and-dagger role, skulking in the shadows of the consulate, pressing her ears against a door or her eyes to a keyhole.

"Of course, that might only have been her cover," Hendricks added.

He saw that I didn't understand this.

"It's called the double take," Hendricks explained. "The agent allows herself to be revealed as a little, insignificant operative in order to conceal the fact that she is actually a very important one. So you have to look again. Hence, the double take."

"But there's no evidence that Marisol was . . ." My question trailed off.

"No, but there was an intelligence report on her," Hendricks answered. "It didn't say a lot, but it didn't have to, because what it says emphatically just by existing is that Marisol was a person of considerable interest to Casa Rosada." He shrugged. "As I'm sure you know, Buenos Aires was a nest of vipers in those days. On both sides, people were being tortured, killed. For most people in the world, politics is not a game."

There was more than a hint of condescension in Hendricks's last remark, the implication that in Argentina Julian and I were playing hopscotch in a torture chamber.

Hendricks placed his briefcase on the table. "Was Julian political?" he asked.

"Political," I repeated. "Do you mean was he an idealist, some kind of an ideologue?"

"Those two are very different," Hendricks said.

"In what way?"

"An idealist is a man with blinders," Hendricks answered. "An ideologue is a man who's blind." He looked at me gravely. "Which was Julian?"

"I'm not sure he was either one," I said. "I don't think he had time to be before . . ."

"Before what?"

"Before Marisol disappeared," I said. "And after that, as you know, he did nothing but look for her."

Hendricks nodded. "Look for her, yes."

Now his eyes gave off the sense of a man who'd seen too much and who regarded those who hadn't as little more than children.

"Who did this friend of yours think he was, hmm?" he asked. "Some superhero? The type your father dreamed of being?" He looked at me as if the bloom of youth were still on my cheeks. "Grow up, please."

He paused a moment, then leaned forward in a way that was decidedly avuncular.

"Do you know what real warriors say about a fictional creation like Rambo?" he asked. "That he would be dead in five minutes. But that during the course of those fateful five minutes, his bullshit heroics would kill every soul under his command."

170

He watched me for a moment, like a man looking for a hidden motive; then he leaned forward and looked at me as though certain of one thing: that for all my privilege, all my expensive education, I could still stand another lesson.

"You cannot know a people if you do not share their pain," he said, "and Julian knew nothing about what was going on in Argentina. He was just a tourist who happened to stick his toe into a river of blood."

He drew an envelope from his briefcase.

"Be glad you've lived a cautious life, Philip," he said. "Because the reckless die young." The envelope slid toward me. "And they kill young, too."

19

In literature, the unopened envelope occupies a privileged place. Most famous, perhaps, is the one Angel does not find in *Tess of the d'Urbervilles,* and the lack of its discovery causes a deeper tragedy to unfold.

As I began to read it, I couldn't help wonder if a further tragedy might also unfold in the report Hendricks had given me.

It was seventeen pages long. It had originally been written in Spanish, but Hendricks had gone to the trouble of having it translated.

The first pages were dully biographical. They recounted the date and place of Marisol's birth, the deaths of her parents, her subsequent border crossings from Argentina to Paraguay, and her final settlement at age six, now an orphan, in the charge of Father Rodrigo, whose parish "presided over various charitable affairs within the region of Gran Chaco."

On page 3, Marisol arrives in Buenos Aires. She is fourteen years old, the recipient of a small scholarship at a Catholic academy, one arranged by Father Rodrigo "as a result of her intelligence and ambition." Marisol continues in this school for the next four years, chalking up impressive grades and glowing testimonials from the nuns, who find her dutiful, obedient, and "quick to take advantage of any opportunity to please." She studies English more assiduously than any other subject.

On page 9, Marisol graduates from the academy, then begins to take courses at a vocational school that focuses on various aspects of what the report calls "clothing." While at the school, she focuses on design.

To support herself, Marisol takes several jobs, all of the sort traditionally opened to the penniless. For a time she is a waitress, but she also serves as an usher at the opera house and as a clerk in its gift shop. She works as a tour guide at one of the city's art museums. While working at the museum, her proficiency in English is noticed, and she makes a little extra money by leading English-speaking tours.

Throughout this time in her life, Marisol continues to take courses at the vocational school. In this way, she is like hundreds of other young women in the city. But now, and for the first time, something ominous appears in the report: "Subject makes contact with the American consulate in Buenos Aires and is employed as a guide."

I knew that it did not take much to fall under the eye of the junta, but Marisol's work as a guide struck me as so unlikely to yield useful information that it would hardly have been worth it for them to keep track of her, much less bother to kidnap and "disappear" her. I found no evidence that she'd made any effort to cozy up to any particular person, some high civilian or military official she might seduce, and from whom, during an evening of sex-hazed pillow talk, she might garner a bit of useful intelligence. In fact, she had never even served as a guide to anyone who could have been remotely considered a conduit for vital information.

The final two pages of the report provided both a chronology that succinctly recorded the previous events and a complete list of the people to whom Marisol had been recommended by the consulate, along with their professions, and their reasons for being in Argentina. Almost all of them were businessmen or people connected in one form or another to cultural exchange. Among the people for whom Marisol had served as a guide, there were no military personnel listed, no diplomats, no high officials from any government. Instead, Marisol appeared to have spent most of her time escorting members of various religious organizations who moved in steady caravans through whatever region was perceived rich in desperate souls, along with low-level representatives from a few small charities. It was such modest figures who made up Marisol's list of clients, hardly the sort that might interest a spy.

So if she had indeed been a Montonero operative, what information had she brought to Vargas, I wondered, and from whom had she received it? The answer was that her information would have been of little value and she herself of little importance as a spy.

Such is what any Casa Rosada agent would have seen on first glancing at Marisol.

But what might he have seen, I wondered, if he'd done a double take?

* * *

The Skype screen flickered slightly, but I could see my father quite clearly. He was wearing a burgundy robe with a velvet lapel, and it struck me that he looked much more like some retired CIA chief than a lowly State Department functionary. Because of that, I wondered if he might sometimes still be captured by the Walter Mitty fantasies Hendricks had mentioned, a man who, in his private moments, assumed an imaginary role far more important than any he'd ever actually had.

"I spoke to your friend, Hendricks," I told my father. "He thinks that Marisol might have been a Montonero operative of some sort."

I half expected my father to laugh at this, but instead he only nodded. "Well, it can be seductive," he said. "The world of intrigue."

I took him through the details of my talk with Hendricks, Casa Rosada's suspicions that Marisol was a spy who had kept her ears open while working for the American consulate. Then I added the odder supposition that she might have been a far more important figure, her lowly guide job merely a mask.

"What might she have been?" he asked.

"She seems to have been associated with a very bad guy," I said. "His name was Emilio Vargas. He was from the Chaco, like Marisol."

My father didn't seem at all surprised by what to me still seemed an outrageous conjecture.

"It's easy to get caught up in a revolution," he said in his most worldly tone. "It's a very heady business. Especially for the young. You start to imagine yourself a Mao or a Lenin, the savior of your country."

I recalled what Harry had said about Julian's book on Chikatilo, how he'd gone to some lengths to detail the killer's elaborate fantasies, the serial killer and sexual psychopath as savior of Mother Russia.

"It has a terrible allure, being part of a secret army," my father added. "It's possible that Marisol could have been swept into something like that. Youth is a minefield, after all. Even Julian was attracted to the idea of being a secret agent."

This was true, of course. Even before our trip to Argentina, he mentioned "secret gears," which I took to mean some sort of intelligence work. But he appeared to drop any interest in such a life after Argentina.

"What part of that sort of work interested him?" I asked.

"Deception," my father answered matter-of-factly. "Disinformation, that sort of thing. Playing psychological games. He thought himself quite clever, you know."

"Very clever, yes," I said.

"He thought he would be best at winning someone's confidence," my father added. "Particularly in a one-on-one situation."

I thought of the times I arrived at the exact time and place of rendezvous only to find Julian and Marisol already waiting for me, sitting at some little table, their glasses half-empty, so it was obvious that they'd been there for quite a while.

"Hendricks gave me the report Casa Rosada had on Marisol," I said. "It makes it pretty clear that Marisol never had contact with anyone who would been of interest to the Montoneros while she worked as a guide for the American consulate."

I stopped cold as the thought hit me, worked it through, then stated it.

"No one except for me, that is," I told my father. "And Julian."

"Why would the Montoneros have had any interest in you or Julian?" my father asked.

"Because we were connected to you, Dad," I answered.

My father said nothing, but I could see his mind turning this over.

"We would have been the perfect targets, wouldn't we?" I asked. "If Marisol had actually been a spy."

"But how would she have known that you and Julian were connected to me?" my father asked.

"Well, for one thing, she heard Father Rodrigo mention you," I answered. "And beyond that, I once heard Julian describe you as something of a mentor. As a matter of fact, he even suggested that you were a little higher up in the department than you were."

"Did he?" my father asked softly.

"Yes, and I also remember him telling her about our house," I added. "He described it pretty grandly, so she might have gotten the idea that you were quite powerful, the center of an influential circle."

"How ironic," my father said quietly. "Since I was never anything but—"

"Julian had a picture of Marisol with Emilio Vargas," I interrupted. "Where would he have gotten it?"

"From someone in Casa Rosada, I suppose," my father answered. He appeared to run a curious possibility through his mind. "He might have gotten it from my contact there."

"You had a contact in Casa Rosada?" I asked, surprised that he'd even lightly touch such cloak-and-dagger operations.

"She was only a clerk," my father added quickly. "She's in her eighties now."

"So no longer a Casa Rosada functionary, of course."

"Not for many years," my father said.

"Where is she now?"

"Why do you want to know that, Philip?"

"Because this contact of yours might have some idea of who Marisol was, what she was doing," I answered. "She might know if any of this is true about her, that she was . . . a deceiver."

My father drew in a long, slow breath. "She went back to Hungary," he said. "You should be aware that hers was not a clean record. You've probably never heard of the Maros Street hospital massacre."

It occurred in Budapest, he went on to tell me, a peculiarly monstrous incident during the last-ditch effort by the collaborationist Arrow Cross to annihilate the few Jews not yet deported from Hungary. Having taken control of the city in the wake of the retreating Germans, the men of the Arrow Cross Party went on a rampage, and among the victims were the most helpless of the city's remaining Jews. The poorhouse on Alma Street was attacked, as well as the hospital on Városmajor. But it was the patients, doctors, and nurses at the Jewish hospital on Maros

Street who suffered the full brunt of Arrow Cross cruelty, a full day of slaughter that included torture and murder.

"My contact played a part in it," my father said at the end of this narrative. "She never denied this. At least that was to her credit."

"What happened to her after she left Casa Rosada?"

"She returned to Budapest," my father answered. "She got a job with the American consulate."

"Her reward for being a spy?" I asked.

My father didn't answer, but I saw the answer in his eyes, all the dirty little deals he'd known about but never approved of, the ratlines and secret bombings and clandestine overthrows.

"Do you know where she is?" I asked.

"She retired and moved into a small town in what is now Slovakia."

I was surprised that my father knew this, as he could tell from my expression.

"We were . . . friends briefly," he told me. "Your mother died long before."

"I see," I said.

"We met in a restaurant on one of my few trips to Buenos Aires," he added. "Each time I went there, I saw her. It was never love." He shrugged. "But she worked in Casa Rosada, and so I . . ."

"Played the secret agent?" I asked.

My father nodded with the sadness of one who had run out of fantasies, a Walter Mitty no longer inclined to daydream.

"Foolish," he said softly. "It was all very foolish."

For a moment he seemed lost in thought. Then, quite

suddenly, like one who sensed himself rather under surveillance, he said, "Anyway, since she was my only contact, I sent Julian to her when he was looking for Marisol."

"It was you who sent him to Casa Rosada?" I asked, surprised that he'd never mentioned this.

"It was a fool's errand," my father said. "But he seemed desperate to find this young woman. She'd gotten under his skin somehow. He was really quite determined. I thought my contact might help him solve the mystery of her disappearance."

"Would she talk to me, this contact of yours?" I asked.

"I'm sure she would," my father said. "For old times' sake, as they say."

"Who did this woman work for?"

"A colonel by the name of Ramírez," my father answered. "Juan Ramírez. He ran a few of the junta's *escuelitas*."

He saw that I didn't understand the word.

"The 'little schools,'" my father said. "There were a great many of them in Argentina at that time. They were places where the enemies of Casa Rosada were taken to be reeducated. That is to say, where they were tortured." He appeared to consider his next move with a strange seriousness. "I could write to her if you like. I'm sure she'd been willing to talk to you."

"Yes, do that," I said. "I'll follow up with a letter of my own." I reached for a paper and pen. "What's her name, your contact?"

"Irene."

"And her last name?"

"Jóság," my father answered. "It's Hungarian, of course. It means 'goodness.'"

Goodness.

How bright a word, I would later realize, to have given so dark a new direction to my tale.

20

When I later located Irene Jóság's village on a map, I saw that it was quite near to Čachtice, where the Bloody Countess had lived and in whose looming castle she had carried out her many torture-murders, her life and crimes the subject of Julian's fourth book, *The Tigress*.

The countess was born in Nyirbator, Hungary, in 1560, the daughter of one of that country's ruling families, and according to Julian, nothing in her early life suggested the monster she would become. Rather, she was quite studious, and by the time of her marriage, she had mastered Latin, German, and Greek, and had read a great deal in science and astronomy—learning that Julian portrayed as part of her perfect disguise.

At the age of fifteen, she married the son of another equally favored family, and in 1575, the presumably happy couple took up residence at Varanno, a small palace, before moving to a larger one at Sárvár, and finally to the castle that was her wedding gift, the looming, often fogbound Čachtice.

The war to defend Europe against the Ottoman encroachment would last until 1606, and during all that time it fell to Elizabeth not only to manage but to defend her holdings against the ever-threatening Ottomans. This she did with great skill and vigor. But it was not all she did, for although the outer walls of Čachtice remained strong, something was crumbling inside them; it was during this period that loneliness began to weather Elizabeth's carefully constructed edifice and, in that weathering, reveal what lay beneath. With her husband at his studies in Vienna, Elizabeth now, for the first time in her life, had real power, that is to say, power on the scale of a man's. She was the lady of the estate, her authority absolute, and like Ilse Grese at Ravensbrück, she began to wield a whip.

It was a weapon she could use with complete impunity, as it turned out, because her husband had by then become chief commander of Hungarian troops in the western war against the Ottoman Empire, a campaign that removed him for months at a time. Thus, with no one to stay her hand, she began first to berate and then to slap her servants, each attack fueling the next, until at last she drew blood and later found that where this drop had fallen on her cheek, the flesh beneath had seemed to bloom. In the blood of servants, she had miraculously discovered youth's eternal fountain.

More of this restorative blood was easy to find, of course, and in the coming months and years, Elizabeth found plenty of it. Enough first to taste, then to sip, then to drink. Enough first to dot her finger, then to cover her face, then to coat her body.

But even the walls of Čachtice were not thick enough to hide what was going on there. The first rumors began to circulate as early as 1602, and by 1604, when Elizabeth's husband died, they could no longer be dismissed, for they were not rumors of infidelity or even of odd sexual practices, both of which were common among the nobility of the time.

It was a Lutheran minister who finally raised his voice so loudly that the authorities were forced to hear it. Even then, however, they were slow to act, and it was not until 1610 that an investigation was ordered, which resulted in Elizabeth's being caught in the act of beheading a teenage girl.

Elizabeth, being of such high birth, was put under house arrest, where she remained until her death in 1614.

During those intervening years, the investigation continued and more than three hundred victims were discovered, Julian reported, though the exact number of young girls who lost their lives in the secret chambers of Čachtice could never be known.

Julian had not been reticent to detail the horrors of Čachtice. There'd been whippings and mutilations. Elizabeth had bitten off parts of her victims' faces and other body parts. She'd taken some of the girls out into the snow and watched them freeze to death. She'd performed surgery and other medical procedures upon them as well. She'd observed the stages of starvation before death. She'd used needles and hot irons. There seemed no end to her cruel ingenuity.

But in Julian's account, the countess's crimes, horrible as they were, were in some sense less cruel than her deceits, her great show of piety, her many gifts to the Church, the changing aspects of her mask. For Julian, it seemed, of all creatures great and small, it was the chameleon that should be most feared, particularly—I thought of both the Terror, La Meffraye, and the Tigress, Countess Báthory—when deceit took the shape of a woman.

* * *

On the map, a jagged road led from the countess's castle to what I imagined to be the far more modest abode of Irene Jóság, and I found myself imagining Julian driving down it, bleary-eyed from another sleepless night, his head spilling over with the horrors of Čachtice.

I could have simply corresponded with Irene Jóság, of course, but by then I'd come to think of myself as something of a detective, and in that guise I entertained the hope that by actually talking to her I might learn something that would clear up the great bramble I'd stumbled into, a thicket of intrigue in which identities changed as well as motives, where I could no longer tell what Marisol had been or whether Julian had ever guessed that she was something other than she seemed.

"You'll miss Paris," Loretta said when I told her that I was heading for Hungary. "Everyone does."

I told her that I was going to Hungary because my father had given me the name of someone who was at Casa Rosada when Julian was in Argentina. Now I added, "Julian went to Casa Rosada looking for Marisol."

"Why would he have gone there?" Loretta asked. "I thought Marisol had nothing to do with politics."

"That's not so clear anymore," I said, then related what Hendricks had told me in London, along with my subsequent conversation with my father, the result being that I was now quite uncertain about who Marisol had been.

"So she might have been anything," Loretta said at the end of my account.

"Yes," I said.

For the first time, I felt a turn in the narrative I'd been living through.

It was clear that Loretta had noticed a dark undertow in my answer.

"Do you think Julian ever knew any of this?" she asked.

"I don't know," I answered.

For a moment I felt that we were both fixed in a space no one else could share.

"Philip, are you still there?" Loretta asked.

Her tone was troubled, and I realized that I'd been silent for a long time, and the silence alarmed her.

"Yes," I said.

There was a brief pause, then Loretta said, "Would you mind if I joined you, Philip? Could you use a traveling companion?"

It struck me that Julian had never had such a companion, and that perhaps this, too, had served to doom him.

Might it doom me, too?

With that question I felt myself curiously imperiled, like a man moving down a river, into a darkness, now afraid that at the end of the journey there might be revelations as fatal to me as they had been for Julian, terrors that he had faced in solitude and isolation but that I had not the courage to face alone.

"Yes," I said, like a man reaching for a life rope. "Yes, I could."

* * *

She arrived in Budapest a week later, dressed in a dark red blouse and floral skirt, glancing swiftly here and there, until she saw me in the waiting crowd.

"Welcome," I said when she came over to me, and meant it.

Even so, she looked at me doubtfully. "Really, Philip?"

"Yes, really," I assured her. "As you guessed, I could use some company."

"But you've always seemed quite self-contained."

"We're not always how we seem," I said.

"Almost never, in fact," Loretta said.

Something in her gaze took hold of me so that I felt exactly as Charles feels when he sees Emma Bovary, how dark her eyes are and how marked with fearless candor.

The intense feeling that swept over me at that moment had to be diverted, so I nodded toward where I had a car waiting.

On the drive into the city, Loretta kept her eyes keenly fixed on the new surroundings. In that keenness, that hunger for things she had not seen before, I glimpsed the young girl she had once been, the one who had traveled with Julian, two brilliant children facing their father's camera as they stood at the bottom of the Spanish Steps or at the Eiffel Tower, pictures she'd framed and hung in the Montauk house. There'd been other pictures, too, those same children walking through the butterfly house in Salzburg or along the shaded trails of the Vienna Woods. They had also strolled Barcelona's Ramblas together and paused to marvel at Sagrada Família.

In each photograph, they appeared splendidly happy, children endowed with as much good fortune as anyone could wish.

Those two bright young faces had changed quite a bit over the years, but it was Julian's that changed the most, and at our last meeting I'd gotten the feeling that it was not just exhaustion that plagued him but some tumorous mental growth that had at last broken through the surface.

When I said this to Loretta, she considered it a moment, then said, "You know, he said something quite disturbing a couple of days before he went out in the boat. He was sitting by the pond. I went out to him. He had that look in his eye, like he was deep in thought. Just as a matter of conversation I said, 'So, how are you doing, Julian?' I expected him to answer the way he usually did, something like, 'I'm fine, Loretta, how are you?' But instead he quoted that line from *The Rime of the Ancient Mariner*. You know, the one where he says, 'A thousand slimy things lived on and so did I.' I took it for a little joke and made nothing of it. Julian often said things like that. Self-deprecating things. But this time, I should have known that he was in a very bad place."

"We let a lot go by, didn't we?" I asked. "There were signs we didn't read."

She nodded. "Yes, there were."

When we reached the hotel, Loretta stepped out of the car and looked at its ornate facade. I could see that she recognized it.

"Julian mentioned this hotel," she said. "I remember it from his letters. 'It has beautiful Zsolnay tiles,' he said."

"They're in the bathhouse," I told her. "In the old days, it was used by the Soviets. It's where they met their agents. Or at least that's what the hotel manager told me. In any event, it gives the place some history."

Seconds later we were in the lobby. I nodded toward the bar. "Maybe a drink before you go up?"

"Yes, that would be nice."

We were soon seated at a small table in the bar, drinks in hand, Loretta casting her eyes about the room with what still seemed like a hint of childlike wonder.

"Very dark here," she said. "Thick curtains."

"It looks like a place where 'certain documents' might have been exchanged," I said, rather as a joke.

"Julian described it in one of his letters," Loretta said. "He said that it looked like an old man still concealing his crime." She took a sip of her drink. "Do you think he came upon this hotel by accident?"

I shrugged. "I suspect the bullet holes near the door and around the first-floor windows might have gotten his attention," I answered. "The manager here speaks English quite well, so I've listened to his history of the place. I asked him about the bullet holes. They're from when the Arrow Cross—the Hungarian fascist party that collaborated with the Nazis—defended the city against the Russians. The Germans had abandoned it by then."

Loretta reached into her bag and retrieved a single photograph. "I thought you might want to see this," she said as she handed it to me.

In the photograph, Julian is seated at the little office alcove on the second floor of the Montauk house, a large window behind him, the pond shimmering in the background. He is holding a book whose title I can't make out, but which seems as battered as the man holding it. His hair is slightly mussed, as it often was in the morning, and he is wearing the blue robe I gave him as a welcome-home gift upon his return from Russia.

"Why this picture?" I asked.

"I thought of it after I talked to you," Loretta said. "It's the last picture of Julian. He set up the camera and took it himself."

"It's an odd self-portrait," I said. "Not very flattering."

"I didn't know he'd taken it," Loretta said. "But when I started to put the camera away, I noticed it and printed it out." She drew the picture from me and looked at it very intently. "It's a warning, a picture like that: 'Don't end up like me.'" She handed the photograph back to me, then looked toward the window, out at the busy street life. "I've often thought that if life were fair, we'd be given a picture of where we'll end up if we continue down the road we're on." She turned, and the smile she offered quickly faded. "That might be enough to save us."

For a time, she was silent, then she said, "So, what's your theory about Julian at the moment, Philip?"

"I don't have one," I admitted.

"I don't either," Loretta said. "I simply think Julian was a condemned man, a man who was sentenced to some sort of inner life imprisonment."

"But for what crime?" I asked.

"That would be the question, wouldn't it?" Loretta asked. She took another sip from her drink. "The crime of Julian Wells," she added. "Still unsolved." She seemed suddenly to shuffle off the weariness of her long flight, perhaps even some part of the long aridity that had marked her life since Colin's death. "So," she said, "where do we begin?"

21

All literature skirts the otherwise insurmountable issue of man's many different languages. Fictional characters roam from country to country miraculously speaking whatever language they encounter. The fictional character is sent from London to Istanbul and gets off the train in a city in which everyone speaks English. Throughout the fictional world, the Tower of Babel ever lies in ruins, so that upon first encounter with an African bushman or a Bedouin trader, all indecipherability vanishes, and our hero immediately engages in a profound discussion of life, death, and eternity, when, in actuality, he would have been struggling to locate the nearest watering hole.

This is to say that it was not within my power or Loretta's to simply head out of Budapest and locate Irene Jóság somewhere in the wilds of Slovakia without assistance. Arrangements had to be made, and several days were required to make them, a time during which Loretta and I strolled the streets of the city, took in its churches and museums and monuments.

By then I'd spoken often enough with the hotel manager to have gained some slight knowledge of the city, at least enough to add a bit of local history to our strolls about the city.

191

"After the fall of the Soviet Union, the Russians were required to take away all the other monuments they'd erected to themselves in Budapest," I told Loretta. "All the plaques and red stars, everything." I pointed to a pedestal upon which rested a single pair of boots. "Of course the Hungarians had already beheaded the statue of Stalin. In fact, they cut him all the way down to his boots."

We turned and walked on for a time, now closing in upon the Danube.

"I remember something Julian once told me," I said. "He said that a traveler enters the world into which he travels, but a tourist brings his own world with him and never sees the one he's in."

"Where did he say this?" Loretta asked.

"In Buenos Aires," I answered.

She walked on without speaking until she suddenly stopped and said, "Then Julian must, at some point, have no longer thought of himself as a tourist there."

"But that's what he was," I told her, then returned to my meeting with Hendricks, how he'd seemed contemptuous of Julian's "quixotic" effort to find Marisol. "And in a way, I think Hendricks was right about Julian," I said. "Because in a sense, he was a tourist. How could he have been anything else?"

"By being drawn into the turmoil," Loretta answered.

"How might that have happened?"

Her expression was pure collusion, as if we two were now in league, testing the same conjectures, exploring the same possibilities.

"I've been thinking of something you said the night you called me and told me you were going to Hungary," Loretta answered. "It was about the report on Marisol, the fact that she might have been a spy. You mentioned that she hadn't been with anyone important as a guide but that she might have gotten the idea that you or Julian could have known something."

"Or some*one*—namely, my father," I said.

"Yes," Loretta said. Her gaze became quite intense. "And I thought, if she actually was a spy, she might have had a completely different idea about Julian. Not as someone who knew something but as someone who might later be in a position to know something."

"I'm not sure where you're headed."

"That she might have thought he had access to information," she answered. "Or at least that he could gain access to it. Information from your father, for example. And so, for that reason, she might have tried to turn Julian. That's the term, isn't it? To 'turn' someone?"

"You mean Marisol might have tried to turn Julian into a traitor?"

She saw how unlikely I thought that was.

"It's the oldest turn there is, Philip," she reminded me. "As a matter of fact, it goes back to Eve."

There was Jezebel, too, and Delilah. The list of female deceivers is very long indeed. Could Marisol have been such a woman? If so, her disguise was quite brilliant, for I had no inkling that she was anything other than an admirable young woman, dutiful and striving, who simply wanted a fighting chance.

And yet, the photograph I'd found in Julian's apartment couldn't be denied. Marisol seated with Emilio Vargas, leaning toward him, whispering in his ear. Might she have targeted a young man who was naive and inexperienced in the ways of intrigue, one already determined to do some great good in the world, romantic and idealistic, a well-connected young American she could "turn"?

I thought again of the photograph, Marisol's lips at Vargas's ear.

Might she have been whispering the name of this young man?

It was only a question, and yet I could almost hear the name she whispered.

Julian, I thought, and on that name, I once again recalled the time he got into an argument with me over some small detail, how uncharacteristically wrong he was, and how, to prove him so, I rushed back to my room to find the evidence. It was just after Father Rodrigo's departure, and I'd left him with Marisol at a small café near San Martín. I'd returned to find them talking very somberly, and at that moment, as I thought now, they had truly looked like two conspirators caught in a moment, to use René's phrase, "of dark conclave."

As if it were a surveillance photograph, I saw Julian at the instant he suddenly caught me in his eye, his expression not unlike that of a little boy caught in a disreputable act.

Had I caught him? I wondered now.

And had the "crime" he'd long ago claimed that I had witnessed been his treason?

* * *

There are times when no alternate route presents itself, so that your only choice is to continue down the road you're on. Now that road led out of Budapest.

By the time I took it, I'd secured the service of a guide. His name was Dimitri, and he was quite young and eager, utterly unlike René. On the way to Irene Jóság's village, he spoke of his great love of English, how assiduously he read the great writers of that language. He was astonishingly impressed to learn that I was a critic and that Loretta was the sister of what he called a "real writer," though he was quick to admit, not without apology, that he'd never heard of her brother.

"What is again the name of your brother?" he asked as he pulled out a small notebook.

"Julian Wells."

"I am sorry to say that I have not read his books," Dimitri told her, "but I am certain that I will very soon search for them."

Loretta promised to send him some of Julian's books when she returned to the States, and when we stopped for lunch, Dimitri responded by gathering her a bundle of wildflowers.

After that we drove on, now through a countryside that felt increasingly dense.

"There's Čachtice," I said when it came into view. "Countess Báthory's torture chamber."

Loretta's gaze grew more intense as she peered at it, but the intensity was combined with noticeable dread.

"Are you sure you want to go to the castle?" I asked cautiously.

To my surprise she was, so Dimitri drove up the winding road that led to the ruin.

It was not overwhelmingly large, and as in the case of many such places, the walls had long ago been pulled down. The tower still stood, however, along with an imposing foundation whose broken stones we walked together, the great sweep of the countryside stretching below us as far as we could see.

It was within these now-crumbled walls that countless agonies had been inflicted upon the countess's victims, Elizabeth growing steadily more vicious as one year quite literally bled into another. Here she had starved and beaten and burned and slashed the bodies of innumerable innocents, while screaming obscenities so vile they shocked even the blood-spattered minions who helped carry out her tortures.

At one of Gilles de Rais's castles, no less a literary figure than Anthony Trollope had paused to reflect upon the screams of the victims, even claiming that they could still be heard, as if sound waves do not dissipate. But dissipate they do, as Julian had pointed out in *The Tigress,* such that the wintry trees that had gathered around the body of yet another child had remained silent and unhelpful while the magistrate's men searched for clues, as if they were bribed witnesses into whose snow-encrusted hands the countess had placed a few silver coins.

"It's creepy here, don't you think?" Loretta asked.

"Yes," I said.

During the remainder of our walk about the grounds and rubble of Čachtice, Loretta appeared quite thoughtful. She gave no hint of what her thoughts were, however, though I suspected that she was considering the terrible possibility that Julian had, in fact, been turned by Marisol, and thus, for a brief time, might have proved himself a traitor. Still, I didn't press her. And it was not until we'd returned to the car and were headed toward Irene Jóság that she opened up to me.

"I remember one day when Julian and I were in that little boat I found him in," she said. "He'd come home after writing *The Tigress* but hadn't started *The Commissar*. We were talking about when we were children. Our travels. How fearless we were in those days. At one point I said that the things I feared most now were the things everyone feared. Getting old. Getting sick. Dying. I could tell that he didn't fear any of those things. So I asked him what he was afraid of. He said that he wasn't afraid of anything anymore. It was the 'anymore' that seemed strange to me, because the way he said it, he seemed to be telling me that he'd already confronted the thing he most feared."

"And triumphed over it?" I asked.

Loretta shook her head. "No, only that he'd confronted it." She glanced up toward the broken towers of Čachtice. "And after that, he was like those ruins. Beyond repair."

Beyond repair.

Since we had no way of pursuing this point, Loretta and I simply continued on, and we reached Irene Jóság's house about an hour after leaving Čachtice.

It was very modest, and with all the growth around it, the tall grass and twining vines, it was barely visible from the road.

"Are you sure this is it?" I asked Dimitri.

"I am sure," he answered.

We got out of the car and approached the house by means of a broken walkway overgrown with weeds and clogged with shrubs that seemed as swollen, as Julian might have written, as bodies in the sun.

I knocked at the door and heard a shuffle of feet inside the house. Then the door opened, and a very small woman appeared. She was dressed plainly, her hair streaked a yellowish white. Her eyes were startlingly blue, and there was a quickness to them that suggested what I had little doubt was a very high intelligence. She didn't wear the usual country clothes of Hungary, but a black dress with lace at the sleeves, so that she looked like a Spanish matron. Clearly she'd dressed for the occasion, and I even noticed a touch of blush on her cheeks along with some bright red lipstick that had missed its mark in one corner of her mouth.

"Ah," she said in an English whose accent was far more Spanish than Eastern European, "the Americans are arrived."

She stepped back rather shakily, waved us in, and directed us to chairs in her small living room.

"You would like something to drink?" she asked.

"No, thank you," I said.

With that, she slowly eased herself into a small wooden chair, and the usual niceties commenced. She asked about our hotel in Budapest but was more interested in my having come from Paris, a city she had romanticized but never seen, and now would never see, which brought us to her various ailments, bad joints and hearing loss, failing eyesight, the travails of old age, a subject that finally turned her mind toward my father.

"Your father is doing well?" she asked me.

"Not altogether well, no," I answered. "The same problems you've mentioned. Aches and pains."

"I'm sorry," she said. "It is better to be young."

We talked at some length about the work she'd done for the Americans, by way of my father, whom she described as having always been very kind to her. He had acted like a gentleman, without airs, she said, a man capable of speaking quite candidly to a simple clerk. She had either read or been told that "the great George Marshall" had had such qualities, and after the arrogance of the big men at Casa Rosada, my father's modesty had been much more than simply refreshing. She gave no hint of the somewhat more intimate relationship to which my father had quite clearly alluded, so I made no mention of it either.

At the end of this tale, she drew in a long breath, then glanced at Loretta. "I did not expect a second guest. This is your lovely wife?"

I had introduced Loretta at the door, but this appeared to have escaped the old woman's attention.

"No, this is Loretta Wells," I reminded her. "Julian's sister."

"Ah, yes," Irene said. "Julian's sister. My mind fades, no? Ah, yes, Julian." She drew her attention over to me. "The reason you have come, as your father told me in his letter. Julian. What a sad young man."

This seemed as good a segue into the purpose of our visit as any, and so I said, "My father tells me that you worked at

Casa Rosada in the early eighties." I looked at the notes I'd taken during the conversation with my father. "For a Colonel Juan Ramírez?"

Irene nodded. "He was a ladies' man, Juan," she said. "Very handsome. He many times wished to take me to his hideaway in Puerto Madero." She smiled. "He was a true fascist. 'You do not live with the Reds,' he said to me. 'You live under the Reds, or you do not live at all.' He would have done anything to save Argentina from the Reds. In fact, he did what all fascists do, which is the same as Reds." She clearly held the two groups in the same disdain. "He was always after the Montoneros. Those he dreams about at night. Killing every one of them. It is for this he lived. He wanted to hunt them down like a fox would hunt a rabbit. With his nose to the ground until he found them. Then he rips them apart."

"But how did he find them?" I asked.

"Names came to him," Irene said.

"From informants?"

She nodded. "He had many people, but it was the big fish, a Montonero, who gave him the big names. Where they lived, too, these other Montoneros hiding in their caves. Even the names of their children he gave to Juan."

"Ramírez turned a high-ranking Montonero?" Loretta asked.

"Yes," Irene answered. She appeared to see this informant in her mind. "Very tall, but an indigene. He was from the Chaco."

"Emilio Vargas?" I blurted.

Irene's eyes widened. "You have heard of this one?"

"Yes," I said. "He was a Montonero torturer."

200

Irene laughed. "This he did to show how bad he was," she said. "It is sometimes necessary to do this. This shows you hate the enemy, that you are ruthless. When he did this, the others say to themselves, 'See how he hates. See how much he is with us.'" She laughed again. "Cruelty was his disguise." Her eyes twinkled with a curious admiration. "But it was only one of his disguises."

For a moment she looked like a little girl watching shapes change in a funhouse mirror.

"Because he had a disguise for Juan as well," she added.

"Why would he need another disguise?" I asked.

"Because he was never really turned," Irene said. "He was always a crazy Montonero."

"Vargas was a double agent?" I asked.

"Yes," Irene said. "Juan was suspicious of this. This is why he puts much pressure on Vargas to prove himself. It is what Juan always did. He works like a thumbscrew, tighter, tighter until his people break. For this reason, Vargas tries to give Juan better and better information."

Her features suddenly grew tense, as if she were afraid that she was being watched even now.

"But it was never good enough for Juan," she said. "So he always asks Vargas to prove his loyalty. He threatens to cut off Vargas's ears, cut out his tongue. This he would do if Vargas does not deliver him the goods. And by this he means people."

"People?" I asked.

"Juan wanted to scare Vargas into giving up a big-time Montonero. So he makes Vargas like a man in the ocean who sees the shark coming toward him. He does not have time to get out of the water, so he takes some smaller man and puts this man between himself and the shark." She laughed. "Juan loved this game. He said to me, 'Vargas will pluck out his own eyes and cut off his ears. He will give me the name of this woman by the time I am finished with him.'"

"Woman?" I asked.

Irene nodded. "A real she-devil, this is what Juan called her. She had kidnapped some children of the junta. She would lure them with little candies. There would be a van, and very quick, they were gone, these kids. She was good at this. She sent them back torn and burned. It was very bad. The eyes gone. More than anyone, the big men at Casa Rosada wanted this woman for what she had done to these children. And it was this woman Juan wished to get from Vargas because it would be a big catch for him, and he would get a big promotion if he found her."

"How did you happen to know so much about what Ramírez was doing?" Loretta asked.

"He wants me in his bed, so he makes himself a big man to me," Irene answered. "He tells me everything, his many stories of the spies and agents. He does this more when he has too much wine." Her eyes squeezed together, as if I were a distant object she was trying to bring into focus. "But he was a clever man, Juan. And when the house was on fire, he got out through a little hole." Her smile was pure contempt. "He speaks only Spanish, and so he goes to Spain. He sits in the park and talks to the old men of the Falange." An odd defeat settled over her. "There is always a place for such men."

She paused like one exhausted by history, then continued with what seemed to be considerable effort, determined to complete her tale. "But enough of this," she said finally. She waved her hand as if to wipe the whole dark era from her mind. "So, Julian. Your father says to me that you want to know what I say to Julian when he comes to Casa Rosada, no?"

"Yes," Loretta answered quietly.

"Well, he comes to look for this woman," Irene said. "Excuse me, please, but I do not remember her name."

"Marisol," I told her.

Irene glanced toward Loretta, then turned to me. "Julian comes to Casa Rosada to find this Marisol." She looked at Loretta. "I am sorry to hear of his death. Such a young man. It is always a tragedy when death comes so soon." With that, Irene turned her attention back to me. "Your father sends Julian to me, but I know nothing of this girl."

"You knew nothing at all?" I asked. "I thought you might have given him a picture of Marisol with Emilio Vargas. I found it in his room in Paris."

The old woman shook her head. "No, I do not give Julian such a picture. I go to Juan. I ask about this girl who has disappeared. I can see he knows this girl, but he tells me nothing."

"I thought he told you everything," I said.

"This I also think," Irene said. "But about this one, he is silent."

"He said nothing at all?" I asked doubtfully.

"He says to me, 'Irene, to know about this one, this is not for your ears.' And he will say nothing more about her. He tells me if this American comes again, to tell him to go home and forget about this girl."

"So who was she?" Loretta asked. "Marisol."

Irene shrugged. "This Juan never tells me, but I think she is big fish, because after a while, he is very big man at Casa Rosada." She smiled. "All of this I would have told Julian when he came here, but he did not ask about this girl."

"Julian came here?" Loretta asked.

"Yes," Irene answered. "Just for one afternoon. We have cold drinks, and talk of the old days."

"And during that time, Julian didn't mention Marisol?" I asked.

"No, nothing of this girl." She looked oddly puzzled that this was the case. "So, I think maybe he knows already what happened to her."

My lips parted in dark amazement.

"Knew already?" I asked. "But he couldn't have known."

"This is how it seems me, yes," Irene told me. "That he has no more questions about this girl."

For the first time, Loretta looked skeptical, though she had perhaps been so all along. But now she made no pretense of believing the old woman's story.

"Then why did he come here?" she asked.

"He comes here to—how I should say?—to say good-bye," Irene answered. "He wished to thank me for talking with him back in the old time, when he came to Casa Rosada." She faced Loretta. "He has much trouble, your brother. There is a heavy weight on him. This I can see. And so I tell him that I know this weight."

She turned her gaze to an old album that lay on a nearby table. "You can hand this to me, please?" she asked.

I stood, walked over to the table, retrieved the book, and gave it to her.

"There is the bad thing I show to Julian and speak to him about," she said as she opened the book and began leafing through its ragged pages.

"Ah, here it is," she said as she motioned Loretta and me to come forward and look at it.

In the photograph, a young woman with a rifle, wearing an Arrow Cross armband, stands beside a priest, staring down at the sprawled bodies of a group of men and women, all of them in civilian clothes.

"That is Father Kun," she said. "He is a priest, but it is his fantasy to be a soldier. He wears always a gun in his cassock and he lines up the Jews and he draws this gun and he says to us, the ones with rifles, he says, 'In the name of Christ, FIRE!'" She looked up from the photograph. "And so I did." She closed the book. "This is my confession, and I tell it to Julian." She smiled. "He says good-bye. He kisses my hand. He says he goes soon to Rostov."

"Because that's where Andrei Chikatilo lived," I said.

Irene clearly did not recognize the name.

"A Russian serial killer," I told her.

She shook her head. "Julian says nothing of this killer," she said. "He is going to Rostov to say also a good-bye to this man from many years before. I know his name from my time in Argentina. He was a Russian agent there."

205

"Julian was in contact with a Russian agent while he was in Argentina?" I asked.

"Yes," Irene said. "This is what he tells to me. He met with this man many times, he says to me. He was a man who knew many secrets from the bad times in Argentina."

"Who was this Russian?" Loretta asked.

"His name is Mikhail Soborov," she answered without the slightest hesitation. "Juan had much fear of him."

"Why?"

She laughed. "Because he is one—as we say here—he is one who knows where the knife is." She sat back slightly. "Did Julian meet with him in Rostov?"

"I don't know," I answered.

Irene shook her head softly and, with that gesture, appeared to slip into some former life. "There was something about Julian that made you wish to speak with him the things you do not speak about with others. When I make my confession to him he tells me that he also has known bad things. He says he is like me."

"Like you in what way?" I asked.

"In his crime," Irene answered.

"Murdering innocent people?" I asked.

Irene shrugged. "This I do not know."

"He said nothing about what this crime was?" Loretta asked.

"No," Irene answered. "But it had made him tired, I think. He tells me that he wants someday to go home."

"Home," Loretta repeated softly.

"Home, yes," Irene said. "He wants to find peace there." She smiled softly. "He said there is a pond."

PART V
The Commissar

22

There is a scene in *The Commissar* where Julian imagines Chikatilo's wife—the mother of his children, the woman who had lived with him all the many years during which he had secretly ridden the desolate rails of a crumbling Soviet Union—at the moment she begins to suspect that poor, pathetic Andrei is something other than he seems:

> *She recalled that cold December day, so near to Christmas,*
> *when Yelena Zakotnova had first gone missing. Had she*
> *ever seen Yelena walking the streets of the village? In the*
> *papers she was a pretty girl, only nine, with dark hair cut*
> *short. From a distance, Chikatilo's wife said to herself, her*
> *killer might have thought she was a boy. "Her killer," she*
> *repeated in her mind, now with a chill colder than any*
> *winter she'd endured in Shankty, because at the very mo-*
> *ment she silently pronounced the words "her killer," she*
> *envisioned Andrei and immediately recalled the spots of*
> *blood she'd seen trailing along the side of the house she*
> *shared with him, the dim light of that shared bedroom,*

her empty bed during the long absences of this man, the
knife he packed with his black bread and cheese.

I mentioned this scene to Loretta over dinner, then added, "It's in all Julian's books. Deceit. The moment when the face of someone you thought you knew changes, and you suspect that there's something terrible behind the mask."

"And you're thinking that Marisol wore this mask," Loretta said, "that she was the 'she-devil' Vargas gave to Ramírez—actually a terror, like La Meffraye, or a tigress, like Countess Báthory."

During the drive back to Budapest, I'd actually envisioned Marisol in this dreadful role, her eyes glittering in the dark way Julian described the eyes of Countess Báthory.

"There are such women, after all," I added. " René mentioned one in Algiers. She was called 'the Blade,' and according to him, she scared the hell out of everybody. Marisol would have been even more frightening because she seemed so completely innocent."

Loretta took a sip from her glass and cast her eyes about the lobby of the hotel.

"So it's a question of moral betrayal," I went on. "Marisol presents herself as this simple girl from the Chaco. She claims that all she wants is an opportunity to better herself. By day she quotes Borges and guides Julian and me around Buenos Aires. By night she goes to some dungeon and becomes a monster for the Montoneros."

Something about this scenario clearly troubled Loretta.

"If any of that is true, then Julian truly had stepped into that world your father warned you about," Loretta said. "That shadow world. Agents, double agents, triple agents. He wasn't used to that kind of complexity. But he would have begun to worry about it, don't you think, if he'd gotten wind of any of what we've found out? He'd have begun to ask himself the same questions about her that we're asking. He would have wanted to know not only where she was but who she was. Because he wouldn't have been sure of anything anymore. Was she a girl with no politics? Was she a Montonero? He might even have come to think that she could be a double agent working for the junta."

"Working for the junta?" I asked.

"Working to catch Vargas, or something like that," Loretta said. "Julian would have begun to consider all kinds of deception."

All kinds of deception.

With those words, I felt life turn again, and on that turn, Marisol became an ever-changing shape. Could it be, I wondered, that the many faces of female evil that Julian had drawn were merely his multiple attempts to capture the yet more elusive moral nightmare that was Marisol?

I thought all this through for a moment, then said, "But if Marisol worked for the junta, why did she disappear?"

Loretta appeared surprised that I'd taken her latest conjecture seriously. At the same time, she clearly began to considerer such a possibility.

"The most obvious reason would be that her cover was close to being blown," she answered. "For that reason her 'handlers' took her out of the game."

"So, in this scenario, Marisol was never kidnapped or murdered at all?" I asked.

It was a dark twist that now produced yet another wholly unexpected turn in my mind.

"That would mean that Julian was looking for a woman who had never been kidnapped at all," I said.

I could scarcely imagine the betrayal he would have felt if he had unearthed such a grim truth about Marisol, how deep it might have been, how thoroughly it might have unraveled him.

The grave effect of that thought must have shown in my features, because I could see it reflected in Loretta's.

"Of course, we have no idea what Julian finally came to think about Marisol," she reminded me.

True enough, I thought, and yet I remembered a night when Julian and I were in La Boca. Julian had stopped suddenly in front of one of the neighborhood's characteristically bright-colored houses. He gave a slight nod toward the back of the house, where an old car rested near a basement window. Its hood was up, and a set of long black cables ran from its battery down into the cellar.

"That's one of the places where the junta takes people," Julian said quietly. "It's a little torture chamber."

"How do you know that?" I asked.

"Marisol pointed it out one afternoon," Julian answered. "She says everyone knows what happens there."

But had everyone truly known that, I wondered now, or was it only Marisol who'd known?

And had Julian, in some dreadful moment of awful recognition, discovered this grim truth?

There is always a moment when the various elements of a mystery must be gathered together like puzzle pieces and rearranged upon the table, each piece seeking its place in the slowly emerging picture. I knew that it was time for the pieces of my story to arrange themselves for that final "reveal," but instead of reaching illumination, I faced an even darker world of shifting loyalties and identities, one in which Julian, so young and naive, could easily have been ensnared.

"What are you thinking, Philip?" Loretta asked.

"I was thinking about Julian," I answered. "That the world had become very dark to him by the time he left Argentina. And that if we keep pursuing this, it may become very dark to us, as well."

"So, do you want to stop looking?" Loretta asked.

"No," I answered. "But I don't know why."

She reached over and touched my hand. "It's because curiosity is the hungriest of beasts," she said. "And so we have no choice but to go on." Her smile had an element of old tragedies about it. "We're like Nick and Nora, Philip. Only a much darker version."

Her touch was soft and warm, and I had not felt such a touch in many years.

"Yes," I said. "We are."

23

We arrived in Rostov early in the morning. Our guide, Yuri Kasov, looked to be around fifty, and had served as Julian's guide and interpreter, as well.

"No problem," he assured us by phone. "I do everything."

True to his word, he subsequently made all the plans necessary to get Loretta and me to Rostov-on-Don, which, despite its rustic name, turned out to be a bustling city of more than a million.

At the airport, Yuri whisked us off to a surprisingly modern hotel, where we treated him to dinner. Loretta struck up a curiously intense interrogation that began with Yuri's first meeting with Julian, progressed through Julian's research, and moved rapidly until she reached her intended point.

"Do you remember Julian meeting a man named Mikhail Soborov?" Loretta asked. "He lives here in Rostov, I believe."

"Yes, I went with him to this man," Yuri answered in an English that became more offbeat by the minute. "At first beginning they are trying to speak Spanish, but the old man, he was no longer to speak it." His smile betrayed a carefully honed cleverness. "I never have expect that Julian to look for such a one as Mikhail Soborov."

214

"Such a one?" Loretta asked.

"Old-time KGB," Dimitri answered.

"What did they talk about?" Loretta asked.

"I don't know," Dimitri said. "They will not talk in front of me. Once Julian, he is said something in Spanish, and the old man, he is getting up and push me out of the room and close the door."

Why? I wondered, but there was no point in asking, since the conversation moved to other topics until the meal came to an end.

But the notion of Julian having some secret conversation with a Russian agent continued to trouble me, and later that night, tossing sleeplessly in my bed, I decided to take a walk.

Outside the hotel, the charmless streets of Rostov swept outward toward the distant Don, a river that did indeed, as Sholokhov said in the title of his famous novel, flow quietly to the sea.

It was mostly a cheerless place, architecturally boring, yet its streets had been walked by an extraordinary number of Russia's great literary figures. Pushkin had a boulevard named after him; Chekhov and Solzhenitsyn had also spent time in Rostov; and a young Gorky had worked on its docks. A city with such rich literary history appealed to me, of course, but I saw little evidence that it had done the same for Julian. In *The Commissar*, he had painted it as a warren of all but indistinguishable streets, a gray labyrinth fed by a gray stream, through which Chikatilo, "the Red Ripper," had made his way like a blind horse, sensing corners, alleys, and dead ends, and always, always, the presence of a waylaid child.

It was the route of this devouring monster that Julian had relentlessly followed. He had written of Chikatilo's birth in the tiny village of Yablochnoye, a little boy whose mother had filled his mind with tales of the Great Famine, including the hideous story that Chikatilo's own brother had been kidnapped and eaten by neighbors. Meticulously, Julian had detailed the emergence of this wounded boy into a biologically complete but inwardly crippled adult, a man who married and became the father of two children by the time he took a teaching job in Novoshakhtinsk, the one from which he was later dismissed amid charges of child molestation.

Julian had spent time in both those places, as was clear from *The Commissar*, but it was in Shakhty (Russian for "mine shaft," as Julian pointed out) that he had stayed the longest, as if attempting to unearth what it was about this grim little town that finally tempted Chikatilo to commit his first murder.

She was only nine years old, and Chikatilo lured her to an old house that he'd bought for the purpose; thus it was a crime, as Julian wrote in one of his stark phrases, "as premeditated by his reason as it was preordained by his madness."

It was the blood of this child that Chikatilo's wife found in the snow in front of her own house and that generated the suspicions she would harbor for decades, little noises that continually sounded like a footfall outside her window.

But loyal wife that she was, Fayina kept her silence as the years passed and the body count rose in towns and villages along railway lines, riverbanks, and the many forests of the Don.

It was here, in Rostov, that Chikatilo had killed two women in Aviator Park, then gone on to kill again in Novoshakhtinsk and from there back to Shakhty, then back to Rostov, where yet another body was found in Aviator Park.

Julian had pointed out Andrei Chikatilo's extraordinary recklessness, the careless abandon with which he murdered, the public arenas that were both his killing fields and his dumping grounds, as if he had come to believe, as all madmen do, that he was in league with the sun and the moon, protected by the elements themselves, shrouded by fog and veiled by rain, perhaps feeling the added pleasure of believing that in all the world he would be the last person suspected of his crimes.

In fact, Chikatilo's only precaution, though Julian came to doubt that even this was a conscious act of evasion, was that he'd finally begun to enlarge the murderous circle that had earlier enclosed him, killing outside Moscow, then in Revda, Zaporizhya, Krasny Sulin, and as far afield as Leningrad.

Julian had visited every murder site, his book made clear, but it was here, in Rostov, that he'd lived during most of his time in Russia, and it was here that he'd written a good deal of it while holed up in a small apartment off Ulyanovskaya Street.

I knew the address because I'd written him many e-mails, encouraging him in his research and subject matter, always adding that one day I thought his accomplishment would be clear. I never knew how he received my encouragement because he never once responded to it. Rather, his next communication would detail some new idiom he'd learned or some new author, usually Russian, whom he'd discovered.

Late in the evening I came to the little street where Julian had lived for many years. It was quite dark by then, but Rostov's reliable street lamps offered sufficient light for me to see the windows on the third floor. How many times Julian must have stood at those windows, I thought, stood and stared cheerlessly out over this deeply foreign city.

The expatriate is well established in literature, of course, but usually the portrayal is romantic—Lord Byron in Italy, for example. One sees the desolate exile less often, and yet when I considered Julian's time in Rostov, I thought of Ovid's banishment to bleak, impoverished Tomis. "My punishment," love's great poet wrote, "is the place." It was unimaginable to me that Rostov and Shakhty and Revda had not been similar punishments for Julian, and had I begun to write about him when I returned to my room later that night, I would certainly have made some comparison between his life in Rostov and Ovid's in Tomis, how isolated Julian must have felt in Russia, and how incalculably alone. The difference was that Julian's exile was self-imposed—thus another sign that he had inflicted some strange punishment upon himself by living in desolate places and filling his mind with torture and murder, by choosing as his sole companions the great demons of the world. In that way, too, I supposed, he wasn't just a good man, but a great one, not just an artist, but one whose art had imposed exile and solitude. Ovid had been forced to live in dreadful Tomis, after all, while Julian, at least, had chosen it.

I said this to Loretta the next morning, and in response she glanced out over the spare little dining room our hotel provided, most of the tables occupied, the air filled with the soft Slavic murmur of the other guests.

"This must have been the loneliest place Julian ever lived," she said. "With no one who spoke English. Or any other language he knew."

At Loretta's mention of Julian's languages, I found myself thinking of the first one he'd learned, Spanish, then of the first country in which he had encountered it.

I thought of Julian and Marisol in a sun-drenched Buenos Aires. But now Marisol was less fixed in my mind, an identity that had been in continual revision, first as businesslike guide, then as spy, then as an Argentine version of La Meffraye, working either for the Montoneros or the junta, but equally evil in either capacity.

It was no doubt my continual reimagining of Marisol that took me back to a particular moment only a few days before I left Buenos Aires. It was my only time alone with her, and she seemed curiously preoccupied. It didn't surprise me when she said, "There are days when one falls out of love with one's life."

"Months and years, if you're not lucky," I told her.

"Why do you say this?"

"Because it happened to my father. He regrets everything."

"And you?"

"My regret is not with anything I've done," I told her. "But sometimes I'm not altogether happy with what I am."

"What makes you unhappy in this way?"

"Well, it's mostly the fact that I don't have any talent," I answered. "I don't sing or act or play a musical instrument.

219

I've read the great books, but I couldn't write even a bad one. Julian, on the other hand, has talent in great abundance." Then, for the first time, I gave full voice to the truth. "I would like to be more like him."

She glanced away, as if from a subject she didn't want to discuss. "And what is Julian?"

I found that I had no answer for her, and this surprised me, the fact that I couldn't pin Julian down, that something about him remained in flux, unsettled.

"He is very smart," Marisol said, then looked out into the traffic. "This much is true." She turned to face me. "But he is like his country. He isn't finished yet. And in many ways, he is still a little boy."

She added a quick smile to this last remark, so that it seemed not a criticism of "his country" but a curiously affectionate statement instead. For that reason, I let it pass and went on to another subject. But now, sitting at a breakfast table in Rostov, it returned to me insistently, and I related the exchange to Loretta.

"Still a little boy," Loretta said. "You know what's clear when a woman says that about a man? That she knows she's superior to him." She seemed briefly to consider Marisol with an added complexity she was still struggling to grasp. Finally she said, "Do you know the moment when Sherlock Holmes realizes that Irene Adler has seen through his disguise?"

I had never read Conan Doyle, so I said, "No, I don't know any of those stories."

"There is a moment when their eyes lock, Holmes and Irene Adler, and at that moment, the great detective knows, without doubt, that this one woman has fooled him."

I imagined Julian in the shock of that recognition, coldly aware that he'd been played for a fool.

"You know," I said, "if Julian ever found out that he was fooled by Marisol, fooled into believing that she was this innocent girl from the Chaco when she was something different, a spy, a torturer, a double agent, it would have wounded his self-confidence, his entire sense of himself."

Loretta nodded. "Yes, it would have."

"Would he have sought revenge?" I asked.

Loretta considered my question for a time before she spoke.

"You've stumbled upon another turn, you know," she said. "The idea that when Julian was looking for Marisol, it wasn't in order to find out what had happened to her or even who she really was." Her gaze revealed something menacing. "Because he already knew."

I immediately grasped where she was headed.

"And so he went looking for Marisol because he intended to . . . ," I said, then stopped because I felt compelled to resist saying what had come into my mind.

I could have resisted it, almost on principle, but I would have had to ignore Loretta's eyes, how very intense they were, filled with the sudden dread that rises when you sense that you are closing in upon a horrible truth.

221

"Because he intended to kill her," I said. I felt a shudder. "Was that his crime?"

I saw Loretta entertain this possibility, then just as quickly reject it.

"But how could that have been Julian's crime?" she asked. "Because he said that you witnessed his crime, remember?" She smiled at the wrong turn my latest conjecture had made. "Julian murder Marisol?" She smiled in utter confidence of the next thing she said. "Surely, Philip, you did not see that."

24

Mikhail Soborov's residence was more of a cottage than a house, and it was in an area that was mostly rural, a part of the Ukraine that had once blossomed with small, independent farmers, the famed kulaks that Stalin had so despised and all but exterminated through planned famine. Julian had made the point that Chikatilo was beaten for bedwetting and for almost every other offense, but the Great Famine was the traumatic event in the Rostov Ripper's life; its tales of cruelty and cannibalism were ones to which the young Andrei responded not with horror or repulsion, but with a vicarious throb of pleasure and excitement that surely must have flooded his soul with dark surprise.

There was nothing at all surprising about Mikhail Soborov, however. In fact, he looked so much the way I expected that in a book he would have been a caricature of the boisterous, big-bellied Slav, hard-drinking and jolly, a Russian version of Falstaff.

"Thanks for talking to us," I said as I took the hand he quite cheerfully offered.

The old man laughed robustly. "In old days, I would have hidden in the woodshed," he said, "or had you killed en route."

"In that case, I'm pleased that things have changed," I said.

"Oh, yes, they have changed," Soborov said with an air of jollity that now struck me as somewhat false, something other than Santa Claus underneath the bright red coat. "In those days my ideals were young, and a man takes on the look of the god he worships, is that not so?"

Rather than wait for me to answer, he turned swiftly to Loretta. "Now, here we have one who has not been aged by disenchantment," he said as he took Loretta's hand and gallantly kissed it. "Now, please. We shall have vodka, the three of us."

But before reaching for the vodka, he cast a hard look at Yuri. "We don't need extra set of ears," he said sternly, and with that closed the door in his face.

When he turned back to us, he was frowning. "They say we are free now in Russia to say what we wish, but I do not trust such 'guides' as this one who comes here with you."

"Why would they want an agent with us now?" I asked Soborov once we'd taken seats in his small living room.

"Because repression is a snake that grows back its head," Mikhail answered in a way that clearly closed the subject. "So, what did Julian tell you about me?"

"Nothing at all," I answered. "I learned about you from Irene, as I said in my letter."

"Irene, yes," Soborov said. "You know that in Budapest, during the war, she shot Jews in hospital beds, no?"

"My father hinted at something like that," I answered. "And when we met her, she showed us a picture. It was quite sad. She feels—"

"Guilt, yes," Soborov interrupted. "Julian once called it the false consolation of those not really harmed."

"What an unforgiving thing to say," I told him.

"For most, time wears guilt away, like wind and water," Soborov said, "but perhaps time more forgiving than should be, yes?"

"Perhaps," I said, since I could think of nothing else.

Soborov peered at me closely. "We never meet, you and I?"

"No," I answered. "At least, I don't think so."

Soborov laughed. "Too bad. You might have learned one of our tricks."

I looked at him quizzically.

"How to make meeting look not planned," Soborov said. "This how it looks with Julian and me. I am just a man at next table. I rise to leave, but I leave keys on table. Julian picks up keys and gives to me. I take keys and say to him that I am like Borges. Blind, like old poet." He laughed. "Code is passed, just like in movies." He looked at me with an almost impish expression. "Too much like in movies, yes?" He waved his hand as if dismissing the subject, and with that gesture, his features became more serious. "This not how I meet Julian, of course."

"How did you meet him?" I asked.

The old man smiled widely. "You always in big hurry, you Americans, but we have not yet had vodka."

With that he left the room, then returned to it a few seconds later with the glasses and a bottle encased in a square of ice.

"Do you know what we say in Russia?" he asked.

We shook our heads.

"That drink only second most important thing in life," Soborov said. "Of first importance is breathe." He laughed loudly. "You get it, yes?"

We nodded.

He poured each of us a glass, then offered his toast. "To peace."

We touched our glasses, and with that the old man sat down in a large chair opposite us.

"So, to Julian," he said. "Because you are Americans, I will tell you quickly. He came to Soviet consulate. He was looking for girl. She had disappeared and he was looking for her. He gets nothing from Casa Rosada, and so he comes to us." His smile was that of an old man being mischievous. "The Reds." He shrugged. "We did not know where this woman is, but perhaps we know someone who does." He appeared briefly reluctant to say more and waved his hand. "Ah, what difference does it make now?"

With this Soborov clapped his hands together.

"All right, then," he said. "So. Have you ever heard of the Dogo Córdoba?"

I had no idea what this was and said so.

"It is dog," Soborov told me. "Especially bred in Argentina." He leaned forward and rubbed his hands together vigorously. "It is fighting dog that is famous for not to back down. The Dogo Córdoba bred to endure great pain. They are champions in the dogfights."

"What does this have to do with Julian?" Loretta asked.

"Because this is where we send him," Soborov answered. "To a dogfight."

I could scarcely imagine Julian at such an event, but by then there were many aspects to Julian's life that were equally hard to imagine.

"They illegal, these fights," Soborov continued, "but there are places, hidden places, or maybe not hidden, but protected by police." His smile was incongruously warm. "And we know what Argentine police doing in other places, no? Things that make dogfights look like country dance." He drew out a handkerchief and swabbed his neck, as if he had returned to the heat and humidity of an Argentine summer. "It was July," he said. "Very hot." Now he turned to Loretta. "They very secretive, of course, the people who go to Dogo Córdoba fights. It is like a secret society. Important people in Argentina come to these special fights. High in government. But also thugs, and of these thugs there is one we keep eye on. He is called El Árabe."

"The Arab?" I asked.

"That is what he is called, yes," Soborov said. "Because he is brown, almost like the peasants. He was very low sort of fellow. He had not much intelligence, but low cunning, this he had much. In this way, like Stalin. He had worked himself into a good job running whole network of *escuelitas*. We knew that some of our people were in his custody, but we did not know where they were. El Árabe was very hard man, maybe impossible to break, we thought, even under stress. But he had weakness." He laughed at the nature of this weakness, then revealed it. "He was like little child when it comes to Americans. A young man like Julian would attract his attention. This is what we think. A young American. Smart. Good-looking. Maybe with money, maybe from good family. We know that such a one would appeal to El Árabe."

Loretta looked as if suddenly struck by a cold breeze. "You tried to recruit Julian as a spy?"

"Not at first, because we think maybe he is spy, or maybe he is 'spy who comes in from cold.'" He laughed. "Either way we wish to keep eye on him."

Soborov paused to take another sip of vodka.

"There was Dogo Córdoba fight in little town outside Buenos Aires," Soborov continued. "In pampas, but not far from city. We know El Árabe will be there because he is great lover of these fights. Can you believe this? After day of torture, this is what he does in order to relax, watch dogs tear each other apart."

He looked at Loretta.

"And so we send your brother there," he told her. "We give him money and he bet like rich man, and this, too, we know, will catch eye of El Árabe."

Now his gaze returned to me.

"I was Julian's 'handler,'" he said, "and so I go with him there because I want to see if he makes contact and report to my superiors if this American has talent for deception we might later use." His face soured. "It was dreadful place, where we went that night. Very dreadful place."

Soborov described the event, how it had been conducted in the sweltering interior of a large shed, the dogs brought in on chains and lashed to the sides of a circular pit whose walls were made of corrugated tin, unpainted and splattered with the blood of previous combats. The crowd was washed with sweat and beer and they screamed to the dogs and across the pit to one another, yelling taunts and bragging about their picks of the night, waving money and sometimes knives.

"It is from hell, this scene," Soborov said, "and at center of pit, there is El Árabe, with his black hair plastered down, yelling at dogs, laughing, and drinking beer."

I recalled a scene in *The Commissar*, a moment when Julian has Chikatilo dream of being a pit master at an orgy of torture, moving about with a riding crop, dressed in a red jacket and high black boots, orchestrating the terrible performance as he strides from ring to ring.

"Julian has been shown photographs of this stupid little bastard," Soborov went on, "and he make it his business to get near him, waving money like the others, but speaking only good American English, which catches ear of El Árabe."

In my mind, I saw this "stupid little bastard" turn at the sound of Julian's voice, his gaze drinking in this young American as if he were a movie star.

"I am across pit, but I see El Árabe speak to Julian, and Julian speak back, then El Árabe turn back to pit and give signal with a big wave of hand for fight to begin."

What happened after that was a fierce struggle between two Dogo Córdobas, white dogs, Soborov told us, and so the blood that swept over their spinning flanks and dripped from their mouths and coated their teeth and ran down their throats was vivid red.

"The Dogo Córdoba is extinct now," Soborov said at the end of this description of the fight, "because so many die in the pit and because they become so unstable, cannot be with another dog without killing it. Because of this they disappear." He offered a rueful smile. "Life cannot be sustained by ferocity alone." He explained: "I hear this and I like it."

He was silent for a time, as if his last remark had come to him unexpectedly and was still resonating through his own long memory.

"Anyway, Julian meet El Árabe many times after this," Soborov said, "in the bars and in dance halls of the tango. He is good at pretending friendship. He can make anyone believe he loves them." He shrugged. "Once he say to me, 'All you can offer to those who love you is the pretense that you love them back.'"

Even for Julian, this struck me as an infinitely sad pronouncement, and to avoid its sting I rushed ahead.

"Did you help him find out what happened to Marisol?" I asked.

"No," Soborov said, "but I think perhaps El Árabe did, because Julian must have discovered something very bad. I believe this because he suddenly change. He has been a good-looking young man; then overnight he is old and looks like one who has, as we say, crossed the Styx. He still has this look when I see him last." His gaze darkened. "A very bad man, El Árabe. Very bad. He feels no guilt, this man. Even after the junta fall, he offers no apology for his little schools. To this day, he is sometimes on television in Argentina, regretting nothing, saying that he enjoyed every minute of it."

"Did he go to prison?" Loretta asked.

"For few years," Soborov said. "Then he is released and after that he is home to his village near Iguazú."

I recalled the town Julian had circled on the map he was looking at on the day he died. "Clara Vista?"

Soborov nodded. "He lives there still, makes interviews, laughs in the faces of those who still seek the disappeared."

He let this settle in. Then, as if trying to lighten the atmosphere, he smiled quite brightly and said, "By the way, did Julian ever finish the book on Chikatilo?"

"Yes," I answered. "It'll be published next year. He called it *The Commissar*, and it's the most thorough account of Andrei Chikatilo yet written."

"Good," Soborov said. "He was a hard worker, Julian. This much can be said of him, and it is not a small thing. I would like to receive a copy of this book when it is published."

"I'll make sure you do," I promised him.

Soborov smiled. "So, have I said to you what you wished to know about Julian?"

"Not really," Loretta answered bluntly.

Soborov was clearly surprised by this answer.

"Irene said that when Julian came to see her a few years ago, he already knew what happened to Marisol," Loretta added. "You're saying that it was this El Árabe who told him?"

Soborov nodded. "Who else could? He was Julian's last contact in Argentina."

"When Julian came here, did you talk about Argentina?" Loretta asked.

"Yes," Soborov said. "We talked of the dogs, and of that girl, the one who disappeared. He said that he found her."

"Found her?" I asked. "He found Marisol?"

"Yes," Soborov answered. "It was the Arab who led him to her, but he did not tell me how."

"Did Julian say anything about who Marisol was or might have been?" Loretta asked.

Soborov looked puzzled. "Might have been?"

"A Montonero, for example."

Soborov shook his head.

"What did he say about her?" Loretta asked.

Soborov considered his answer for a moment, then said, "He said only that a trick is played upon her."

"What kind of trick?" I asked.

Soborov took a surprisingly casual sip from his glass. "He was always speaking in . . . what is the word when it is about a little thing, but it is really about big things . . . what is the word for speaking in this way?"

"Metaphorically?" I asked.

"That is it, yes," Soborov said. "Not really about one thing, about many things." Now he shrugged. "So when I ask him what is this trick, he does not answer me directly. It is something he cannot speak about, he tell me." He put down his glass. "So all I know is that he has a name for this trick." His smile bore the weight of the dark view of things he seemed to have glimpsed in Julian's eyes at that long-ago moment. "It is called 'the Saturn Turn.'"

PART VI
The Saturn Turn

25

"The Saturn Turn," Loretta repeated quietly.

We were seated in a small park near our hotel. It was late in the afternoon and there were few people around. Children were in school and workers were at their jobs. A few older people walked about, along with an occasional mother pushing a stroller. Overall, the scene was quite peaceful, and this allowed my mind to roam rather freely until, for some reason, I hit upon Aeschylus, of all people. It was not a line from any of his plays that came to me, however, but the fact that he had written his own obituary and how odd that obituary was. In it, Aeschylus mentioned nothing of his fame, nothing of his plays, nothing even of his life, except that as a young man he had fought at Marathon. That, it seemed, was the thing of which he was most proud, the one thing about himself that he wanted remembered.

Julian, of course, had left no obituary, much less an explanation of why he had chosen to take his own life. Stranger still, while Aeschylus had proudly noted his fighting at Marathon, Julian had chosen to destroy the last words he'd ever written, as if dreading their meaning.

When she spoke, it was clear that Loretta's mind was tending in a completely different direction.

"I was just remembering something Julian once said," she told me. "He had just gotten back from Swaziland, where he'd gone to write an article. We were looking through the photographs he'd taken there. People in terrible conditions, all of them man-made. He looked up from one particularly grim picture and he said, 'It all comes down to people in the end, Loretta. All the global policies and grand schemes. They all come down to what we do to people, whether we help or harm them.'"

On that thought, I was with Julian again, sitting in Grosvenor Park, peering up at the great eagle that was mounted at the top of the American embassy. He was staring at that eagle when he spoke.

"Ambrose Bierce called diplomacy the art of manufacturing a plausible lie," he said.

I laughed at this, but Julian didn't. Instead, his gaze darkened and a shadow settled over him. "To play that trick really well, Philip," he added, "is a master crime."

I related this odd exchange to Loretta, who listened to it very carefully, as if combing each word for some telling detail.

"Maybe Julian learned that in Argentina," I added.

Loretta nodded and touched my hand. "On to El Árabe," she said.

For the next few days, we turned the small desk in my hotel room into a makeshift research center. Loretta's Spanish was far better than mine, though neither of us was in any sense fluent. Still, by working together, and despite online translations that were often close to indecipherable themselves, we got the gist of the many articles we found on El Árabe.

Just as Soborov had told us, El Árabe was anything but shy when it came to publicity. He'd been sentenced to ten years for his *escuelitas* activities and had served seven before being released.

Upon release, he'd moved to the small town near the great falls at Iguazú, an area of Argentina where it is possible not only to see both Paraguay and Brazil but to easily slip across their borders. He had not been shy about stating the obvious:

> I wanted to be close to the border in case the little men of
> Casa Rosada want to try me again on some trumped-up
> charge. I live here in peace. I do not hurt a cat. I sit on
> my little porch and I say to the world, "I take the dirty
> name you call me with pride, for I am El Árabe, and I
> regret nothing."

As became clear from the many interviews that Hernando Vilario—which was El Árabe's real name—had granted in the days following his release, he not only had no regrets, but he was actually proud of what he'd done.

> You only have to look at Russia under the Reds to know
> what men like me saved Argentina from. The people of
> Argentina should put statues of us in the park, because we

are the reason they do not live under the Red flag. Would they like it better under Castro? With the old cars and the falling-down capital and the eight-hour speeches in the hot Havana sun? They should thank men like me, the men who saved them from such a thing. Instead they put us in prison, and we are made to fall on our knees and deny the great thing we did. We stopped the Reds in their tracks, and for this all Argentina should be grateful to us.

He had repeated these pronouncements in almost every interview since his release. He had also appeared on radio and television, and with each appearance, according to one editorial, "he becomes more bold and outrageous. He grows fat on ill repute and displays his crimes like medals."

As the years passed, less and less notice was paid to him, though he clearly took every opportunity to regain the public eye. Once, he even ran for election in the small district in which he lived. He was soundly beaten, but his campaign of "blood and fire" was vociferous enough to get him yet another brief burst of attention.

After this election, Loretta and I discovered, he had more or less faded from public attention until another series of articles appeared in a paper called *Hoy,* a small Buenos Aires weekly. They were written by one David Leon, and their tone, though not sympathetic, was curiously tinged with what Loretta called "a little mist of understanding." Not enough to obscure El Árabe's deeds, she went on to tell me, but careful to place them within the context of Argentina's tumult, the raging battles that had rocked the country, the kidnappings and assassinations, the economic instability, all of which had combined, he wrote, "to inject in every vein a liquid, icy fear."

"This is our man," Loretta said as she handed me the first of Leon's articles. "This is the man who can help us meet El Árabe."

In the photograph on the front page of Leon's series of articles, Hernando Vilario stood on a large veranda, his back to a sprawling jungle, naked to the waist and staring straight into the camera as if it were a gun. The brutality that came from him seemed the sort that must have been forged in man's early caves, hard beyond measure, merciless, and without remorse. But to this otherwise dreadful portrait, he had added a string of wooden beads. They hung from his neck, so brightly polished they glinted in the sunlight.

They might have come from anywhere, but the last time I had seen such beads, they had belonged to Marisol.

I didn't mention this to Loretta, however, because I saw no reason to. Even had I known absolutely that they were the same beads Marisol had worn so many years before, I still had no idea whether El Árabe had violently yanked them from her neck or whether she'd given them to him sweetly, tenderly, her eyes glittering with their shared work, a little gift in appreciative commemoration of their partnership in crime.

26

We arrived in Buenos Aires on a clear, bright day, not unlike my first visit. That was many years before, but as the cab made its way down Avenida 9 de Julio, I recalled that time not as something that had vanished, but as a time whose still-obscure events were now adding a fierce purpose to my life. Of course, I also knew that part of that new purpose involved Loretta, who sat beside me, gazing out at the streets of the city.

"You look like you did the first time I saw you," I told her now.

She looked at me. "Hardly."

"No, seriously," I said. "I once read that fear is the last reflex to leave us, but with you, I think it will be curiosity."

She studied me a moment, then said, "You know, Philip, I think that's the nicest thing anyone ever said to me."

We reached the hotel a few minutes later. It was on San Martín, the plaza where Julian and I had often awaited Marisol and down whose wide stairs we had escorted Father Rodrigo to his bus.

"We should take a walk once we're settled in," I told Loretta.

"Yes, let's."

And so we did.

It was late in the afternoon and the air was turning cool and the shadows in the park were deepening. The lights had already been turned on. Not far away we could see the bus station.

"It's the same everywhere," Loretta said. "The orphaned poor gather in train and bus and subway stations. Julian said that he thought they unconsciously hovered near some means of escape."

Below, I could see the same dusty boys who had huddled in those same littered corners the day we saw Father Rodrigo off to the Chaco, where undoubtedly yet more such children were to be found.

"I gave Julian a copy of *The Wretched of the Earth* the night he left for Argentina," Loretta said. "Franz Fanon's classic. Then I told him something an old African man had once said to a friend of mine. They'd met at one of those desert refugee camps that had cropped up all over Africa. The old man had lived all his life in the bush. He was missing several fingers. He'd amputated them himself, he said, with a machete. He held up the stubs and wiggled them a little in my friend's face. Then he said, 'Do not avoid suffering.' That was the message I had for Julian, that he should not avoid suffering."

I smiled sadly. "And as it turned out, he didn't."

Loretta returned an errant strand of hair to its place. "Just for the record, and because we must surely be near the end of this, I want you to know that I've enjoyed being with you, Philip. I've enjoyed traveling with you and talking with you and listening to you."

"I feel the same, of course."

She laughed. "You know, in a book, this scene would be quite a maudlin moment, don't you think?"

"Yes, it would," I said softly. "But in life, those moments are often the best."

The next morning we ate breakfast, then made our way to the address David Leon had given us for *Hoy*.

Loretta had gotten in touch with him while we were still in Budapest. She had found their exchanges quite warm, Leon more than willing to speak with us about El Árabe, a man he described as not only a sociopath but one who thought everyone else a sociopath, too.

The oddity in Leon's description of El Árabe, however, was the fact that he appeared to be extremely intelligent. Soborov had portrayed him as something of a buffoon, capable of low cunning, but little else. Leon's articles presented a far different assessment, one in which El Árabe seemed much closer to the Mr. Kurtz of *Heart of Darkness*: keen-minded, resolute, with something curiously immortal in the nature of his malice.

David Leon was younger than I'd expected, a man in his thirties, tall, lean, with jet black hair that almost perfectly matched his glasses. He was dressed in a white shirt, jeans, and an olive green corduroy jacket.

"Good to see you after so many e-mails," he said to Loretta when we arrived at *Hoy*, then turned and offered his hand to me. "And you must be Philip?"

I took his hand. "Thanks for seeing us," I told him.

His office was a cubicle in a sea of cubicles, and so he suggested that we move to a conference room down the hall.

"It is more private there," he said.

The conference room was also rather small, with a square table, scarred with use, and dotted with coffee rings.

"It is a historical artifact," Leon said as he ran his fingers on the table. "It belonged to José de Costa. He was imprisoned by the junta. A great reporter. One of the disappeared. It was while I was seeking to discover his fate that I came across El Árabe. He knew nothing of José, but he spoke of many other things. He is a great river of talk."

"So it seems," Loretta said.

We all took seats at the table. I had brought Julian's old briefcase, and while Loretta and Leon continued to speak, mostly about their earlier correspondence, I took out a paper and pen.

"You are a journalist?" Leon asked me.

"No," I answered, then started to say that I was a book reviewer, but found that I could no longer describe myself in that way. What was I? For the first time in my life, I didn't know, an unexpected fact I found curiously exhilarating.

"As I told you in my first e-mail, my brother was going to write a book about his experience in Argentina," Loretta said, clearly in an effort to get me off the hook. "He evidently ran into Hernando Vilario at that time."

She had already told him a great deal, I knew. In her correspondence with Leon, she'd described Julian's life and work, how he'd searched for Marisol after the disappearance, contacted

243

both Casa Rosada and the Russians. She'd also told him that Julian was studying a map of Argentina before his death and that he'd circled the very village in which El Árabe now lived. She'd related the details of our talk with Soborov, as well—everything he'd revealed about his interaction with Julian and Julian's subsequent meeting with El Árabe.

Now, she said, "So, as you know, we're here because we want to talk to him."

"As I told you, this is not difficult," Leon said. "Hernando loves the attention. Especially from Americans. He is a big fan of the American Western. There is a picture of John Wayne in his house. I have already arranged for you to see him. You could fly there or take a bus. It is a long ride by bus, but not a bad trip. You will see our beautiful countryside."

"We want to be well prepared before we talk to him," Loretta said, "so we'd appreciate anything you could add that you think we should know."

"Know?" Leon asked. "He is a monster. This you already know. But he is a monster who is at least without deceit. When he was arrested, he spit in the face of the government. At his trial, he spit at the judges and made no apologies for his *escuelitas*."

Leon walked to a metal cabinet and withdrew an ancient carousel projector.

"It was El Árabe's. He took many pictures," he said. "He was proud of them. 'My gift to you,' he told me."

Leon walked to the front of the room, pulled down a screen,

turned off the room's overhead light, returned to his seat, and reached for the button that controlled the carousel.

"This will not be easy," he said.

When the lights went on again, I felt that I had been gutted both spiritually and physically. In fact, mine had been a reaction so visceral that I'd had to hold my stomach and close my throat. At the end of it I was pale and felt that my legs had gone numb beneath me. There is a kind of revulsion that moves you beyond what some men do, to what some men are, and it is that that drains and exhausts you and leaves you with nothing but a need to escape the whole human race.

"So," Leon said as he turned on the light. "That is El Árabe. Do you still want to meet him?"

"It isn't a question of wanting to meet him," I said. "We need to meet him."

Leon rose, walked to the front of the room, and drew up the screen, all of it done quite thoughtfully, as though he was turning something over his mind.

When he returned to his seat, he folded his hands together on the table, fingers laced, like a man with a pronouncement. "Steel yourselves, then," he said. "For, no matter what evil you have known before, you have not known such a one as El Árabe." He turned to Loretta. "It is strange, is it not, that your brother was associated with such a man?"

With Leon's question, how little I still knew of Julian struck hard. But truth is truth, and the fact remained that the pieces of Julian's story were still scattered. It was as if Loretta had been right long ago when she'd said that the pebbles Julian had strewn along the forest floor might lead only to more pebbles.

"El Árabe will be expecting you," Leon said as he turned to me. "Good luck."

Leon had wished me good luck quite cheerfully, but as Loretta and I left his office I found something final in his good wishes. For it was luck I would need, surely. In fact, it was all I had left, because I'd reached the very end of what I could discover of Julian beyond what was in his books. I had read and reread those books, along with his notes and letters. I had gone to Paris, Oradour, London, Budapest, Čachtice, Rostov, and now Buenos Aires. I had interviewed the slender list of people who seemed to have made a contribution to Julian's work, his guides and his sources. I had talked to my father and to Loretta and even to myself, surely the three people, other than Marisol, who had most figured in his life. I had done all this, but I still had not cracked the door to my friend's most secret chamber or gained any notion of why he had rowed out to the center of the pond, nor what I might have said to stop him from what he eventually did.

"So," I said to Loretta wearily, like an old gumshoe on his way to a final rendezvous, "the last witness."

27

Our meeting with Hernando Vilario was not scheduled until the day after our arrival at Iguazú, and so Loretta and I decided to visit the great falls. I'd made the same trip with Julian years ago, the two of us flying out of Buenos Aires on a stormy afternoon. We'd stayed in Iguazú a couple of days, then returned to the capital.

A good deal had changed at Iguazú since then, changes no doubt necessary in order to make the place more attractive to tourists. Now a small train took visitors into the jungle that surrounded the falls. As we disembarked, I noticed that they were playing the theme from *The Mission,* a film whose dramatic opening scene had ended with the startling image of a crucified priest being swept over the Devil's Throat.

For a time we walked silently through a jungle that was now equipped with cement walkways and steel railings, safe for old people and children.

"The music back at the train reminds me of what Julian said about the difference between tourists and travelers," I said.

Loretta peered out to where the roiling waters of Iguazú could be heard but not yet seen.

"This is the last time he was a tourist," I said. "When we got back to Buenos Aires, Marisol was waiting for us. We all went to a restaurant in La Boca and had dinner and wine. Julian had never looked more delighted with his life. Everything had come so easily to him."

A thought appeared to strike Loretta. "I know you felt rather dull in comparison to Julian. We both did. But were you jealous of him, too?"

It is strange what can be unearthed if the time is right and the inquisitor is dear, and at that moment I felt it rise like a gorge in my throat, the awful truth of things.

"Yes," I said, and with that admission I felt a crack run through the portrait of my long friendship with Julian. I recalled all the times I might have influenced him, might have taken advantage of his weariness, his long bouts of despair, and even his penury—I might have used all that to nudge him in a different direction. I had even silenced any criticism of his work that might have made it leaner and sharper or reined in the wild sprawl that had sometimes marred his books. He might not have listened, but the fact remained that I had never offered him the slightest direction. With Loretta's question, I had to wonder if I had done this not because I thought it would do no good, but because I'd preferred him to remain where he was, tucked into a shadowy corner of the literary world, preferred him to remain what he was, a writer whose subject matter would doom him to an inconsequential place. Had I said nothing because I secretly delighted in all the now-darkened lights that had once shone on him, took pleasure in his failure?

"My God, Loretta," I breathed. "Was I not his friend?"

She saw my eyes glisten as all the many deceiving layers of my feigned friendship fell away.

She drew me into her arms. "Now you are," she said.

28

The road to El Árabe led out of the bustling little town that bordered Iguazú and into the deepening jungle that surrounded it, burrowing into the depths in a way that did indeed remind me of Conrad's *Heart of Darkness*. Kurtz had gone far upriver, to the Inner Station, as Conrad had so metaphorically called it, deep into the savage heart of things, and there, amid that splendor, created a landscape that in all the world had most resembled hell.

I was busily going on about this when Loretta finally stopped me.

"Julian said something about goodness," she told me. "I hadn't thought of it before, but it was actually the last thing he said to me."

She had gone down to the sunroom, where she found him in his chair, with the map of South America spread open on his lap. She asked him what he was doing and he said that he was remembering a place where he learned something about evil.

He had a pen in his hand, she said, the point touching the map, where, as she later saw, he'd circled the village of Clara Vista.

She asked him what it was that he had learned. His answer was surprisingly simple, though ultimately unrevealing. "That goodness is evil's best disguise," he said and added nothing else.

"Goodness is evil's best disguise," I repeated as we moved ever deeper into the Paraguayan jungle from which El Árabe had made his many cruel pronouncements. I found myself imagining that his house was similar to the ravaged abode of Mr. Kurtz, surrounded by a fence of bare wooden poles topped with dried-out human heads.

El Árabe's home was not emblematic of the dead soul who lived inside it, however. In fact, it looked more like a small woodland cottage of the sort one might see in more temperate climates. The vines that would otherwise have hung like thick green drapery from the roof had been cut back, and no vegetation crawled up the walls or slithered up the supporting posts of the side porch. For this reason, the cottage appeared curiously European in the way that any sense of wildness had been clipped away.

I could see three wicker chairs and a brightly colored hammock that took up almost the entire width of the porch. The windows were large, and their orange shutters were open; inside I could see unexpectedly feminine curtains, white and lacy, softly undulating in the warm, lazy air.

The house itself was built from concrete blocks, painted to a glossy sheen. There was no front porch, just an earthen walkway leading to a door bordered by an assortment of plants potted in identical terra-cotta pots. A short storm fence stretched around the back of the house. Over the fence, I could see an old woman busy at a clothesline, hanging T-shirts, jeans, and a few oversized dresses with large floral patterns of the type I'd seen on the women in the town.

I glanced toward the front of the house. So the moment has come, I thought. I looked at Loretta. "Ready?"

She nodded. "Ready."

And thus did we close in upon the Inner Station.

We had gotten only halfway up the dirt walkway that led to the house when the door suddenly swung open and a short, round man stepped out into the bright sun. He was perhaps seventy years old, but with jet black hair, quite obviously dyed, combed straight back and glinting in the sunlight.

"So the Eagle has landed," he said with a laugh.

He was wearing light blue Bermuda shorts and no shirt, and his nearly hairless belly shook with quick spasms as he laughed. "Welcome to my house. As we say, and I hear often said also in the American movies, '*Mi casa es su casa.*'"

With that, El Árabe thrust out his large hand. "I am a great fan of American movies and John Wayne. Come, you will see." He stepped aside and waved us in. "Please, come, come. I will have my housekeeper make drinks for us. You like mai tai? Margarita?"

I could not imagine having a drink with this man, and yet I could find no way to refuse it. He was my last contact, the end of the line, and if I learned nothing further, I could go no further.

"Whatever you have," I said, and glanced at Loretta.

"Yes," she said with a quick smile. "Whatever you have."

"Ah, good, we shall have drinks, then," El Árabe said as if he was certain we would refuse them and now felt relieved that we hadn't. He walked to the window and called out to the old woman in the back, "*Vaya. Los invitados quieren algo de tomar. Margaritas para todos, por favor.* With that he turned back to us. "She is slow, poor thing," he added sorrowfully. "But in time the drinks will come." He swept his arm out toward an adjoining veranda. "Out there it is cool. We sit and talk and wait forever for the drinks." He laughed heartily. "You like my house?"

The living room was small, and El Árabe had decorated its walls with pictures not only of John Wayne but perhaps twenty other American movie stars, their studio photographs in cheap plastic frames. I caught Humphrey Bogart, Spencer Tracy, Alan Ladd, and John Wayne as I made my way outside.

"No women," I said to him as I stepped out onto the veranda. "I would have expected, say, Veronica Lake or Ava Gardner."

El Árabe waved his hand. "I am a man of action," he said with another broad laugh. "I admire other such men. Men with, what do you call it, the steely stare." He laughed again. "I would wish to be the strong silent type. The Gary Cooper. But, as you see, I talk too much." He grinned impishly. "And I am not tall." He indicated the wicker chairs. "Please, rest. It is a long way from Buenos Aires. Did you fly?"

"Yes," I answered. "But once in Iguazú, we rented a car."

"Iguazú, yes," El Árabe said. "So not a long drive this morning. Was it easy to find your way?"

"There aren't many roads, so it's hard to get lost," I said.

"Not many roads," El Árabe said. "Not like in America, with the many, many highways."

"No, not like America," I said.

Out of the blue, El Árabe asked. "So, my English is good, no?"

"It's very good," I told him.

"From the American movies," El Árabe said. "I watched them when I was a kid. I still watch them. I like to practice all the time my English. But here it is hard. Here there is nothing. I am surrounded by such ignorant ones. They vote always for the Reds." He leaned back slightly. "Do you speak Spanish?"

"I'm afraid not," I answered.

His gaze slid over to Loretta. "And you, señora?"

"Only enough to get by," Loretta said. "My brother spoke it quite well."

"Your brother, yes," El Árabe said. "You have come to speak of him. I understand this from Leon. He has died, your brother."

"Yes," Loretta said.

"So young," El Árabe said sympathetically. "Unusual in America. But here, they die like flies. We know death. We know pain. It is never far from us. At night we hear its voice in the undergrowth. There is much devouring one of the other here." He turned to Loretta. "As your brother knew."

El Árabe looked like an actor who'd blown a line, and who, in doing so, had skipped ahead in the play, dropping five pages from the script and thus arriving too early at a place too far along.

"Margaritas!" he called, and looked back at us. "She is slow, as I said. But she is good at the few little things she does.

254

In Buenos Aires, they would not tolerate so slow a servant. But here, time has almost stopped, and we move slowly, like the sun." His grin was rapier thin. "I am also philosopher. I have many thoughts. But no one wishes to hear them." He laughed. "The world would have to change too much to give me honors. El Árabe is despised. El Árabe is a murderer, a rapist, a torturer." For the second time, his gaze hardened. "But who did I do these things to, eh? I will tell you. To people who would have done the same to me, to you." He waved his hand. "Even now, they wear the T-shirts with the face of Che. Who was a murderer, this famous Che, with the movie-star face and the movie-star fame, a man who would have caused the deaths of millions."

He didn't wait for this to settle in before he surged on, his eyes fiercely widening as he continued. "And you have read what Castro said to Khrushchev?" His gaze leaped from me to Loretta, then back to me. "You have read this? During the crisis with Cuba? With the missiles? He told that fat old Russian to kill all the Americans. To drop all the bombs. He said he would sacrifice Cuba for such an annihilation."

He shook his head at the monstrousness of it. "I am what you call 'small potatoes' compared to this one who would have killed millions. As Stalin did. And Mao." He thumped his chest. "I, El Árabe, was never such a killer as these two Reds."

It would have been a passionate attack on ideological extremism had El Árabe's own hideous acts not been equally extreme, but I felt it prudent to say nothing about this.

"I gather that you know why we've come here," I said.

El Árabe nodded, then looked at Loretta. "Leon told me about your brother. He said you believed he was perhaps going to write about me in his next book."

"Perhaps," Loretta said. "Just before he died, he took out a map of Argentina. He had even circled the name of this village."

This information seemed not to surprise El Árabe in the least.

"As you see, I am not hard to find," he said. "I hide from no one. I wish only that those Reds who now stink up the halls of Casa Rosada do not cross the border." He pointed to an old hunting rifle that leaned against the far wall. "I would fight, but I have nothing but this—what do you call it?—this . . . popgun. Even so, they do not come. Even so, they fear me. Do you know why? Because I know their secrets, these men at Casa Rosada. I know they are not so holy as they say they are. They know my crimes because I have not hidden them. But I know the crimes they hide."

He smiled in the way of one who could easily prove his point. "Guilt makes men tired and skinny." He patted his full belly. "I have no such problem."

A rattle of pots and pans came from the other room.

El Árabe shook his head. "It is hard to think with such commotion," he said.

I glanced toward the kitchen, where I could see the woman stumbling about, her hands shaking violently.

"She probably has Parkinson's disease," I said. "Or something like it."

El Árabe waved his hand; then his eyes shot over to Loretta. "Your brother had come to me before. Back in the old days. He

was looking for a girl. He thought I might know where she was."
He stopped and stared at me sullenly and with such a sense of
volcanic violence that I felt a cold streak of genuine fear.

Now he burst into a raucous laugh.

"See what I can do?" he asked. "An old man, and I can still
fill a heart with fear." He laughed again, a great, self-satisfied
laugh that shook his belly violently. "With this look, too," he
said and seemed to clamp down upon me with his eyes, so that
I felt like little more than a small animal in a steel trap. "This
one could really shut them up. Even when they were screaming,
it would shut them up."

He laughed again, and quite suddenly his entire demeanor
changed. It was as if a cloud had parted to reveal a wholly different person, one whose every aspect had been clothed in shadow
but which now became clear in the light.

"Shall I speak French to you, my American friends?" he
asked in perfect English. "Should I speak German?"

The transformation continued, and all the earlier features
of his disguise fell away; he was no longer the slick-haired thug
but was what he immediately claimed to be.

"Better that I should speak the Spanish of Castile," he said,
"for I am Spanish, and this peasant patois I speak to such a one
as that wretch in the kitchen is not my native tongue."

"I see," I said quietly.

"As Julian knew, a great spy must be a spy from birth," El
Árabe said. "He must have played a role all his life."

He was now as refined a worldling as could be imagined
in any novel of intrigue. All his boorishness and vulgarity had

257

simply dropped away like pieces of an old costume. Beneath it, there was no swagger, no bravado. I could almost imagine him in evening dress, having brandy and a cigar in the staterooms of Madrid, exactly the sort of suave foreign agent my father had dreamed of being.

"It takes intelligence to play a buffoon, and I fooled them all. Even Julian was fooled by my disguise. But those days are gone and there is no need for me to play this trick." His laugh was no longer of the belly-jerking sort but was now the soft chuckle of a man in his club. "Julian. You have come to speak of Julian. What a naive young man he was, looking for this girl." Now his laughter turned cold and mirthless. "He came to me because the Reds had sent him. They had told him I was in charge of many evil things, and so I perhaps might know of this missing girl." He cocked his head and glanced from one side to the other. "Shall I tell you about your friend, your brother?" he asked. "He was looking for this girl, but shall I tell you what he found?"

Warily I nodded, and Loretta whispered, "Yes, tell us."

And so he did.

258

29

At the end of *Heart of Darkness*, Marlow is drained by the tale he has just related, emptied not of energy but of belief. It is as if the darkness he describes has dialed down the light in his soul.

So it seemed also with Loretta, at the close of El Árabe's tale, and so it certainly was with me.

"Do you believe what he told us?" she asked a few minutes into our drive back to town. We had been facing the road in complete silence.

"Every word," I answered.

She looked at me. "Why?"

"Because it fits," I said.

I thought of a moment in *The Secret Chamber*, when La Meffraye stands on the ramparts at Machecoul, staring down at the thirty men that the Bishop of Nantes has sent to arrest her master. From that height she considers the crimes in which she was complicit, and their consequences, and she knows, absolutely, that she is bound for hell.

"Julian could see nothing but darkness after that," I said softly, now thinking of how hideous it must have been for him, the scene he'd witnessed at El Sitio.

"I remember something I said earlier," Loretta said. "That if Julian ever saw an atrocity, it would have unstrung him."

"And it did," I said.

Loretta clearly understood that something had also unstrung me as well.

"El Árabe's last question," she said.

With that simple reminder, I was there again, sitting on the veranda, listening to El Árabe. But now there was the added element of foreknowledge, and I found myself imagining as much as recalling his narrative, tasting the dust in the air, seeing the swirl of the dogs as they tore into each other, feeling the small droplets of blood that shot out from the ring, and hearing Julian's voice over the roar of the crowd.

"That one is a killer."

El Árabe turned to him. "American?"

Julian nodded, smiled. "A bankrupt one if I keep betting on the wrong dog."

El Árabe grinned, pulled a red handkerchief from his pocket, and swabbed his bare chest. "Bet on John Wayne in the next match. With him you will get back your money."

Julian laughed. "John Wayne, really?"

"He is my dog. I am big fan for John Wayne." He swayed slightly and hitched his pants. "Howdy, Pilgrim," he said, and offered his hand.

"Julian Wells," Julian said as he took it.

"Where you are from?" El Árabe asked between swigs of beer.

"New York."

El Árabe reached for a bottle, opened it, and thrust it toward him. "We drink to friendship, eh? America and Argentina." He pounded his chest with his right fist. "Brothers."

Julian took a long pull on the bottle. "Brothers," he said.

They were two actors, I thought, playing out the scene in my mind: Julian, the naive American with a vague lust for adventure; El Árabe, the crude peasant infatuated with American cowboys. Encased in their roles, they acted their way through the next few hours, Julian betting on El Árabe's dogs and almost always winning, so that as the evening deepened, his roll of cash grew thicker, a fact El Árabe was careful to notice because he needed Julian to think him not only a peasant buffoon, easily outwitted, but also a man who could no less easily be bribed.

"You got much money now, coño," El Árabe cried over the noise of the crowd. "You should be careful you don't lose it."
Julian laughed. "How would I lose it?"

"Not lose, maybe. Someone take it. Not everyone is a brother. Not in this bad place."

Julian swayed slightly, as if drunk. "It doesn't look so bad here."

El Árabe wagged his finger. "Very bad. Very bad people in this place. You maybe not go back to Buenos Aires tonight."

"I have to. I have no place to stay."

"You stay with me. I protect you. Morning, you go back to Buenos Aires." He threw his arm over Julian's shoulder. *"You safe with me. Brothers, no?"*

Julian's head lolled to the left. *"Too much beer."*

El Árabe laughed. *"We go home now,"* he said.

I imagined them almost as comic characters in a melodrama, the tall young American and the squat little Argentine, a drunken Don Quixote and a malignant Sancho Panza struggling toward the old truck where El Árabe had already caged the few dogs that had survived the fights—"quick killers," as he called the ones that emerged from their struggles with treatable rather than fatal wounds.

In the truck, Julian had fallen asleep, or pretended to, and I saw him slumped in the dusty darkness, his body jerking with the bump and sway of the road.

"Okay, we are home now," El Árabe said. *He opened the door and drew Julian out into the weedy driveway of his house. "You never sleep in hammock before, no? You like it. Very good. Stars. Cool air."*

Either passed out or feigning unconsciousness, Julian had slumped into the hammock that hung on the wide porch of El Árabe's house, arisen groggily the next morning, reached for his money, and found it missing.

"I know what you look for," El Árabe said with a loud laugh. "You think maybe I steal money from you, no?" He reached into the pocket of his soiled jeans and pulled out a roll of cash. "I keep it for you. We are brothers, no? We do not steal from each other." He laughed again. "Maybe from others we steal, and maybe to others we do bad things, but I do nothing bad to Pilgrim, and Pilgrim, he does nothing bad to El Árabe."

Thus was sealed a bond that deepened over the next few weeks as both Julian and El Árabe continued to perfect their roles, playing off each other with such skill that there were times when the subtext of deception seemed almost to disappear, nights of less drinking and more talk, which at last brought them each the long-sought moment.

"It's all just a way of forgetting," Julian said quietly. He took out a cigarette and lit it. "All this drinking." He drew in a long breath and released it slowly. "It is because of a woman. She is missing."

"You will find another," El Árabe said. "You must think of something else."

"I can't."

Then, in a sudden burst that El Árabe found either absolutely brilliant if meant to deceive him or absolutely stupid if it was real, Julian had revealed everything: how he had met Marisol,

263

her work as a guide, how she had later disappeared, his long effort to find her, how he'd gone first to Casa Rosada, then to the Russians, who had set him up to meet El Árabe, all of it in a cataract of impassioned narrative that had finally impressed El Árabe in its anguished sincerity.

El Árabe remained silent for a time, then quite softly he said, "It is possible this one you spoke of, this missing woman, it is possible she is still alive, no?"

"No, it's not possible," Julian said. "We both know what happens to these women."

"Not to all, maybe," El Árabe said. "Maybe some of them are kept."

"Kept?"

El Árabe shrugged. "To some men, it is a waste to kill such a woman," he said. "Better to keep her for a while."

Julian's gaze glimmered with hope. "Keep her where?"

El Árabe smiled. "They are called 'escuelitas.'" He offered Julian a look that could not have been mistaken. "Perhaps she is still at one of these places. Do you wish I look for her?"

"Yes."

"And if I find her, do you wish to go to this place?"

"Yes," Julian answered. "Yes, I want to go there."

Time passed, and during that time Julian had revealed ever-deeper confidences. He had come to Argentina, he said, in search of a life's work. Such had been his chief hunger when he came here, he told El Árabe, a furious need to do some great good work, a need his host had found both naive and comical. But Julian's sincerity had won El Árabe over. He'd been a fool, but a lovable fool, a man who wanted to help the ones who live in the dust. More than anything, he now sought Marisol.

"*Because you fuck her, no?*" El Árabe asked. "*Those little indigenes, they fuck hard and fast.*"

"*I never touched her.*"

El Árabe laughed. "*You think she is so innocent, this woman?*" He drained the last beer of the evening. "*Maybe not so innocent, my friend. If she was so innocent, she would not have disappeared.*"

"*No, she was absolutely innocent,*" Julian insisted. "*There was no reason for her to have been taken. She wasn't involved in politics. All she wanted . . . and she said this to me . . . all she wanted was a fighting chance.*"

"*If this is so, I will find her for you,*" El Árabe said.

It took him only a week to find the *escuelita* to which Marisol had been taken, and though she was no longer there, he felt certain that by talking to the commissar of the camp, he would be able to find her.

And he did.

"*Okay, so we go there tomorrow,*" El Árabe said.

"*Where is it?*" Julian asked,

*"There is a dog farm on the pampas. They breed
there the Dogo Córdoba. They have also a barn and stalls.
This they have made into an escuelita."*

They left Buenos Aires the next morning, driving first along the
wide boulevards, then out into the suburbs, and finally down
a dirt road to a location El Árabe called El Sitio, which means
only "the place."

It was a farmhouse of sorts, though it was unclear
whether it had once been occupied or whether it had been
constructed only for its current purpose. Its windows were
boarded up and left unpainted, which made the structure
seem like an immense crate. It had a corrugated roof that
was streaked with rust.

*"They keep them here," El Árabe said with a crude smile,
"the ones they are educating."*

The heat inside this building was stifling, of course, and so, El
Árabe explained with a wink and a grin, there was no need for
the women to have clothes.

Julian remained in the truck, El Árabe said, while he went
in search of the commissar, who was in a nearby shed where
preparations for "the day's lessons" were under way. Those
preparations involved hooks and ropes and the fetching of the
commissar's favored whip, a *chicotte*, made of rhinoceros hide
and imported from the Congo.

From his place inside the truck, Julian had a clear view of the farmhouse and the line of upright wooden poles, each fitted with handcuffs, that stood to the side of it, and toward which, while El Árabe discussed the whereabouts of Marisol with the commissar, a naked woman was pushed and shoved and prodded by two men in green uniforms, each wielding a *chicotte*.

I could only imagine Julian's thoughts at that moment, how he must surely have realized that the same outrage had been committed upon Marisol. Naked and caked in her own filth, she must have been led to those same poles, cuffed and left to bake in the sun, while the men took their lunch break under the nearby trees. Like the woman he watched from the interior of El Árabe's truck, Marisol must have waited as the minutes passed and the men leisurely smoked their cigarettes, then rose and came toward her, as these men now did toward this unknown woman, slapping their *chicottes* against their dusty brown boots and, as the whipping commenced, beginning to laugh.

The beating lasted for several minutes, El Árabe said, with long pauses during which the woman was left to hang in the sun. Through it all Julian sat in the stillness of the truck, staring through its dusty windows as the whips sang in the air, along with the cries of the woman and the laughter of the men.

"She was covered in blood by the time I got back to the truck," El Árabe told us. "She was hanging down so low her long hair almost touched the ground, and her back, legs, and arms were raw. The whips almost skinned her."

But it was what El Árabe saw inside the truck that chilled the air around me as I listened. He had passed the bloody girl who slumped almost to the ground, her wounds now boiling in the noonday sun, and given the scene hardly any notice. He had, after all, attended many such sessions. Nor had he paid any mind to the second woman, also naked and filthy, who was at that very moment being led out by two other men. He had noticed the commissar strolling toward the broken-down corral, but that had had no interest for him, since he had already ascertained Marisol's whereabouts. It was Julian, and only Julian, upon whom El Árabe, with an unexpected feeling, had fixed his attention.

"He was sitting exactly where I'd left him a half hour before," El Árabe told us. "He said only, 'Was this done to Marisol?'"

From the corner of my eye, I saw a terrible question form on Loretta's lips. "Had it been?" she asked.

El Árabe nodded. "And worse," he said. "But I did not tell this to Julian. I told him she was simply brought here and shot. It would have been a bad thing to tell him more than this. He was blaming himself. He was saying it was his fault she was dead. I could not tell him more. This would have made it worse for him. So I told him only that she was dead. 'They dumped her,' I said to him. 'She is dust.'"

Julian had gone quiet, El Árabe told us.

"Pain can make men wail like women," he said. "But in Julian, there was only silence. He was alive, but he was dead. I took him back to Buenos Aires. All the way, he did not speak. I left him at his hotel. He never came to me again."

For a time, no one spoke, and we heard nothing but the woman still fumbling about in the kitchen, along with the occasional bark of a dog or the call of a bird.

Finally, I said, "So Julian never saw Marisol?"

El Árabe shook his head. "And this is good, for it was very bad, what had been done to her. Very bad, the torture. Even the ones who live do not recover."

Another stark silence followed. Neither Loretta nor I had been able to move, so we were still frozen in place when the woman at last came out onto the veranda, dragging one foot behind her, causing the tray that bore our drinks to jerk as it trembled in her shaking hand. Her head was down, her hair was unkempt and streaked with dull gray. It was long enough to shield her face, but suddenly, with a wildly trembling hand, she drew it back to reveal the only thing I might recognize among the web of wrinkles and behind the drooping eyelids: her startlingly black eyes.

In a novel, it would have been Marisol, of course, this sadly broken woman. And I would have risen and gathered her into my arms and brought her to some safer, kinder place. There she would have lived out her days, sitting beneath a mango tree, enjoying the breeze from off La Plata. I would have occasionally come back to see her, and at some point she would have recalled Julian in his youth, our bright days in Buenos Aires, and together, as the sun set over the great trees of San Martín, we would have found the small measure of peace this life affords.

All these sweet, consoling things would have happened in a book, but as Julian knew, life takes a different turn.

"Maria," El Árabe said, "say hello to my guests."

She gave no response, but merely placed the drinks on the little wooden table in front of us, spilling them slightly as she did so. Then she turned and struggled back into the house.

When she'd finally disappeared into the shadowy interior of the house, I drew my eyes over to El Árabe.

"Why was Marisol disappeared?" I asked. "Was she a Montonero?"

El Árabe shook his head. "No. She was a nothing, just a girl from the Chaco."

"Then why was she taken?"

El Árabe grinned. "It was a mistake, but life, it is full of little twists and turns, no?"

"That's not an answer," I said firmly. "Why was Marisol taken?"

El Árabe shrugged. "She was betrayed," he said. "A boy she grew up with in the Chaco. In that orphanage there. They have a picture of those two together, those two indigenes. Marisol and that other flat-nosed peasant."

"Emilio Vargas?" I asked.

El Árabe nodded. "He was a weasel, that Red. And he lied about this girl. She was just a guide or something. But this Vargas, he feeds her to the wolves. Who knows why? Perhaps he is getting even with her because she does not fuck him in the old days. Men are scum in this way. One thing I know, he was there when it was done. Laying it on her himself. Making a big show of it." He shrugged. "It was Vargas who caused Marisol to be killed. But that is not how Julian saw it. And for that reason he thought himself her murderer."

270

"Why would Julian have felt responsible for what happened to Marisol?" I asked.

"This he told me, and this I know."

"What did he tell you?"

El Árabe appeared quite amused by the tricks embedded in the scheme of things, and I could see the true cruelty of this man, how he loved, more than anything, to watch a helpless creature dangle.

"Tell me what Julian told you," I demanded.

His smile was a paper cut. "Perhaps you should ask your father."

30

My father?

This could not be the ending, I thought. In a novel of intrigue it would be too obvious—the story of a son's quest to find out what he could have done to prevent his friend's suicide ends up circling back to the father. As a literary route toward dark discoveries this one was way too familiar, trod, as it were, by Oedipus.

Yet, I could see the question that remained open each time I looked into Loretta's eyes: *What did your father do?*

I had considered what I was going to say to him many times on the flight back home with Loretta. During that time, the stakes had steadily increased for both of us, Loretta needing to know what Julian had discovered, I needing to know the part my father had played in whatever that discovery had been. Life was a warren of secret chambers, I decided, everyone on the plane a harbor for dark things. All the old clichés of spy fiction took on a hard reality: hall of mirrors, nest of vipers. My father had always wanted to be a character in a tale of intrigue. Now he was.

"He doesn't have to tell you the truth," Loretta warned me when we parted at the airport. "He doesn't have to tell you anything."

"I know."

"So be careful, Philip," she added. Her tone was tense and her eyes held a feline sharpness. It was clear how much all this had come to matter to her, our search, now in dead earnest, for Julian's crime.

"Because in a way, this is an interrogation," she added.

This was true, of course, and if my father chose to remain silent, then the story would end with an ambiguity no novel of intrigue, or even the cheapest thriller, could permit. We would know what happened to Marisol. But we would never know why it had happened, or why Julian had blamed himself for it, or why at the end of his life he'd still been wanting to confess to a crime for which he had long ago pronounced himself guilty.

But what was Julian's crime?

And why had he died without revealing it?

The answer to those questions now lay with my father.

He looked much weaker than when I'd last seen him, and in the flesh, rather than on a computer screen, he seemed far more frail.

"Ah, Philip," he said. "Welcome home."

He was sitting in his chair when I arrived, as upright as possible, and as he watched me settle into the chair that faced him, his mood seemed one of cheerful expectation.

"So," he said, "tell me about your adventures."

All my life I had wanted him to be eager to hear my tale. All my life I had felt somewhat inadequate for never having one to tell him. Now the one I brought him was incomplete, with missing pieces he alone could provide.

"Well?" my father said eagerly. "You must surely have some stories."

I felt like a man who had reached the final chapter of a book he had been reading for a long time, one of those vast nineteenth-century tomes in which many fates shift and veer, only to reach what in the last pages seems to be their predestined ends.

"Yes, I do," I said quietly.

Then, like a wily cop in a bleak interrogation room, I laid the groundwork for what was to come. I offered a brief summation of the route I'd traveled, through Julian's books, then on to the places I'd gone and the people I'd met, first René and Oradour, then on to Irene in Budapest and Soborov in Rostov, a trail that finally wound its way back to Argentina, where I'd confronted El Árabe in a little house tucked into a corner of Paraguay near Iguazú Falls.

The last of my tale had taken me to the brink, but I found that I could not cross it, and only said, "He was a cruel man, El Árabe."

"They come out of the woodwork in a place like Argentina during a time like the Dirty War," my father said. He appeared to grow somber for a moment, then, by act of will, to lift his own heavy spirits. "But you've had quite a time of it," he said. "Travel to exotic locales. Talks with various odd ducks, even a Russian spy. It's like the books I used to read."

"A lot can be learned from those books, I suppose," I said, rousing myself for another reluctant effort to confront my father.

"Deception, for one. False identities and wrong turns. That one may smile and smile and be a villain." I paused, then added, "That goodness is evil's best disguise. Julian said that. In fact, it was the last thing he said."

My father stared at me silently for a moment, then said with perfect calm, "What do you suppose he meant by that?"

"I don't know," I said, now moving with small steps toward the trapdoor, the steps beneath it, "but I think it was something he learned in Argentina."

"Yes, he did change after that." His gaze dropped to his hands, then lifted slowly up toward me. "That girl who disappeared."

"Marisol," I said.

The trapdoor opened and I took one step down.

"We found out what happened to her, you know," I told my father. "She was arrested by the junta. She was tortured, then killed."

"I thought as much," my father said.

"But we never found out why," I said as I made my slow descent. "She wasn't political after all. That much is clear. She was just a girl from the country."

My father said nothing, but I thought I saw a sad glimmer in his eyes, and with that I made the rest of my journey down.

"Julian thought it was his fault," I said. "He blamed himself for her death."

"Why?"

"I don't know," I answered. "And when I tried to get that particular answer from El Árabe, he said I should ask you."

My father's body tensed. "Me? Why would he say that?"

"I don't know that either," I told him.

He looked at me closely. "But you think I know, don't you, Philip?"

When I didn't answer, he sat back slightly, as if some invisible interrogator had pushed him.

"Do you think I was working for the junta, Philip?" he asked. "That I was one of their agents? Because I'd have to have been one, wouldn't I, in order to know why Marisol was killed?"

"I suppose you would have, yes," I admitted.

"Is that what you think?" my father demanded sharply.

"I only know that Julian blamed himself," I said, "and that when I tried to find out why, El Árabe—"

"Pointed his finger at me," my father interrupted. "Yes, you said that, Philip."

He was clearly offended, and in the grip of that offense, he lifted his head like a proud but wounded warrior and glared at me.

"Do you know why she was killed?" I asked flatly.

"No, I don't," my father answered sternly. "How could I?" His eyes sparkled with affront. "I was nothing!" he cried. "You may have some fantasy that I was the puppet master in Argentina and that Julian was—what?—my pawn?" A hot breath blasted from him. "But I was nothing! I have always been nothing. Why else would I have played that silly little trick with Julian?"

There are moments in life that resemble the sound of wood cracking beneath you, and I had reached such a moment.

"What trick?" I asked.

My father seemed caught in a seizure of self-loathing. "Passed over and passed over. Again and again."

"What trick, Dad?"

"The butt of jokes," my father hissed vehemently.

"What silly little trick with Julian?" I demanded more firmly.

"Like some character in a novel," my father raged on. He paused for a long moment, drew in a smoldering breath, then stared at me coldly. "But life is not a novel, Philip. Do you know why?"

"Because people die," I said, paused a single, lethal second, then added, "especially people like Marisol."

My father's expression suddenly turned grave. "What are you talking about?" he asked. "Why do you keep going back to this girl?"

For the first time, he appeared to glimpse a dark shadow moving toward him, that pale rider we all fear, not the one that brings our death, but the one that brings the truth about our lives.

"What are you talking about, Philip?" he asked again, and it seemed clear to me that he honestly did not know.

"Something Julian once said just came back to me," I answered. "A thought from Thoreau. That although the little boys kill frogs in play, the frogs die in earnest."

My father stared at me silently, waiting, with some small but building hint of foreboding in his eyes.

I leaned forward slightly.

"Julian wanted to know why Marisol had been arrested," I said. "He wanted to know what evidence they had that Marisol was anything but a young woman who was just a guide." I paused, then released the arrow that contained all I knew. "El Árabe told Julian what that evidence was. It had come to Casa Rosada by way of an agent named Emilio Vargas. A double agent, actually, because Vargas was pretending to work for Casa Rosada, but in fact he was working for the Montoneros. He was also a friend of Marisol's from childhood, from the Chaco. He was under surveillance when Marisol went to him. I saw a picture of them together, but I have no idea why she went to him, because evidently she hadn't been in touch with him for many years."

"Then suddenly she went to him?" my father asked.

"Yes."

"When?"

"Not long after we met Father Rodrigo," I answered. "I know it was right after that because in the picture she is wearing a bead necklace that Rodrigo gave her."

I could see my father's mind working desperately, though it seemed less in an effort to get off the road we were on than to move farther down it.

"Of course," he said, as if some dark veil had torn. "Of course that's what she did."

For a moment, neither of us spoke. But during that time, though he said nothing, I saw a frightening change come over my father, saw the stony facade crumble, his mask fall away, so that he suddenly looked like what he was, a man in the act of loosening the cord that had bound his soul for so long.

Finally, my father said, "Julian felt responsible for what happened to Marisol because he was responsible, Philip." He straightened himself slightly, like a man before the bugle sounds, prepared, as his forebears had been prepared, to receive the blow.

"And so was I," he added. He seemed to rethink some painful issue of his own. "I've always believed that only the bravest of us have the courage to confront our wrongs." He stared at me brokenly. "Like Julian did." He let this final thought rest a moment, then added, "And the time has come for me to confront mine."

It had begun with the most innocent of inquiries, my father told me, one made when he and Julian walked the grounds of Two Groves one morning. Julian had come downstairs early and found my father alone at the kitchen table, drinking coffee. With his usual perceptiveness, Julian had found the scene quite sad and pointedly suggested an early morning stroll. With that, the two of them made their way out of the house and into the small orchard that surrounded it. After a few minutes of inconsequential conversation, Julian asked, "Do you think one person can change things?"

"It was a silly question," my father told me, "and at first I didn't take it seriously. It was a young man's question, and a very naive young man's at that."

But as the talk progressed, Julian's seriousness became increasingly obvious.

"He wanted to do something great," my father said. "To use that shopworn phrase, he wanted to 'make a difference.'" He shrugged. "Because he knew how my own career had gone, he doubted that he could do anything truly good at, say, the State Department. He wondered if there might be some other way.

He was simply exploring things with me, considering different avenues. That's when I said, 'Well, perhaps you should become a spy.'"

To my father's complete surprise, the idea appeared to catch.

"Maybe it was the romance of it," my father said. "Or maybe he truly began to think that somehow, in the secret corridors, he would be able to learn things that would eventually allow him to do some important good in the world." My father lifted his hands in a gesture of helplessness. "It appealed to me, how much Julian ached to do something good."

His gaze suddenly became quite intense. "A man shouldn't grow old wanting vengeance against his life, but that's exactly what had happened to me and I knew it. I didn't want it to happen to Julian. I didn't want him to be consumed by the raging disappointment that was consuming me."

It was an anger he had fiercely repressed, of course, though there'd been moments when I'd seen it in the way he grappled with a tangled coat hanger as if it were alive and thwarting him, as if to kill it.

"I was a little man trapped behind a desk," my father said, "dreaming my secret-agent dream."

"Walter Mitty," I said softly.

My father nodded. "And so I suggested Argentina as a place Julian should visit. I did this for the right reasons. I wanted him to see the real world. Get out of the cocoon his intelligence and good looks had provided for him." He sat back slightly and passed his hand over the blanket that covered his legs. "And given what

Julian had said about being a spy, it was also a place where we could play a little game."

He stopped and looked at me brokenly.

"It was never more than a game, Philip," he said, pleading his case before he'd even made it, "a little boys' game."

He decided to give Julian a harmless cloak-and-dagger assignment, he told me. If Julian liked the taste of the work, then perhaps he could pursue it. And if he didn't, then it might at least cool his zeal for whatever he thought the life of a secret agent was.

"Part of that assignment, of course, was to tell no one," my father said. The sadness in his voice deepened. "We swore this to each other, and clearly Julian kept his promise. Now I am breaking mine."

My father had considered several small tasks Julian might carry out while in Buenos Aires. None of them appealed to Julian, however, and so he pressed my father until he finally came up with a mission that had a suggestion of romance in it.

"Simply because—stupid, stupid—simply because it involved a woman."

Here he paused like a man at the jagged edge of a bottomless abyss.

"Marisol," I said, and with that word, I pushed him over it.

My father nodded. "Julian was so young, you see," he explained in a tone that now seemed stripped of all but regret. "So, in my own stupid way, I thought, What could be more thrilling than a secret assignment involving a young woman?" He seemed now on the brink of his own devastating revelation.

"She was just a guide," he added. "Just a young woman with a job, who wanted . . ."

"A fighting chance," I said.

My father drew in a long breath, then continued.

"It was just a little exercise in deceit," he said. "It had nothing to do with Marisol."

My father could see that I had no idea where he was going with this.

"The idea was for Julian to try his hand at acting," he told me, "like Loretta on the stage. Julian was to test himself, to see how good he was at . . ." His eyes took on a terrible sense of his own foolishness. "To spy, you must make the target trust you and believe you. You must be able to make a lie credible, so your target will accept the lie you tell."

"And Julian's target was Marisol," I said.

My father nodded. "Because she was innocent, you see. She wasn't in the least political. She'd been vetted by the consulate. They knew she was just a simple country girl. And so it was safe."

"What was safe?"

"It was safe to deceive her."

Julian was to pick his time, my father said, and pass on a bit of information, something she would find doubtful but which he would make her believe.

For Philip, sole witness to my crime.

I recalled the meeting with the old priest, Julian's remark about the likelihood of his being arrested, then the far more intense conversation I'd later come upon, Julian and Marisol in that little outdoor café, Julian animated, Marisol grave. I never knew the substance of what had passed between them. Now I did.

"Julian told Marisol that he had information about Father Rodrigo, didn't he?" I asked. "That he was going to be arrested. Not just a suspicion, but actual information from the consulate, as if he were a secret agent."

My father's sad smile held nothing but the dreadful fact of his own great miscalculation.

"Yes," he said. "And I'm sure that Julian had no idea that she would tell anyone. It was just a game." He shook his head despairingly. "Little boys. We didn't think that she would tell anyone other than Rodrigo, and that would not have mattered. What was the worst that could happen? She would believe a harmless lie and nothing would happen to anyone."

"But she told Emilio Vargas."

My father nodded. "Evidently, yes."

"She loved that old priest, and so she went to someone she thought could help him," I said.

My father lifted his arms and gripped the arms of his chair. "An old friend from her childhood, apparently," he said. "Someone she thought she could trust as much as . . ."

"Julian?"

My father looked like what he was, a man confronting the wrong Julian had faced so many years before.

"Until you mentioned this man, Vargas, I'd never heard of him," he said. "But now that you've told me about him, I know exactly what happened because I've known other men in his situation. You have to deflect attention away from yourself. And because you are a traitor, you have to give up someone else as a traitor. When Marisol went to him and told him what Julian had said, he saw his chance. He could finger her as a 'source' at the American consulate, say that she'd come to him as a fellow Montonero, and then he could turn her over to Casa Rosada."

He eased back into his chair and, with that movement, seemed to deflate.

"It's a classic play, Philip," he told me. "The trick is to make sure that the one you give up is as innocent as a child, one who can be devoured like Saturn devoured his children, without their ever knowing why." He paused, then added, "That's why, as a ploy, it's called the Saturn Turn."

These two little boys, my father and my best friend, had played a lethal trick, but Marisol had died in earnest.

"Julian never forgave himself," I told my father "He was good in that way. He thought only of the consequences of his acts, never of their intention."

"I hope you can forgive me, Philip," my father said.

"I do," I assured him. "But as Julian must have known, it's Marisol who can't."

When he gave no response to this, I said, "But then it's always like that, isn't it? You said so yourself."

I was surprised that I felt neither ire nor bitterness as I quoted him: "It's always the little people, too small for us to see, the little, dusty people, who pay for our mistakes."

I left him a few minutes later, expecting to face the night alone, but to my immense relief, I found Loretta waiting in the lobby of my building.

"It's a lovely evening," she said. "How about a walk through the park?"

We left the building and headed out into the night. She could see that I was shaken, but she asked no questions, and thus left it to me to decide when and where to speak.

We had already walked some distance into the park and taken a seat on one of its benches before I did.

"One night I came upon Julian and my father at Two Groves," I began. "They were alone for a long time in the study. It was very late and I'd gone upstairs to bed. But later I came down again and found them there, talking. They both looked rather surprised, and a little jarred, by my sudden appearance. They waved me in and we all talked a while, and I went back up to bed soon after. But it was in their eyes, Loretta. Conspiracy." I drew in an unsteady breath. "It was just a game," I said, then in a sudden rush, I related everything that my father had just told me. "He and my father promised each other never to mention Argentina. Like little boys with their blood oaths. And so he never did." I shrugged. "And I suppose that's what he couldn't bear any longer, the fact that he had this crime bottled up inside him and couldn't release it."

Loretta looked doubtful. "That's why he never confessed? Because he promised your father?"

Her question stopped me cold. No, of course not, I thought. Julian would not have held to such a childish oath. Nor would my father have cared if he'd broken it. After all, my father had just confessed his own complicity in Julian's crime.

So why had Julian never confessed, and why had he chosen death over that confession?

I recalled how, in light of his own father's death, Julian said that a little boy required a hero, someone he could look up to, someone who could guide him. Later still, he had concealed the identities of the men who massacred the villages of Oradour. When I asked him why he'd done this, his answer was simple. What would be the good, he asked, of telling some little boy that on a particular day in a particular place his father had been complicit in a great crime?

Had I been that little boy?

"No, Julian didn't confess because of me," I said to Loretta. "He didn't confess because I was still a little boy to him."

Then I told her how I'd reached this conclusion, the fact that Julian must have been profoundly influenced by his own father's death, how he must have come to think of my father as central to my life, how he'd known that he could not confess his crime without revealing my father's complicity in it. He had protected me as he'd protected the children of the soldiers who massacred the villagers of Oradour. It was all of a piece, I told her.

At the end of this, Loretta simply stared at me doubtfully.

"It's all too neat, Philip," she said. "And it's all too simple. That's natural, of course, because when a man you love kills himself, you want it to be about one thing. Just one thing you could have changed. But for some people, it's not one thing. It's everything." She looked at me pointedly. "Julian killed himself because he was like Marisol," she told me, "the victim of a Saturn Turn."

When she saw I didn't understand this, she continued.

"His simple goodness turned on him," she said. "Life used it against him in the same way Vargas used Marisol's innocence against her." She shrugged. "The meek never inherit the earth, Philip."

I thought of poor, benighted Swaziland, Africa's last kingdom. Julian had gone there some years before, then written an article about the conditions he'd found, how, while their king ordered fleets of luxury cars and flew about in a private jet, the people lay on their stomachs lapping water from fetid pools, picked chicken heads and pig's feet from the dumping grounds of the nearest abattoir, and brought this muck back home to cook in battered pails—a people whose life expectancy was thirty-one. In the final passage of his essay, Julian had written of the red-dirt townships and the plywood shanties, the motionless pools of poisoned water, the mud hovels and rusty sheds, where life comes for the people of Swaziland, as it has always come for the truly innocent, "with a knife in its hand."

As Loretta had now made it clear, that same life, fixed in a Saturnine gaze, had at last come for Julian.

"I don't want to be alone tonight, Loretta," I confessed.

If she'd had the smallest hesitation, the look in her eyes would have betrayed it. But I saw only that she'd grasped the full meaning of what I'd said.

"Perhaps not ever," she said.

I knew that it was not an ending Jane Austen would have written, orchestrated by the peal of marriage bells, all happiness assured, but even so, I took Loretta's hand.

"Perhaps not ever," I repeated.

She smiled. "Do you know what you would have said to him if you'd been in the boat?" she asked.

I shook my head. "Not yet," I told her.

But by the time we reached home, I did.

After

He folds the map and puts it on the table beside his chair. Beyond the window, he sees the flat gray waters of the pond. The boat, its yellow paint long faded, rests beneath a weeping birch.

He rises, walks to the window, and looks out.

In the distance, a small breeze rustles the leaves of the birch and skirts along the green lawn and gently rocks the purple irises that grow beside the water. He has seen so many grasses, so many flowers. The lavender fields of France, the cloudberries of the Urals with their little orange petals, the feather grasses of the pampas swaying like dancers.

He will miss these things.

He considers the act, then its consequences.

He will make it clean.

There will be no fuss.

He turns and gives a final glance at the map. He has studied so many maps. He thinks of the water bearers of the world, almost always women, hauling their jerry jars to the river or the lake. His mind is like those jars, worn and dusty, scarred by use, but still able to hold its heavy store of memory.

And yet there is something he forgot.

He walks to the small desk in the corner, opens the notebook, and tears out the top sheet. He folds it carefully, without hurry, then sinks it deep into his pocket.

It is disturbance you must look for, the old trackers told him. Not prints. Not trails. But disturbance in the spear grass, a sense of reeds askew. Those will lead you to the one you seek.

He looks about the room for any hint of such disturbance, finds none, and with that assurance, walks to the door, then passes through it, and moves out onto the lawn. He feels the breeze whose movement he had sensed before, cool upon his face, a pressure on his shirt, a gentle movement in his hair.

He hears a bird call, glances up, and sees a gull as it crosses the lower sky. When was it he first saw the sunbirds of the Sudan, their sun-streaked, iridescent feathers?

He shakes his head. It doesn't matter now.

He draws down his gaze and with a steady stride makes his way to the boat. It is heavy, and he has been weakened, though less by his final work than by this final decision.

But the decision has been made.

The boat is weighty but he pulls it into the water. What was the lightest he ever knew? Oh yes, it was made of bulrushes. And what was the other word for bulrushes? Oh yes, it was tule.

The boat rocks violently as he climbs in, but he rights himself, grabs an oar, and pushes out into the water.

How far to go?

The center of the pond. Far enough that he will appear small and indistinct in the distance so that she cannot tell what he is doing, nor get to him before he can complete the task.

Seventy feet from shore now. Perhaps eighty. He has not rowed in a long time. Even now his arms are aching. But that will be over soon. He knows that he has grown weak in the Russian wastes, but he is surprised by just how weak he is. Or has his secret always worked upon him like a withering disease?

One hundred feet out from shore.

Enough.

He takes the paper from his pocket, unfolds it, and reads what he has written.

"It's your final dark conclusion, isn't it?" I ask. "And it was going to be the first line of your next book."

He turns to face me. His features bear the mark of life's many cruel tricks.

"Because there is no answer to our *zachem*," I add.

He nods.

"Write it," I tell him softly. "Go home and write it."

He remains silent, still.

"The world has plenty of noise, Julian, but not many voices."

He watches me steadily.

"And because there are so few, each one matters."

I lean toward him, hoping for more persuasive words. When none comes to me, I shrug. "That's my argument. The simple fact that we need people who remind us of the darkness."

His smile is slight and, like everything else, difficult to read, impossible to know.

"That is your job, Julian," I add. "And you need to do it."

With a curiously resolved movement, the renewal of some almost vanished strength, Julian returns the paper to his pocket and once again takes up the oars. I know, because I know him, that he is thinking of his book.

The wind touches the far trees. On the near bank, a dragonfly shoots over the still waters.

I follow the soft beat of the oars.

Second by second, the house grows nearer.

Even so, I cannot be sure that he will make it home.

For life, as Julian knew and his life and words and crime declared, is, at last, a Saturn Turn.